PENGUIN BOOKS

JEZEBEL

Megan Barnard is a former literary agent and editor turned full-time writer. When she's not writing, she drinks coffee, travels widely, and shuffles towering stacks of books around so they don't kill her or her husband. She lives in Maryland with her husband and her pup, Pippin.

JEZEBEL

MEGAN BARNARD

PENGUIN BOOKS

PENGUIN BOOKS

An imprint of Penguin Random House LLC
penguinrandomhouse.com

LIBRARY OF CONGRESS CATALOGING-IN-PUBLICATION DATA

Names: Barnard, Megan, author.

Title: Jezebel / Megan Barnard.

Description: New York : Penguin Books, [2023]

Identifiers: LCCN 2022059182 (print) | LCCN 2022059183 (ebook) |
ISBN 9780143137672 (paperback) | ISBN 9780593511794 (ebook)

Subjects: LCSH: Jezebel, Queen, consort of Ahab, King of Israel—Fiction. |
Women in the Bible—Fiction. | LCGFT: Bible fiction. | Novels.

Classification: LCC PS3602.A83355 J49 2023 (print) |
LCC PS3602.A83355 (ebook) | DDC 813.6—dc23/eng/20230222

LC record available at https://lccn.loc.gov/2022059182

LC ebook record available at https://lccn.loc.gov/2022059183

Printed in the United States of America
1st Printing

Set in Fournier MT Pro
Designed by Sabrina Bowers

First, to Tyler. For our ordinary, extraordinary life.

For my dad, the biggest dreamer I know.

And for Katie, who knew Bel first.

———+———

Once, before her name was a slur,

there was just a woman called Jezebel.

Mostly, this is for her.

JEZEBEL

PROLOGUE

When I slid from between my mother's legs, I screamed so loudly the dogs began to howl. The midwife picked me up and gave me to my mother's waiting arms, but still I screamed, shaking with such fury that a bead of sweat rolled off my mother's nose and into my mouth, so that my first taste was bitter salt.

"Why is it crying so loudly?" my mother said, cringing away from my flailing limbs.

"It's a girl," the midwife said patiently. "Girls always cry more than boys."

My mother did not ask why girls cried more. She just held me away from her body as I continued to scream. Suddenly, the midwife, who had been about to take me from my mother and give me to the wet nurse, backed away.

"She has been marked," the woman said, pointing to my waving hands. In the center of my right palm was a red mark, pointed like a star.

"It is a gift from the goddess," said my mother's maid, who had been cleaning up the blood on the floor. Her hands were clasped together, eyes shining. "She shall be blessed."

"No," the midwife said sharply. "It is a curse and must be removed."

My mother looked from the midwife to the maid. "It's small," she said. "Surely it doesn't matter?" Still, she held me out to the midwife, who flinched. "She must stop screaming; it will wake the king."

"She is screaming because she is cursed," the midwife said. "She will not stop until we remove it." She gestured to my hand, which was ruddy and plump. My fingers were fisted over the mark, protecting it like a clam that did not want to give up a pearl.

"She is blessed by Astarte," the maid said again. "The goddess will punish her if you remove the mark."

"The king will be angered if we leave it," the midwife said, picking up a sharp knife and slicing through the cord that bound me to my mother. The knife was still bloody in her hand when she reached for me. My mother hesitated, but she, more than any other, understood what it was to anger a king, so she handed me over, covering her ears so she did not have to hear me scream.

I did scream, though. I screamed when I took my first breath, and I screamed when the midwife sliced the skin away from my hand, and I screamed when she sewed it back up again, pulling the skin so it folded over the red star and made a mounded hill in my tiny palm.

I can still feel that puckered skin, all these years later. I believe the maid was right, that it was a blessing from Astarte taken from me, perverted.

After all, it was that mound of skin, that hidden star, that led me—Jezebel—to this. A dry, hot wind whipping through my hair. The city, a jewel, spread out before me. A man, whose pale eyes find me as a dog begins to howl.

I meet his gaze and smile.

PART I

◉◉◉◉◉◉◉◉◉◉◉◉◉◉

Ahab . . . did more evil in the eyes of the Lord than any of those before him . . . he also married Jezebel . . . and began to serve Baal and worship him.

——I KINGS

CHAPTER 1

I grew up fascinated by the images of the goddess Astarte. Her face was everywhere in our palace, in the city of Tyre. Carved into ivory tiles, etched into blue glass, embroidered into vibrant hangings that showed her and El, her husband. She was the queen consort of El, but secretly, I thought of El as *her* king consort. After all, it was her image, not El's, that adorned our city, for she was the mother of all.

I can still remember being very small, trying to be still and quiet as my mother braided my hair. Mother had never touched my hair before, but that day she sat me on a low stool and began to weave her fingers through it. Her hands were surprisingly gentle, and the motion should have calmed me, but I could barely sit under the weight of my mother's strange attention. I clenched the edges of the stool, trying to be good, and stared at the embroidered hanging of Astarte on the wall opposite. Her form was beautiful, with hips and breasts so full they seemed to drip with the life she created. She was unsmiling, and her hair was braided like mine, eyes wide and heavy-lidded.

"Who is she?" I jabbed a pudgy finger at the wall so sharply that my mother squawked, and her hands yanked my hair.

"It's the goddess Astarte. You know this, Princess," my nurse, Shapash, said from across the room, eyes wary as she looked at my mother, as if expecting a rebuke.

I frowned at her, imagining that my dark eyes were burning coals that could explode with fire whenever I wished. I hated how formal she became in my mother's presence. And I could not bear, even at such a young age, being treated like a fool. "I *know* it is Astarte. But who is the woman? Didn't her face come from a real woman? Who is she?"

"It doesn't matter," my mother said, continuing to braid my hair, her hands deft as she wove the strands into each other. "She gave the goddess her likeness. That is all that matters."

"But what was her name?" I insisted, squirming around in my seat so that I might look at my mother. "Was it you?"

"Of course it wasn't me." My mother laughed as she did at almost all my questions. "We don't know her name."

"But I want to know who she is," I said, my voice starting to tremble, though I didn't understand why. "Won't her name be written down in the books of kings, like Father's?"

"Of course it won't." Mother's voice was edged in annoyance, like a crab about to snap at my soft flesh. "She was a woman who did her duty, as all women before her. As I did and as you will."

"But you are queen." I turned to look at my mother's kohl-rimmed eyes, at the gold bangles on her wrists. Her body was as shapely as Astarte's. "Your name will be written down beside Father's."

Mother laughed. "My name will be forgotten, just like yours. It is simply the way of things. Now"—she clapped her hands together, and the bangles clanked against each other—"I'm going to rest before the festival tonight."

Shapash sat me back down on the stool so that she could finish the braids my mother had left hanging loose, and I stared once again at Astarte—at the nameless woman—and clenched my teeth together to prevent myself from asking more questions that were called foolish. I was Jezebel, princess royal of Tyre. I would never become faceless, not even if it made me blessed. My name would be remembered. It would be written down in the manner of kings.

◉◉◉◉

I was six years old when I realized that I was not, in fact, a goddess like Astarte.

My father had called me "little goddess" for as long as I could remember, and I knew he was right. Only a goddess could run as fast as I, keeping pace with the ships as they came into the harbor, speeding faster and faster until the world spun. Only a goddess could eat like I could, devouring figs and olives, stuffing my belly with lamb, and consuming so much melon its pink juices ran down my chin. But the true sign of my divinity was my anger. Only a goddess could feel the anger pulsing through my ruined palm, coursing through me like a thunderstorm that broke open the sea's depths.

I often burned people—my mother, my brother, the servants—with my eyes, which I knew were full of fire hotter than a forge. When I looked at them that way, they flinched from the burn, which felt right and just.

On the day I learned I was not a goddess, I was arguing with Baal Eser about who would become king. "You're wrong!" I screamed, hands in fists, trying to burn him and simultaneously turn him into an ugly snail with my divine power.

"I'm not," he said calmly, which made me even angrier. Normally he would cower before me when I was angry. Who was he to stand upright before me and speak such lies?

"I am the oldest," I said. "The oldest will become king."

Baal Eser looked at me with pity, making my whole body feel as though it were on fire. "Women don't become kings."

"I know *women* don't become kings," I said, throwing the words back at him, wishing they would cut his smooth face like the sharp edge of a shell. "I am not a *woman*. I am a goddess."

Baal Eser gave a startled laugh, and I howled and dove for him. I would tear him limb from limb for questioning me. Baal Eser ran from the room, and I gave chase. I was fast, faster than the wind, and I would catch him. It was exhilarating to run with such anger inside me, and I felt as though I might take flight at any moment. I chased him down the long corridors and into Father's council chamber, but I did not care. It made little difference to me where I killed my brother. I heard startled noises from behind us but ignored them, swinging my arm out, my fist connecting with the soft flesh of his stomach. I saw the fear in his eyes as I dove on him, ready to break him into pieces, but just then I was lifted into the air. I thought I had finally done it—achieved flight through the strength of my anger—but soon I realized I was not flying but being held. I swung my fist out again, and it connected with something solid.

"Wait for me to continue," my father said, his voice strange and muffled. I turned slightly and saw that I had bloodied his nose. I should have been afraid, should have been terrified to have hit the king, but all I could feel was triumphant. "I need to speak with my daughter." He threw me over his shoulder like a sack of grain, and I beat my fists against his back as he carried me, howling, from the room. He walked quickly out of the palace and down the broad white steps that led to the sea, then flung me into the water. It was a shock to feel the cold water all around me, and for a moment I was afraid. But the anger and fear drained out of me as I sputtered and swam to the surface. My father stood in the surf, head dripping, wiping water and blood out of his face.

"You have a strong bloodlust, little goddess," he said, face pleased. "But you can't just pummel your brother into dust because he angers you. And you *cannot* punch the king in the face."

"I didn't know it was you," I said, my dress, purple silk, floating around me pleasantly as though I were a sea spirit.

"You should not punch anyone," he said. "Bloodshed is not for you. Not for women."

I bared my teeth at him as he repeated what my brother had said. "I am not a woman. I will be the chosen king of our people," I said, looking up at Tyre. Our palace sat atop a hill, shining white in the sun, the city falling out before it like a fine carpet.

"Jezebel," my father said gravely. "You cannot be king. Girls do not become king."

The anger returned as swiftly as it had gone. I stared at him, trying to burn him, but he just returned the stare and did not move. "Why won't you burn?" I shouted, balling my fists as my palm grew hot.

"You're trying to burn me?" Father's lips lifted in a smile.

"Don't smile! I am a goddess, and I shall burn you!" I screamed before my father picked me up and threw me into the surf again.

"Daughter," he said when I had spluttered my way to him once more, "you are not a goddess, and you shall never become king of Tyre."

The sea was cold around me, and at his words I felt a sorrow so great I keened. Father waded out to me, and he held me close when I jumped into his arms, stroking my sodden hair.

"I want it," I said, still sobbing. "I want Tyre."

"I know," he said softly. "And yet, you cannot have it. But I shall get you your own kingdom. A land you can rule as queen."

"Queens are not important," I said. "They are not remembered."

"What about Astarte?" my father said. "She is the queen of heaven."

"I can be a queen like Astarte?" I pictured her raised chin and long braids, her direct gaze.

"You can," my father said. "*If* you learn how to control your temper. You don't hear stories of Astarte attacking her brother, do you?"

I pursed my lips but *couldn't* think of any stories like that. "He made me so angry," I said, as Father set me down.

"The next time someone makes you so angry, think about standing in the sea." He motioned to its dark expanse. "Think about the sand shifting under your feet, the coolness of the water around your body. And if that doesn't work . . ." He smiled at me. "Come down and throw yourself in."

Father turned then and went back up to the palace, leaving me standing in the sea. I wanted to follow him, but I felt suddenly weary, as if my father's words had peeled my godhead away from me, leaving me naked as a baby. I looked down at my left hand. It had a long, red mark on it from the sand, and I dashed it into the water over and over, but each time I brought it back to the light it was still marred. I slowly crawled out of the waves and sat on the shore, thinking of the images I'd seen of Astarte. Her skin had no marks upon it. Because the skin of a god could hold no marks.

My ruined palm began to throb, and I opened it to look at the mounded skin there. I should have known long ago—if I had truly been a goddess, no knife could have pierced my skin and taken my star from me.

Shapash had been the one to tell me the story of my birth. She had been there, a silent witness as they had cut my skin open and hidden what should have been mine. The story of my birth was my favorite, as important to me as any story of the gods. For my whole life I thought Shapash told the story because it was important for a goddess to know the truth of her birth. But perhaps instead she had been trying to tell me, in her own quiet way, that I was not and had never been—could never be—a goddess.

I pounded my fist into the sand, wishing I could destroy the beach I sat on, regain my immortality—the godhead my father had taken from me—but my fist made only a small impression, one the waves quickly smoothed away to nothingness.

Slowly I got to my feet and began walking back to the palace. Usually, the sight of it sprawling on the hill above the beach brought only pleasure, but now the white walls seemed to loom, casting shadows I had never seen before.

Sapphira was sprawled on my bed when I returned, and I was glad it was only her and not Baal Eser or my nurse. If I had seen either of them, I would have tried to attack them, or perhaps begun to weep. But Sapphira was always understanding, always wise. She would know what to do. She would be able to soothe the thoughts swirling through me.

I crawled into bed and lay beside her, so our limbs were touching. We had lain this way our whole lives, from the very hour of our births.

"Have you always known I am not truly a goddess?" I said, my voice so soft she would not have been able to hear me had she not been lying by my side.

Sapphira took my right hand in hers. She was the only one I ever allowed to touch it. She didn't say anything for a long moment, and I felt my heart begin to beat fast, not in anger, as usual, but in fear.

Perhaps Sapphira thought me a fool too, just as my brother and father did. Did my whole court mock me? *Not* my *whole court*, I realized suddenly. *Father's whole court. Baal Eser's court.* I would be sent away. Sent far from Tyre because I was not a goddess or a king. I was only a girl.

"Shapash always said you were born when the night was dark, but you screamed so loudly you woke the whole palace, even the dogs," Sapphira said. "I was born the same night, just before dawn brightened the sea. But I was not born screaming."

I nodded. We both knew the story well. Shapash had told it to us before we could even understand what a story was. "The midwife handed me to Shapash even as she tried to stop my mother from dying. Shapash said I was so pale and cold she did not know what to do; I was too weak to even suckle at her breast." Sapphira nearly chanted the words, the rhythm of them as familiar to both of us as our prayers. I had pictured the scene many times, the darkened room lit only by gold-flickering lamps, the deafening silence of a baby who did not cry.

"She was called by the midwife to try to help my mother, so she set me down quickly, in the basket she had already laid you in, assuming because of how small and silent I was, I would die. But I didn't. When she came back to the basket hours later, she found you clutching my hand, laying right by my side, keeping me warm. Alive." Sapphira held my hand tightly. "A goddess is one who gives life," she said quietly.

Shapash had said that anytime they tried to take Sapphira from me I would begin to howl until she was brought back, but . . . "She thought I kept you alive?" I said.

"Shapash said if you hadn't kept me warm and kicking, I would not have had the strength," Sapphira said quietly, squeezing my hand. She didn't say anything else, and I didn't press her. Instead we just lay side by side and breathed in time with each other, as we had since the night we'd been born.

◎◎◎◎

There were few children for me to play with in the palace. Not that there weren't children—the nurseries were full, and my brother had many playmates—but most other children did not like me. Perhaps I had told too many of them that I was a goddess and they had believed me, or perhaps they simply knew of my vicious temper and stayed away, but for whatever reason, it was usually just Sapphira and me together, running through the palace, swimming in the sea, playing elaborate games where I pretended to be the goddess Anat, killing my enemies with Sapphira by my side, fulfilling whatever role I called on her to play.

Even though we were both twelve now, Shapash did not allow us into the city on our own, but we often ran down to the shore when she took her afternoon nap, thinking us asleep as well. We were walking down one day when I heard Sapphira sniffling behind me. I turned—shocked—as I could not remember ever seeing Sapphira cry before. I cried sometimes, when I was angry and could not escape down to the sea, but nothing made Sapphira cry. Not stubbing her toe or being denied sweet cakes or even being scolded by our nurse.

"Did Donis try to trip you again?" I said, swinging out with my fists as if I could hit the troublesome boy from here.

Sapphira shook her head and wiped her eyes on her sleeve. When she spoke, her voice was so soft I had to step closer to hear her. "Last night Father and I ate with my older brother and his wife," she said.

I scowled. I hated eating alone and had shouted at Sapphira's father yesterday when he had come to take her to her brother's house, but he had only laughed.

"I was helping Nikkal with the baby," she said, "and suddenly I heard my father saying that before too long I would have my own baby to take care of."

I stared at her, shocked. Sapphira and I had not even gotten our monthly bleedings yet. How could her father be thinking of marriage already? "Did you tell him no?" I said. "That you don't want to get married?"

Sapphira shook her head. "He did not mean now," she said. "Nikkal could see how upset I was, and she said that Father was only beginning to think of it, that it would be years before he found someone suitable for me." She looked down at her hands. "But I'll have to get married someday."

Her words alarmed me. Most women got married, of course, but not Sapphira. Never Sapphira. A marriage would take her away from me, and I would never allow that to happen.

"But you can't leave me," I said. "We have been together forever."

"I don't want to, Bel," she said, a tear dripping off her nose. "But I am not a princess. I cannot shout at the king or tell him what to do, as you can. I must obey my father."

I raised my chin. "I *am* a princess. And your father is only a palace administrator. I will ensure you stay with me. And never get married and have babies like Nikkal." I wrinkled my nose. Sapphira sniffled again but gave me a small smile. I took her hand. "Don't worry. You will never have to leave me. Unless I order you to," I said with a grin, which she returned. I turned back toward the palace. "Let's go to the temple and speak with the diviner. Perhaps she will be able to see our futures and tell us how we might stay together forever."

Sapphira sighed. "We were just at the temple earlier today," she said. "Why don't we just go down to the shore instead?"

"No," I said. "This is important. We must ask the gods about our future."

"Our *futures*, Bel," Sapphira said, but her face was resigned as she turned back toward the palace.

"We have one future," I said, turning my head so I could not see the doubt in her eyes. "Together."

"But what if my father finds someone for me to marry? How can we prevent that? Everyone must marry eventually, even you."

"I am princess royal of Tyre," I said. "I can do anything. Especially if the gods are with me. That is what we are going to the temple to divine."

I knew Sapphira did not care much for the temple and the gods. She had told me once that the gods could have saved her mother and didn't and so she didn't feel the need to be particularly devout.

The temple of Astarte was full of worshippers each morning and evening, but when we entered at midday, it was quiet. A few priestesses prayed in front of the statue of Astarte, but otherwise we were alone. I could feel the power in the space from the moment I entered it. I knew by then that I was not a goddess—had never been a goddess—but sometimes when I entered the temple, I felt again the power I had known when I thought myself divine. And even if *I* did not have that power myself anymore, the gods did, and they could grant it to their worshippers as they willed.

I walked to the statue of Astarte and stared at her face for a long moment. I could still clearly remember the moment when I had learned that I was expected to be as nameless as the woman who had given her likeness to the goddess. I shook my head slightly, as if a gnat had buzzed near my ear, and looked back at Sapphira, who stared around the temple too, but without the interest I knew was in my gaze. I turned back to the goddess. I would not go into a nameless future. And where I went, Sapphira would follow.

"I would speak with the diviner," I said to a priestess who had just risen from her prayers.

The priestess bowed respectfully to me but said, "Highness, the diviner has been called to another temple. And . . ." She hesitated as if anxious, then said, "The diviner is only for the king's use."

"I am the daughter of the king," I said, my palm beginning to throb in anger. "And I wish to speak to the diviner about my future."

The priestess looked around, as if hoping another would step in, but the others had fled. She hesitated before saying, "The diviner has been teaching a new girl the arts. She is young yet, but she is skilled."

I nodded stiffly at the woman, who went to get the apprentice, leaving Sapphira and me alone in the temple. I knelt before the statue of Astarte and filled the prayer bowl with a dark wine the color of the sea, then gently tipped the wine out onto the altar until only the inscribed prayers that filled the white bowl were dark. "Sapphira and I must remain together." I hesitated, then added, "And I must never become nameless." My voice was loud, echoing against the stone walls of the empty temple.

"Highness?" The priestess I had spoken to appeared from the back of the temple with a girl who looked a little older than us, perhaps fourteen or so, with hair the color of polished bronze, a delicate face, and wide, grey eyes. "This is the priestess Tanith."

"Highness." The girl bowed to me. "I will help you as I can. Do you wish to speak to all the gods or just one?"

"Astarte," I said, looking again at the statue's face.

"Then we should use the entrails of a dove," Tanith said, glancing at the statue of Astarte, which had a dove carved near her feet. "I shall go and get one."

"Bel," Sapphira said, as we watched Tanith turn into a darkened hall, "I love doves. I do not wish for one to be killed just so we can see a hazy future that probably won't even come true."

"The goddess asks for sacrifice," I said as Tanith came back into the room, holding a silver knife in one hand and a pure white dove in the other. "You don't have to watch." I put my arm around Sapphira. "I will watch for both of us."

Tanith brought down the knife on the dove and did not flinch when a spurt of blood sprayed onto her robes. I could smell the blood, salty and metallic, like strong iron in a forge. I thought of the doves that often came to my balcony and let me feed them, but I stiffened so that the tears that had filled my eyes did not fall. I was twelve, no longer a child who wept when she discovered she was not divine. I would not weep over a necessary sacrifice either.

Tanith quickly disposed of the bird's body, leaving its entrails steaming on the altar. Sapphira lifted her head and watched with distaste as Tanith sorted through them calmly, as if they were no more than cool stones on a shore.

"You wish to know your future?" she said, looking at me, and I nodded, but Sapphira looked surprised.

"We didn't tell you why we came," she said, voice quiet.

Tanith smiled gently. "I could say that the gods told me, but in truth, anyone who asks for me is looking toward the future." She looked back to the entrails, and when she spoke again her voice held a different timbre, richer and deeper than it had been before. "You will be married to a foreign king," she said, and I nodded, trying to keep my face even, though the thought made my stomach roil uncomfortably. "But," Tanith added, face softening, "you two will find a way to stay together. For all your lives you will be together. Except"—she looked directly at me—"except at the very end."

I felt Sapphira tremble beside me, but I just laughed. "We will be together our whole lives," I said, squeezing her hand. "Why worry about the end now?" In truth, it did not feel possible that we would ever have an end. What mattered was that we would not be separated, that we would find a way to stay together.

"Divination is not a precise art," Tanith said. "The future is always changing."

I turned to Sapphira and smiled. "It does not matter how the future changes. I will find a way to ensure that you stay with me forever. The gods have willed it. *I* have willed it," I said. "And I am princess of the greatest kingdom in the world. Trust me."

Sapphira hesitated for a moment, then nodded. I turned back toward the young priestess. "You have my gratitude," I said. I looked at her long white robes, the wise look in her eyes, and for a moment I wished that I could become a priestess too. That I could spend my moments as close to the power of the divine as mortals could get. "You are young, to be a diviner already," I said, curious about this girl who wasn't much older than we were.

"I was raised in the temple," the girl said, feeding the entrails of the dove into the nearby brazier. The smell was pleasant for a moment, but it turned bitter as the entrails reduced to black ash. "They found me in a basket on the temple steps when I was just a babe, so they took me in and raised me for the goddess." The look Tanith gave the statue of Astarte was tender, like a daughter to a mother. She looked down at her robes then and saw the blood that had spattered. "I just cleaned these," she said with a sigh, touching the red stain. She looked back at us. Suddenly she did not seem so mysterious and wise, but just a girl like us.

"We were going down to the shore," I said. "Would you like to come with us? You can get the stain out more easily if you soak it first." Sapphira glanced at me in surprise. I rarely invited anyone else to play with us, but the girl didn't seem to notice the look and merely smiled.

"I would like that. I was about to go to the shore when you came in. But of course I waited for you—Your Highness—" she said, suddenly seeming to remember who I was.

Usually I preferred such formality, but for a girl who stood so close to the gods—closer than I would ever be—it did not feel necessary. I waved my hand. "You may call me Jezebel," I said. "When it is just us three together."

We ran down to the shore together and played in the waves for a time, splashing each other and laughing. It was strange to be three instead of two, but I enjoyed the older girl's boisterous spirit, her knowledge of the gods. I loved the stories of the gods, thought I knew them all, but Tanith knew stories I had never heard of, stories of Anat, Astarte. She even taught us a few lines from a poem I had never heard before.

> As soon as El spied her
> He unfastened his scabbard and laughed.
> He put his feet on his footstool,
> And wiggled his toes.

"I don't understand," Sapphira said. "Why is he wiggling his toes?" We lay on the sand, tired after our play in the sea, and Sapphira wiggled her toes in imitation, flicking up a spray of pale sand.

Tanith gave a short laugh, though a blush touched her cheeks. "He is . . . They are about to . . ."

"He is about to bed her," I said, having figured it out immediately, though I had as little experience with such things as Sapphira.

Sapphira made a face. "I do not wish to ever bed anyone," she said. "It does not sound pleasant."

Tanith shrugged. "I would like to, but I won't. I will remain a virgin all my days for Astarte."

"Which foreign king will I be married to?" I said, turning toward Tanith. Both of their faces sobered at my question, and I knew we were all thinking the same thing, that I would be with a man whether I wanted to or not. I had not thought until that moment what it meant that Sapphira's father was thinking of finding a husband for her. My father would surely be making the same preparations, preparations for me to leave home. Leave Tyre.

"I do not know," Tanith said softly. "The signs were not . . . they are not clear, not in that way."

"But I will marry a foreigner. Someone not of Tyre."

Tanith gave a sharp nod.

My palm began to throb. I did not know why I was suddenly so upset. I had known, ever since I'd learned I would not rule Tyre, that I would marry a foreign king. Someone who would bring Tyre wealth or power or peace. But I had been only a child at the time, and the future had felt so far away that it had not felt possible. Not until Tanith saw the signs of it in the steaming entrails.

Tanith looked at me, and there was kindness in her grey eyes. "You are the princess royal of Tyre," she said softly. "You will not be married to some coarse brute. You will marry someone who will robe you in purple and line your wrists with gold."

I looked down at the purple sash across my waist, the gold bangles on my wrists, and gave a bitter laugh.

"Perhaps you will be married to the Pharaoh of Egypt," Sapphira said. "They are a kingdom of great learning. They have had many great queens."

I thought of the Egyptians I had met at court. Their men were not as attractive as the men of Tyre, but they had strong faces and smooth skin that gleamed and smelled of almond and cassia. "I would like to see the pyramids," I thought of the stories I'd heard of the great structures that pierced the very sky. "I would like to create a great nation," I said slowly. "One like Tyre. A place I will be remembered."

"You will be a great queen," Tanith said softly, and I wanted to ask whether it was something she had divined, but I felt afraid, suddenly, to know, to have the weight of a great kingdom upon my shoulders. I looked around the sea, at the ships that dotted the harbor, toward the market full of purple silks and expensive spices, almond oil and doves as white as the one Tanith had sacrificed hours before. How could I ever create a kingdom as great as Tyre?

"You will not have to start at the beginning," Sapphira said, seeming to read my thoughts. "You will be sent somewhere of great beauty and great learning. You will simply make it greater still."

I watched the shining water and tried to believe them. To let my fear slip away as the sea did with the tides.

CHAPTER 2

I threw down my pen so hard the reed snapped in two. I had been trying to write one of the stories my nurse often told of Anat, but no matter how tightly I held the pen, I could not get the letters to form the shapes I needed.

"You must work more carefully, Highness." My tutor picked up the remnants of my pen and handed me another. "The letters will always look clumsy if you are not careful."

"It is impossible," I said, not wanting to tell the tutor that I had been working on the letters for hours, but that no matter how I held my pen, the mound of skin that rose from my palm got in my way and made the letters bounce about. I had even tried to use my left hand for writing, though it was forbidden by the gods, but no matter which hand I used, the shapes were still clumsy.

"Watch Sapphira," the tutor said, gesturing to my friend, who sat beside me. Sapphira's tongue poked out as she concentrated, which made her look decidedly childish, but her writing was beautiful. Her hand was gentle, and she held the pen as lightly as a feather, not with white knuckles as I did.

Sapphira glanced at me, and I saw sympathy in her face, so I looked down at her writing instead. The black ink glistening on the page reminded me of the sun shining on fish scales. Sapphira had the best writing of anyone I knew. She had the hand of a princess.

As I looked at the page, an idea formed suddenly, sparking in my thoughts like the quick dive of a bird, and I stood so sharply my stool scraped upon the ground, making everyone look at me. "I need to speak with my father," I said, leaving the room even though my tutor called after me.

We had our lessons in a small space off the scribes' workrooms, and their heads lifted as I strode by, but they kept writing, dipping their pens into pots of black ink, making tiny, precise cuts to correct mistakes in the skins they wrote upon. The scribes were not allowed to speak as they wrote, but the rooms were never silent— full of the scratching of pens against papyrus and skin, ink bubbling in tin pots, and sheaves being moved as the scribes checked their notes. Being a scribe was a great honor in Tyre, and being a scribe of the king was the greatest honor of all. They were charged with writing down the days of the king and his family, marking each war fought, each trade made, each child born. I knew that the announcement of my birth was written down on papyrus somewhere, and I wondered if that sheaf of papyrus told the whole story—of blood and knives and a gift from the goddess stolen from me. The memory made me want to howl, and the thought quickened my steps. By the time I found my father, I could feel my ruined palm throbbing like a second heart, a ruined, broken thing that could only remind me of what I had lost.

Father was alone in his rooms when I approached, head bent over a sheaf of papyrus. His neat, elegant writing on the paper only made me angrier as I compared it to my own clumsy strokes. I did not wait for him to notice me but marched up to him.

Father did not look up as he said, "What is it, Bel? Shouldn't you be in your lessons?"

"I left," I said, and he finally looked up, crooking one eyebrow.

"You are not allowed to leave your lessons," he said. "I am busy. I cannot play with you now."

"I'm not a child," I said, raising my chin. "I am thirteen. I did not come to play, but to make a request of the king." He leaned back in his seat as if weary but nodded at me to continue. "Each day you read the recordings of the scribes." I touched the papyrus in front of him. "You have long said that it is one of the most important things you do, to know that your days are being recorded properly."

"And so it is," he said gravely.

"It is important," I said. "Because it is how our family will be remembered long after we are dead." He nodded. "I need my own scribe," I said quickly. "So that my days are recorded properly."

Father looked at me for a long moment then laughed, throwing back his head as he did when he was truly amused. "You are a child and a girl," he said finally. "You do not need a scribe. Scribes are for the king. Go back to your studies before you are punished."

I gritted my teeth and bared my palm before him. "I cannot return to my studies because I cannot write. On the day of my birth, I was marked by the goddess. When the mark was sewn up, it ruined my hand so that I cannot grasp the pen properly."

My father's face softened. "We do not know that it was a mark from Astarte. It could have been a curse."

"It was a gift," I said. "And I am now punished for removing it, even though I was a just-born babe who did not hold the knife in my hand."

Father rubbed his thumb over my palm. "Does it hurt?" he said suddenly.

"No," I said, surprised because no one had ever asked how it felt before. "It does not hurt, but . . . sometimes it feels . . . angry." I could tell Father did not understand what I meant, and I blew out a breath of irritation. "I cannot write properly for myself. Not as befits a princess. A future queen." I lifted my chin again. "You will soon marry me to some king in a distant land," I said, trying to keep my voice steady even as the thought of leaving Tyre made me want to weep. "I will need to write letters: to you and Mother, to others of importance. It will reflect poorly on Tyre if the letters look like they were written by a child."

"I cannot spare any of my scribes," he said slowly. "They are all needed for me, for Tyre."

I dug my fingers into my palm. I did not want to cry before my father, but his words made me feel as though I had already been married off and sent to some distant land, no longer *of* Tyre. I took a deep breath so I could calmly tell him the idea I'd had, without anger. "Sapphira will be my scribe," I said. "She has the most beautiful writing I've ever seen. And she would like to see places other than Tyre." I tried to stay calm, to not show my father how much I wished for this.

"Sapphira?" my father said slowly. "I suppose she could be taught by the royal scribes easily enough . . . but what about her father? He will want to marry her off soon."

"Give him gold and a few purple robes." I flicked my hand. "That will surely satisfy him." Father laughed again, the sound deep and full like the beat of a drum, but it only angered me even more. "You let me be mutilated," I said sharply. "You did not protect me as a father should. Therefore, I will be given Sapphira as my scribe. She will write down the accounts of my days and then perhaps you will not be punished for stealing the goddess's blessing from me." I marched from the room, keeping my head high but my face turned away, so my father could not see the tears in my eyes from the throbbing anger in my hand—from the knowledge that I had been cheated of my true birthright.

◉◉◉◉

In the two years since Sapphira had become my scribe, I had refused to write in my own hand and my tutor had stopped trying to force me. Instead, I spent my writing lessons in the room where the scribes kept their recordings. It was small but overflowed with clay pots full of scrolls and baskets of animal skins marked in the scribes' careful hands. The room smelled of musk and the sour tang of ink, but it was worth it to sit there so that I could read what was written down. I wanted to know how to become a great ruler, one worthy of renown. Many of the recordings were stories and songs of my own father's reign, but many more were stories of the kings before Father, their exploits and achievements.

There were no stories of women. My mother's name was not written down, even in her wedding song. She was only called "princess." My father's other wives and concubines were not mentioned at all. They and their children might have been nothing but dust.

I'd asked my tutor which queens of renown he knew of, but he only looked at me stupidly and said, "Your mother, the queen."

"But what has she done of renown?"

The tutor blinked nervously. "She has given the king a son and heir," he said. "And graced the court with her beauty."

I must be remembered for more than my sons, I thought as I wearily climbed the stairs back to my room. The day had been too hot to swim this morning, and I had spent all of it cloistered in the room of writings. I was suddenly desperate to wash the smell of animals from my skin, and since Sapphira was in a late lesson with her tutor, I was alone for the evening.

When I walked outside, I found a cool breeze had blown up from the water. The evening light made blue shadows on the white buildings as I walked down the hill and through the market. Merchants were calling out their wares, and I could smell the sweet musk of cedar and almond blossoms. I stopped at a stall that was selling silk dyed a deep purple. I rubbed the silk between my fingers, and it reminded me of how it felt to drag my hand through the water when I was out sailing.

"Your Highness." The merchant selling the silk bowed to me.

I often walked through the market with my father, and many of the regular merchants knew my face. Father often said that there was no better way to truly understand a land than walking through its market. If it was full of luxuries like silks, spices, and soft-faced women buying gold jewelry, then the people were prosperous and happy. But if it was full only of necessities like flour and oil and fish that sat too long in the sun, then the king needed to take note. I knew that other lands were rife with famine and drought, or, like Israel, our neighbor to the east, always fighting in the name of their god, but it was difficult to picture a market that was not bustling and cheerful, full of music and the scents of cooking meat.

I rubbed the cloth between my hands again before leaving the market and continuing to the shore. I passed the huge vats the fishermen used to collect the sea snails that made the purple dye Tyre was famous for, but the stench was overwhelming, so I walked past them and toward a cove I knew would be deserted.

The tide was coming in, quickly erasing my footprints, but I liked watching them disappear, as though I were a goddess who walked without leaving a mark on the ground. The sun had mostly set, with only a thin line of pink showing between the horizon and the sea. When I finally dove into the waves and the cool water enveloped me, I closed my eyes, wishing I might never leave.

The sun sank, and I swam until the moon rose behind the palace. It was full but red, and it made the white stone look as though it were splattered in blood. The sight made me shiver. I turned away from it and continued to swim until the current grew so strong, I became tired of fighting it.

I'd waded back to shore and was wringing water from my dripping hair when I heard someone calling my name. For a moment, I was frightened, as I could only see the figure of a tall man through the mist, but finally I realized it was my father, dressed simply in a robe and sandals. Before he had become king, he had been a priest of Astarte, and he still wore plain clothes as often as he could.

I did not smile as he approached, feeling wary. When I was young, Father often swam with me, but of late he'd been too preoccupied with the court, and distance had grown between us. "I thought you would be here when I could not find you at the palace," he said, taking off his sandals so that he might wade in the surf. He breathed in deeply and looked out to the sea before glancing back at the palace. The moon had risen higher now, and the bloody light that had shone on it had gone.

"It was too hot to swim this morning," I said.

Father nodded but did not say anything for a long moment. I had just licked the salt from my lips when he said, "It has been decided." I stiffened and looked up at the city shining above us. "You are to marry Ahab, the prince of Israel."

I shook my head to clear the water from my ears, sure I had heard him wrong. "No," I said, feeling my palm begin to throb. "No. You cannot send me to Israel."

He sighed. "Bel, you have known your whole life that you cannot remain in Tyre."

"I am not a child," I hissed, heat rising in my face. "I know I cannot stay," I said, remembering the heartbreak I'd felt when I'd learned I would not become king of Tyre. "But surely it would be more advantageous to have me marry one of the princes of Egypt or Greece." I thought of the conversation Sapphira, Tanith, and I had had three years ago, when we had been only twelve. We had agreed that I would be sent to a land of learning, of culture. Somewhere beautiful. None of us had ever mentioned Israel. Compared to Tyre, Israel was barely more than a collection of huts planted in the earth. We had invented an entire alphabet before their first king had even drawn breath.

Father shook his head. "Israel has a great army," he said. "They may not have the wealth of Tyre, but they are growing quickly. A marriage between us will strengthen both of our kingdoms."

"They are in constant war," I said. "How will you feel if I am slaughtered before I am even able to have an heir?"

"Don't be foolish, child." Father shook his head. "King Omri wants peace."

"And Crown Prince Ahab?" I said. "I have heard of his exploits in battle. They say he rips out the throats of his enemies with his teeth."

Father laughed. "All great warriors have such stories told about them. They say I razed Tyre before I took the throne." His eyes glinted dark in the moonlight.

"You killed the king," I said. "And all his family."

Father's mouth tightened. "The king had lost control of Tyre. He was ruining the country. I did what needed to be done." He shook his head as if trying to shake off biting insects. "Besides, that was long ago. Israel and Tyre are at peace. And you will marry their son."

"What if I refuse?" It was a childish question, but perhaps my father would bend to my will.

Father's face grew grim. "I am king," he said. "My will is law."

"Please, Father," I said, wishing for once that I had my mother's gift of smiling eyes and soft words. "I would have you consider someone else, a prince of—"

"It has been decided, Jezebel," Father said, cutting me off. "I will not speak of this for a moment longer. You are going to Israel."

"No," I said, the words leaping from me as my palm throbbed. "I will not—" He slapped me across the face before I could finish the words. I nearly fell to my knees, giving a cry of pain, though I was shocked more than anything else. My father had never touched me in anger before.

"Listen to me, Bel," he said, taking a step back, a flicker of regret in his face even as he continued. "I have given you a great deal of freedom. I have allowed you to make demands of me and speak when you should not. But you are *not* the ruler of Tyre. You are a girl, and you must learn to listen to the will of your king."

He had never spoken to me so harshly before, and for a moment I thought I might begin to weep, so I turned and ran from him, back to the embrace of Tyre: my city, my home.

◎◎◎◎

I walked through the market, still open even at this late hour. It was full of golden flames from lanterns and candles, and someone played a flute while several couples whirled and danced. The light caught on the gold in the women's ears and made their brightly colored robes seem as vibrant as jewels. I leaned against a wall and watched the dancing until the lights and people blurred together in the tears that had filled my eyes. I had known I would leave Tyre, but I'd hoped I would be sent somewhere like it.

I left the market and wandered the streets, the moon making the white buildings shine softly. I thought of what I knew about Israel. It was a land of constant wars and bloodshed. The king had visited once when I was very small because he wanted Tyrian stonemasons to build him a great palace in Samaria, the capital city of Israel. I wondered now if even then my father had known he would sell me to this king and his son because of the sharpness of their blades.

As I walked, I passed schools and temples, thinking of the scribes still busily at work in my father's palace. I walked down one long road and was confident that it contained more places of learning than in the entirety of Israel. I stopped outside a temple of Astarte and put a hand on the cool stone. I thought of how the woman who had given her face had been nameless, how my mother had laughed and said I would be the same.

I walked the streets for hours, until the sun began to rise and made the white palace turn as pink as the inside of a shell. I was nearly at my rooms, head bowed, when I saw my mother coming toward me. Her eyes were bright, and her cheeks were flushed even at the early hour.

"Bel!" she said, voice high and full of laughter. "Have you been out dancing too?" My mother was beloved in the court for her laughter, for her winning ways. She went to parties most nights, drinking and throwing dice with her favorites.

"Do you know that Father has arranged for me to marry Ahab, the prince of Israel?" I said suddenly.

Mother arched an eyebrow. "Has he decided, then? I knew he was in talks with King Omri."

"Why wouldn't you tell me?" I said, voice rising in anger. My mother and I had never been especially close—to me she had always seemed foolish, childish, even when I was a child myself. But still, she was my mother; she was supposed to look after me and my welfare.

"What was there to tell?" She lifted a hand to her lips as she yawned, her tongue stained purple with wine. "I did not know anything had been agreed upon. And I am not interested in the mighty dealings of kings," she said with a smile.

I felt as though she had just dealt me a blow. "You don't care where I am to go? That I am to be sold to Israel? Because of their shining swords and mighty army, instead of Egypt or . . . or anywhere else?" My voice broke, and I fled from her to my rooms, slamming the door behind me. I went to my balcony and looked out on the city sprawling below me. The fishermen had flooded the harbor, their sails high in the wind. Women were rising from their beds, beginning to bake bread and walk to the market. Scribes were filling their pens with ink, and goldsmiths were heating their forges to create the delicate jewelry that adorned the nobility of Tyre. The vats near the harbor were already bubbling with the purple dye that had made us so famous around the world, and beyond them, the horizon melded with the sea so that it looked like a smooth expanse of blue glass.

I jumped as a soft hand touched my back. I turned, expecting Sapphira or my maid, but saw instead my mother. She was no longer smiling, but her eyes were still bright, as though she could not help the joy that overflowed from her. She was lovely to look at, with lithe limbs and a delicate face, eyes that were pale gold in the morning light. I had been taller than her by the time I was ten, and when I looked at her, I did not recognize my own face anywhere in her features.

"I was fifteen when I married your father," she said. "Surely you knew that you would be married soon?" Her voice was not reproachful, but it made me angry, as though she thought I was a child who did not understand what it meant to be princess of a great nation.

"Of course I knew," I said, shaking her hand off my shoulder. "But I thought I would be married to someone who . . . befits my station. A nation of importance, of learning. Not Israel."

Mother laughed, and though I knew it was not meant unkindly, I still bristled at the sound. "I was the cousin of the previous king of Tyre," she said. "After your father took the throne, I was married to Ithobaal to keep the peace between our houses. Your father was a priest of Astarte before he took the throne. I wouldn't have eaten a meal with him before he killed the king, and by the next harvest I was his wife and expecting his child."

"You were *cousin* to the king," I said stiffly. "I am princess royal of one of the greatest nations in the world. And I am to be sent to *Israel*, Mother," I said, turning toward her. "They have no temples to Astarte, few schools, few artisans. I won't be able to look at the sea from my window," I said, voice growing hoarse.

I turned back to look at the harbor, assuming Mother would leave, but she spoke again. "I have been to Israel," she said softly. "When Omri was crowned, your father and I went. And you are right. It is a harsher place than Tyre. They do not have our schools or temples, and their people are tired from the constant wars. But when I was crowned queen of Tyre, the city looked nothing like it does now. The market was small, and the palace was only half-completed. And now look at it." She smiled and spread her arms wide at the gleaming streets below us. "You will be queen, Bel. You can improve the country as I have improved Tyre. And," she added, voice soft, as she ran a hand over my hair, "I stayed in the queen's rooms while I was in Israel. There is a balcony where you can still glimpse the sea, even if it is in the distance."

I stayed where I was for a long time after she left, watching the sun touch different parts of the city, trying to fix it in my mind, wishing I could engrave it onto my skin so that it would stay as unchanging as stone.

Finally, I rose and went to my father's rooms. I did not knock, and when he saw me standing in front of him, his face grew fierce as though he thought I would try to change his mind again. I longed to scream at him, to beg him on bended knees to send me anywhere else, but his harsh treatment of me the night before had cowed me. I had seen him whip a man who had questioned him bloody, had stood in the room when he'd beheaded a man who had disobeyed his order. I knew he would not kill me, but I did think he would tie me to a donkey and send me to Israel regardless of what I wanted. Such was his right as my father. As my king.

"Since you command it," I said, trying to keep my voice even, my head bowed, "I will go to Israel. But soon"—I lifted my eyes to his, matching his gaze—"no one will remember Israel for what it was. I will build schools, temples, markets. Its people will turn to my will. Soon, they will tell stories about *me*. They will sing my name in the streets and call me blessed. Jezebel, they will say. Jezebel. Jezebel. Jezebel."

CHAPTER 3

I noticed him before I noticed Ahab, the man I was to marry. He was tall, as tall as I was, with dark hair and skin so pale I wondered if he ever saw the sun. His eyes were large and dark and roved over me with such intensity it was nearly indecent. For the briefest moment, I wondered if *he* was the prince, but then I saw the man in front of him and knew instantly that this was my future husband. He was short and dressed so richly I wondered that he did not fall over from the weight of the gold.

I too was dressed in purple and gold, with bangles on my wrists and jewels in my hair, but while Ahab looked foolish, I wore the adornments with the carelessness and experience of great wealth. I might have been traded away to an uncivilized king and his short prince, but I was still princess royal of Tyre. I lifted my chin as I stopped before the prince and bowed briefly, then straightened, forcing him to crane his neck to look at me.

"Princess Jezebel." The man beside Ahab must be the king, Omri. He was the same age as my father but looked much older, with stooped shoulders, dark spots on his face, and hair as white as seafoam. I realized with some relief that the trumpets that had accompanied me through the city had finally stopped and that I could hear him speak, though my ears did ring slightly.

He kissed my cheek, and I could smell something sweet on his breath, milk, perhaps, or honey. The scent reminded me of a nursery, a child, but I did not back away. Instead, I smiled and said, "My father, King Ithobaal of Tyre, sends his greetings."

"His greetings and his daughter," the king chuckled, and I straightened so that the gold in my hair caught the light.

"Indeed." I smiled broadly. My mother often said my mouth was too wide, that when I smiled fully, I looked like a wild dog about to lunge for the throat. "My father is pleased to join our two kingdoms in marriage. It is a great honor." I did not say which kingdom it was an honor for, and perhaps Omri did not understand, but I could tell Ahab did, because he flushed and his lips tightened. So. Perhaps I was not who the prince of Israel wanted for a bride. I flicked my gaze to him and rolled my hips. It was a brief movement, but I saw the way his mouth tightened, the way his eyes dropped from my face to my breasts. Good. He should know that I was not some timid woman who knew nothing about the ways of men. If I wished for him to want me, he would.

"Go and get settled," the king said with a wave of his hand. "I hope you will be comfortable here."

I let my eyes rove around the throne room for a moment. The palace was unimpressive compared to the one I'd grown up in in Tyre. The room was trimmed in gold, but clumsily, by someone who did not have the skill of Tyrian craftsmen. The throne itself was barely more than a chair, and even the king had only a strip of purple across his chest, unlike my purple robe. I let the silence linger for a moment longer, then said, "I'm sure I will be." Neither Ahab nor Omri seemed to notice the slight, but I saw the tall man behind them smile briefly as he brushed his long hair out of his eyes. I saw his ink-stained fingers and realized that he must be the king's scribe, the one tasked with writing his conquests and achievements. I smiled at Omri one last time before leaving the room, promising myself that soon the scribe would be writing my name, as well as the name of the king.

◎◎◎◎

I woke early the next morning because my throat was so dry. I reached for the cup of water by my bed, but it tasted strange, metallic and almost salty, and I was confused until I realized I was tasting my own blood. My lips must have split in the night. I stepped out of bed with lips stained red and walked out onto the balcony. The palace was built on a hill like Tyre, but instead of looking down onto clean streets, merchants, and sailors coming in from the bright sea, I looked onto a dirty city. The hills surrounding it were covered in olive groves, but even their green leaves looked dull compared to home. I looked down to the level directly below mine and saw a street dog—thin as a blade and obviously terrified—being chased out of the palace by a servant with a torch. The sight made my throat tighten. I whistled, and Topaz, who had been asleep on my bed, trotted over to me. I touched her soft grey ears but didn't look down at her for fear my eyes would fill with tears. Instead, I squinted at the horizon until I could see the distant shimmer that was the sight of the sea my mother had promised. It was barely visible, but it took away the ache in my throat and helped me straighten my shoulders and turn back to my room.

The room had been furnished for my comfort, with a large bed covered in pure white linens, rugs for my feet, and walls inlaid with ivory and precious stones. I walked closer to the wall, wondering what story it held, but saw only leaves and flowers carved into it. I touched a delicate almond blossom but did not feel pleasure in its sweetness. In my room at home, the walls and ceiling had been carved with the stories of the gods—Anat the warrior, with her crown of bone, the genitals of her enemies belted at her waist. I wondered if this passive ornamentation was meant as an insult. Was the king telling me that I was just a wife now, or were the women of Israel truly so delicate? I turned back to the balcony and watched people moving on the street. I saw a woman who carried a basket on her head and a baby on each hip. Her arms were as lean and muscled as a sailor's, and her face was as steady as Anat's. I turned from her and touched the almond blossom again. An insult, then. I turned away from it, desperate to see something from Tyre, from home, and I caught sight of my conch shell. A maid had placed it on the low table beside my bed, and I picked it up, turning it under my fingers. It was the only unbroken conch I had ever found during walks with my father as a child. It was pale pink and smooth as silk inside, but spiky and ridged on the outside. I smoothed my finger along its interior until Topaz whined at my feet, and I turned reluctantly to her. She wanted to be fed. I called out, and a moment later servants appeared in the room, one helping me to dress, while another fed Topaz.

Sapphira entered the room, and I felt some slight relief as I looked at her. Tanith had been right. We had not been parted.

After I told my father that I would go to Israel, I had returned to my rooms, utterly exhausted. I had found Sapphira there, waiting for me. I knew as soon as I saw her face that she had heard where I was to be sent.

"I have told him I will go," I said quietly. I felt my face crumple as I spoke the words, and I turned away from her, crawling into my bed. She climbed in beside me, and we lay side by side as we had since we were children. "Israel," I said. "Israel." I repeated the word, trying to make it sound less foreign, less rough on my tongue. Sapphira did not try to placate me. She knew words would not be enough. "You'll come with me," I said. It came out as a command, even though I meant it as a question. She'd always said she would never leave me. But *Israel*. Neither of us had planned for that. Yet I did not know what I would do without her.

"Yes," Sapphira said softly.

"It will not be as we imagined," I said, suddenly wanting to make sure that she understood.

"We will be together," Sapphira said, cutting me off and folding her hand into mine. "*That* was what we always imagined."

And she had done as she'd promised, traveling with me to Israel without a complaint or word of regret.

"How did you sleep?" she asked now, breaking into my thoughts, returning me to my new room.

"Well enough," I said, knowing that if I began to complain about Israel, I would never stop. "I can look at the sea from my window," I added, trying to think of something pleasant to say.

Sapphira's dark eyebrow arched, but she only said, "The wedding feasts start tonight. As you know, each of the next seven days is full of feasts and ceremonies. Then on the seventh day, you will be wed to Ahab."

"Yes?" I said, wondering why she was repeating this to me. It was all anyone had talked about for months.

"You need to be well rested," she said. "If there's something wrong with your rooms that is keeping you from sleep . . ."

"I slept fine," I snapped, breaking my lip open again. "My lip just keeps bleeding because of this damned dry air."

Sapphira's face softened. Finally, she said, "I know it's not home, Bel." She held a little glass jar out to me. "Here's a salve for your lips and hands. It'll help relieve the cracking until you get used to it here."

I took the salve, smoothing it onto my lips. It was red as clay and soothed my skin so that I sighed with relief.

"Seaweed," Sapphira said, nodding to the jar. "I thought it would smell like home."

I nodded but didn't say anything, just placed it on a low table where I kept other oils. "I would like to speak with the king's scribe."

Sapphira looked surprised. "If there's something you need written, you only have to ask," she said, pulling the reed pen from where she kept it behind her ear.

"I know," I said. "But it is the king's scribe who will write our wedding song. I want to make sure it's done properly."

Sapphira nodded, though I could tell she was displeased. "I'll send someone to fetch him right away."

I was sitting at the small table by the wall, trying to break open the skin of a pomegranate, when a deep voice startled me: "Your Highness." The king's scribe was standing near my breakfast table, boldly close. "It's better to eat the seeds one by one," he said, holding his fingers out in imitation. They were long, and the tips were still stained black as they'd been the day before. Sapphira, who was sitting beside me, raised an eyebrow but said nothing.

"Do you never wash?" I said, waving my fingers before dipping them into the bowl of water at my table. The water turned pink from the juice of the fruit, and for a moment I was overwhelmed with feeling. It reminded me of the sunrise hitting the white walls of the palace at home.

"After a while, the ink won't wash away," he said, breaking me from my reverie. I found the accents of other Israelites difficult to understand, but his voice had a depth that the others didn't. It was melodic, like each word he spoke was a poem, a song. He dipped his hands in the bowl, but when he lifted his fingers, they shone as black as though he'd placed them in ink instead of water.

"That does not happen to Sapphira," I said, looking at her fingers.

"I am careful," she said quietly, an almost imperceptible smile on her face. The scribe flushed, and I wondered what it would be like to wear ink as he did, to be constantly reminded of his triumphs—his failures. The thought made me uneasy, so I said, "You stand too close," and he shifted back a step. "Scribe—" I started, then looked at Sapphira and felt ashamed. I began again. "First, tell me your name and title."

"I am Elijah the Tishbite," he said, inclining his head. "Head scribe of King Omri of Israel."

His words were full of importance, but his voice was mild, as if he did not care overmuch for what he said.

"Elijah. I wish to see the song you wrote. The wedding song," I added when he looked confused.

His eyebrows rose, but I could not tell if it was in question or reproach. It was maddening to look at him and not understand his thoughts. Most men—men like Omri and Ahab—had never had to hide anything. Surprise, lust, anger—all were acceptable on the faces of kings. But the man in front of me—Elijah—wore his face as smooth and blank as a woman's. An important trait in a scribe, I supposed, but one that needled me.

"I have not finished it." Elijah took a skin of leather from the deep pockets of his robes but did not hold it out to me. "The ceremony has not yet begun, and neither has the feasting—"

"I am aware of when my wedding begins," I said with annoyance. "It will be sung on the seventh day, and I wish to read it before I am too occupied," I said, trying to smile prettily, the way my mother did.

"The king does not ask to see songs before they are sung. *He* trusts me."

The man emphasized *he* as if it were all that mattered, and it galled me. I stood, and my gold bangles caught the light and shone in his eyes. He shifted so that he was no longer blinded, and I saw something like amusement in his eyes, which needled me even more. I held out my hand. I did not need to say that *I* did not trust him. When he saw that I would not give way, he sighed and finally held the skin out to me.

He had written with a strong, clear hand. I could see by how he'd labored over the piece that he took great pride in his work: there were already fine marks in the leather where he had cut out words or phrases. His writing was much more pleasant to look at than my own, and I felt a swell of jealousy over his beautiful script as I touched the edge of the leather. I took my knife out of my pocket, thinking only to mark a troublesome phrase with the point, but the scribe obviously thought I meant to change it, because he said, "No!" and closed his fingers around my right hand. Sapphira gasped when he touched me, knowing that I did not let anyone touch my ruined hand, much less a man I did not know. I saw fleeting fear in Elijah's face, but still, he did not release me. I could have simply turned the knife and pared away one of his fingers for his daring, but I was pleased by his devotion to the song, so I merely stared at him until he released his grip.

"I have been laboring over it for months," he said flatly.

"I do not wish to ruin such craftsmanship," I said, flashing my teeth. "But it can be improved." I could feel rather than see Sapphira's smile, and I could tell she was happy that I was badgering someone other than her over a song. Elijah's eyes sparked with annoyance, but I ignored his obvious anger. "Here." I pointed to the line. " 'Forget your people and your father's house.' "

"The king requested that line," Elijah said. "I cannot change it except at his will." But he frowned as he said it, and I thought he knew it wrecked the rhythm of the line below it.

I sat back for a moment, knowing I could not change a line the king had requested, then quickly pointed to another. "Here you say 'city.' Name it. Name Tyre." Elijah bent his head, and I could feel the warmth of his body near mine. Finally, he nodded. "You end it well," I added, as a sop to his vanity. " 'I will perpetuate your memory through all generations.' "

"The memory of the king," Elijah added, even as his eyes swung to the beginning of the verse, which mentioned the princess of Tyre.

"Of course," I said. "Who else would deserve such acclaim?"

He smiled suddenly, a quick flash of strong, white teeth, and I thought of the smile Omri had given me the day before, teeth yellow as sand.

"I don't know many women who can read," he said.

"Then you don't know many women."

"I grew up in the country," Elijah said. "No one there could read. Man or woman."

Perhaps I should have been ashamed, but instead I was annoyed, as though he were trying to catch me out. I knew plenty of women in Tyre—women who worked, women who were servants—who knew how to read. "How did you become the king's scribe, then?" I said, more to change his line of thought than out of any real interest.

"I was raised by my mother," he said. "My father was the bastard nephew of the king. Omri arranged for me to be sent to school to learn to become a scribe." I realized as he spoke that it must have been his royal blood that made him so easy and informal with me. Elijah turned toward Sapphira. "And how did a woman become a scribe?"

I was about to rebuke him, but Sapphira just smiled. "I have the most beautiful writing in Tyre," she said. "And the princess and I grew up together. As princess royal of Tyre, she does not have time to write her own letters or reports. I do it for her." Sapphira held a sheaf of papyrus out to Elijah.

"It is indeed fine," he said. "Though I do not think it is better than mine."

"You use too much pressure when you cut away words," Sapphira said quietly, glancing at the song Elijah had handed to me.

Elijah raised an eyebrow. "And you—"

I waved my hand, cutting him off. I was not interested in a competition between the scribes. "And what did they teach you here?" I said, curious myself at how his writing was so beautiful.

Elijah turned to me slowly with a frown. "I was apprenticed to a master scribe by the time I was ten years old. I was taught all the usual things: how to make ink from charcoal and gum, how to fashion a pen out of reeds and hold it lightly between the fingers."

I fisted my hand even though he could not have known about the mounded skin there, my white-knuckled grip.

"We learned how to scrape an animal skin clean so that we could write on it, how to make cuts with a knife so small it was impossible to see." He looked at the silver knife lying on the table. "Mostly, though, we wrote from dawn to dusk." He flicked his hand. "I rubbed the skin on my thumb raw from holding the pen." He touched his thumb, and I pictured him as a child, a boy, crying, perhaps, from the pain in his hands.

Sapphira opened her own hand, and I was surprised that it was full of calluses. "It does hurt, at first," she said softly.

He nodded, and I saw his shoulders relax, as though this moment of kinship was enough for him to let down his guard.

"And did you also learn?" Elijah said to me, looking at my knife.

My hand began to throb, but I said simply, "We were all taught to write."

"And yet you have your own scribe." His voice lifted at the end, as if he were questioning me, and my hand throbbed more.

"It befits my station," I said simply, not wishing to reveal my ruined hand.

He nodded but didn't look convinced. "What was the first thing you learned?" he asked us.

For a moment I was not going to answer his brazen question, but I wanted to speak of my home, of Tyre, so I said, "We learned to write the story of Anat." I closed my eyes and recited: "'Once there was a goddess called Anat, who wore a crown of bone around her brow. She was the bravest of all the gods and rescued her beloved brother from the death god, Mot.'" I'd been young when I had first written the story down and had not yet known the shame of my deformed letters, had only marveled at the shining ink spreading across the page.

"Anat," Elijah said, clapping his teeth together strangely, as though he'd never heard of.

"The goddess Anat," I said, emphasizing the smoothness of her name. "Surely you know of Anat?"

"I know of only one God, Yahweh."

"One god in Israel," Sapphira said. "In Tyre, there are many."

"We grow up with their stories. Astarte, the mother of all. Her husband, El. Anat, Mot, Melqart." I pulled my medallion over my head and gave it to Elijah. "Astarte," I said, enunciating each syllable, as one would to a child.

Elijah passed his thumb over her face. "She looks like you," he said quietly.

The gentleness in his voice felt like pity. I ignored his words, shifting instead back to his scrolls. "I should like to see everything you write for the king."

Elijah hesitated. "The king rarely asks—"

"The king is used to the daily doings of his kingdom and how they are recorded," I said. "I wish to become familiar with them. I wish to know what the scribes are writing about me. About my family." I smiled my too-wide smile. *Let him think I am going for his throat. Let him fear me.* "I only ask that you come to my rooms each evening, so that I might read what you have written that day. You will make any corrections I require."

He must have heard the dismissal in my voice, but he did not hand over his scrolls as I expected, nor did he bow and go. Instead, he ran his fingers over Astarte's face again before handing the medallion back to me.

"You will not be punished for it, if that is your concern," I said, clenching my hands into fists behind me. I thought of how my mother's name had not been in her own wedding song, how she would be remembered for only her son, and my palm began to throb. I would not follow the path of my mother and the women before her. "I will tell the king that it is my wish."

Elijah hesitated but finally looked me in the eyes. "I follow the will of the crown," he said as he bowed to me.

CHAPTER 4

I found the days of ceremony and feasting that surrounded the wedding tiresome. Each day my maids dressed me in fine robes adorned with gold and jewels, painted patterns on my skin and lips. After the fifth day, the kohl around my eyes had begun to irritate my skin and my head felt heavy from keeping my chin up under the weight of the gold. By the seventh and last day of the wedding, I was weary of all the festivities. I did not complain, though, not even to Sapphira, who I barely spoke to during those days. We had different duties for the wedding. I had to sit through hours of prayers and dancing and feasts, and as my scribe, Sapphira had to quickly note down each moment so that she could write it properly later. Each night we both fell into bed too tired to speak.

On the last night of feasting, I found myself once more beside Ahab and decided I must make him speak to me. I had questions I wanted answered, and he was not attentive in the way I expected, in the way in which a Tyrian man would have been. When I spoke to him, he answered me in grunts or sighs, and his eyes were constantly traveling around the room, as though looking to rest his eyes on anything but me. When he did speak, it was only to Elijah, who sat on his right. I thought it strange that a scribe should sit at the table with us during a feast. Even Sapphira did not sit near me, but instead roamed around the room, pen in hand, eyes watchful.

"Why does your scribe sit so near my lord?" I said, hoping that the question might startle him into speaking to me.

"Where else should he be?" Ahab said, without looking at me.

"My scribe is too busy recording the day to sit," I said, catching sight of Sapphira, who stood at the corner of the room, carefully watching the crowd.

"He is my cousin," Ahab said. "I want him here."

"I do not need to walk around the room to do my duty," Elijah said, cutting across Ahab and leaning toward me. "Perhaps your scribe is less skilled."

I gave him a flat look, deciding whether I would speak to him at all. "How are you to record the day correctly if you do not note it now?" I said finally. "You could be making errors."

"I do not make errors," he said. "I remember everything perfectly."

I turned toward Ahab, making my voice soft. "I would like to see what your scribe writes, my lord," I said with a smile, putting a hand on his knee. "In order to make sure it properly reflects your glory."

"It is not necessary," Ahab said with a deep sigh, as though already weary of me. "I trust him." He clapped a hand affectionately on the scribe's shoulder.

I lowered my eyes, trying to appear the submissive wife. "I trust your judgment, my lord," I said. "But in Tyre, my father always had my mother review the scribe's reports each evening, to be sure they properly reflected him and his family." It was an outright lie. My mother, as far as I knew, had never once read a report of one of my father's scribes, but I was not willing to blindly trust what this Israelite was writing about me. "I only wish to—"

"Yes, woman," Ahab said, cutting me off. "If you wish to read his reports, then send for him in the evenings, after the day's events are done." I saw the look of irritation he threw at Elijah, but I just sat back in my chair, pleased that I had gotten my way. I would be recorded properly in the kingdom's writings, no matter how annoyed it made their prince.

I shifted slightly so that I was closer to Ahab's ear. "Have you ever been to Tyre, my lord?" I said, hoping to keep him talking to me.

"No," Ahab said, without looking at me. His avoidance of my gaze made irritation prickle under my skin. He should prostrate himself with gratitude for our marriage. No matter what my father said, I knew Israel was getting the better bargain. "I have no wish to go to such a wicked place."

"Tyre is not a wicked place," I said with a laugh, even as my blood boiled. I wanted to drag my nails across his cheek for his words about my home.

"You worship false gods," Ahab said casually, as if just saying the words made them true.

"What do you know of our gods?" I said, trying to keep my voice light.

"I am not as stupid as you think," Ahab said stiffly. "I have been taught of your gods—Astarte, El, Anat, Mot." He pronounced their names properly but with disgust. "I am not interested in learning more." His voice was firm, but he seemed to have forgotten me an instant later, his searching eyes flitting across the room again before he gave an almost imperceptible sigh and turned back to a piece of meat glistening with fat on his plate.

I took a sip of wine and studied my new husband carefully. He looked as I'd imagined, with a square, weathered face though he had not yet reached his thirtieth year, and muscled arms and legs as thick and strong as an old tree. He did not act as I'd imagined, though. His voice when he spoke was soft: not quite diffident, but not commanding in the way of kings. He did not have a boisterous crowd of men around him either. I was used to soldiers who drank and cursed and belched moving in a crowd around their commander, but Ahab, when he spoke at all, spoke quietly to Elijah. They were obviously close, perhaps not as close as Sapphira and I, but good friends who laughed and jostled each other with long familiarity.

I did not realize I was staring at him until Elijah returned my stare. Feeling disconcerted, I returned my gaze to Ahab but could not find much more in his face than I had already discerned. Even though he was Crown Prince and would be king of Israel, he was not where the power lay. I looked toward Omri, who was as surrounded by courtiers as Ahab was not.

Before I had come to Israel, I had sent a trusted maid ahead of me. I knew Omri would have spies among the maids who would serve me in Israel, and so I made sure to have my own to report of the doings of the court. Dido had a sweet, soft face and had been my maid since I was a child. She was smart and devoted to me, and because she looked so young and naive, people tended to speak openly around her as they wouldn't for someone else. Dido had arrived in Israel in enough time to send me several detailed letters explaining how Omri ran his court and the history behind it.

Omri's lips were purple with wine, and his laughter was loud and raucous—the childlike laugh of a king who had held power for many long years. There was no queen at his side—Ahab's mother had died some years ago, and Omri had not replaced her, preferring—I had learned—to spend time with his concubines in the women's quarters. Dido had mentioned briefly that Omri had a group of men he called his advisors who were often with him, and I looked now for them. I had learned how to sniff out the powerful from growing up among my father's court, had made a game of trying to discern ministers from princes and generals, and the powerful in Omri's court were easier even to find than in my father's. They were not the men who were clustered around him, clinging to him like dogs desperate for scraps. They were not at the head table with us at all, but rather they sat at a round table apart from the rest of the feasting crowd, speaking quietly among themselves. There was a certain severity in their features, and their backs were straight and forbidding, blocking anyone else from approaching them. The powerful often sat like that, ignoring anyone beneath their notice. Omri glanced at them every so often, as if seeking their approval, and once, when a striking man with a beard as white as seafoam nodded at him, the flush on Omri's cheeks grew.

I was unsurprised that Omri was such a king, one who needed approval from others for the things he did and said. It was why his nation floundered while Tyre flourished. My father had advisors, of course, but he did not look to them for approval. His decisions were his alone, and he stood or fell from them on his own.

Still, I thought. *It is good to know where the power in Israel really lies*. It was the advisors I would have to convince to make my plans a reality. For I did have plans for Israel. Sapphira and I had talked of them long into each night as we had prepared to come. My ideas for turning Israel into a great nation started with temples and slowly included granaries and markets, schools and new palaces. I knew what I could do would be limited as long as Omri was king and I would not make the mistake of trying to change everything at once. Instead, I would act with the slow, sinuous movement of a snake, mesmerizing them before I struck.

I turned away from Omri and back to Ahab. As distasteful as it was, I knew what would give me a foothold in Israel: an heir for the prince. I had no desire for a child, but I would grow fat and round and slow for a time if it would give me the power I wanted over the nation. The power to make it like Tyre. A kingdom in my own image.

Even as I thought of my night ahead with Ahab, I realized that the sun had fallen and evening had crept in. I was not the only one who noticed the change. I saw several of Omri's advisors look between me and Ahab. One of the men who had clustered around Omri licked his lips, then leaned in to whisper in Omri's ear. Omri turned toward me and smiled, mouth dripping with grease from the fowl he'd just bitten into.

I felt a leap in my stomach. Not fear, exactly, but . . . unease. I knew that some men were brutal when they bedded virgins. I did not want the pain, but I did want the child who might come of it. A hand gripped my shoulder, and I knew it was Sapphira. She had, as always, known my thoughts.

"I think it is time for the feast to end. Our prince and princess are surely tired and must want their beds." Omri glanced at his advisors, and the white-bearded man gave another short nod before Omri turned away and gave me a flirtatious smile.

I could feel Ahab's arm grow rigid beside me as his father spoke, and I wondered if it was from pleasure or anger. I saw him glance once more to the corners of the room before giving a small shake of his head and rising. He turned toward me, offering me his arm, and Sapphira squeezed my shoulder one last time before I went to bed my new husband.

◎◎◎◎

I was not unprepared when the time came to bed Ahab.

I have heard the stories of our temples, that the priestesses taught the women of Tyre the art of seduction. That every woman was required to become a temple prostitute to appease the lust of our gods and their followers. What idiocy. Our gods do not need the flesh of mortals to be satisfied. And Omri, like all men, asked my father for proof of my virginity. If such a thing was asked of the princess royal, it was asked of every woman in Tyre.

But yes. I knew more than the women of Israel. How could I not? They went to their marriage beds fearful and trembling, with only the knowledge of the sounds their parents made in the dark. If they were lucky, they had seen a buck mount a goat.

In Tyre, we did not leave our women alone and unknowing in the dark.

One of the few things my mother had ever taught me had been about pleasing men. "It is good to please your husband," my mother said. "But if you make him please you as well, that is far better."

I frowned. "Wouldn't it be better to be done with it?" I was young when she taught me, and the thought of pleasing a husband was far from my mind, a distant chore only to be endured.

Mother smiled. "Some think so. But, Bel, listen." She grasped my chin, forcing me to look into her eyes. "Every man remembers the power he felt when he made you groan. He remembers it every time you look at him like this." She looked down, her eyes demure and hooded like a cat's. "He remembers your sighs and thinks he is in control. But you are the one who can ask for anything with only the sounds of your breaths in the dark."

I remembered her words that night when Ahab entered the room. "Won't you come to bed, my lord?" I said to my husband, unafraid.

It was that lack of fear, I think, that they could not forget. Later they would whisper, *She didn't tremble as she spoke, but lidded her eyes like a snake and slipped off her robe to expose her nakedness without fear.*

I wonder if all that came might have been avoided if I had trembled. If what they wanted was for me to be like their women. To be afraid in the dark.

◉◉◉◉

When I woke the morning after the wedding, Ahab was gone and my whole body ached. I wished, desperately, for a swim in the sea. I wished to taste salt on my lips, to close my eyes and float, knowing that no matter where the tide pulled me, I would open my eyes and see the white walls of Tyre.

I rubbed my hands over my heavy eyes and saw the ink that spiraled over them. My maids had painted me with it on the first day of the wedding. I wondered if the designs that were painted all over my body—blossoms and stars, waves and a crescent moon—made me look strange to the Israelites. More foreign than I already was. The thought made me feel prickly with discomfort, so I quickly rose and left the prince's chamber, calling for Sapphira as soon as I entered my rooms. Sapphira appeared from the inner chamber and gave me a questioning look.

"It was fine," I said briskly. I knew I should have blushed like the new bride I was, touch wonderingly at the red marks his lips had made on my neck, but I had too much to do to think longingly of my new husband. "There was some pain, but not much. Yes," I said as I saw Sapphira's mouth open, cutting off her next question. "I made sure the maids saw the blood on the sheets this morning."

Sapphira nodded. It was the true proof of my virginity for the king. "Did you . . . are you in pain?" Sapphira asked.

"No," I said. I knew what she was asking. "Ahab was . . . distracted." I had been surprised by that. I knew men were often rough with virgins, but Ahab's movements had been distant, his eyes far away the whole time. I could tell that he had not wanted to feel anything, but I had used the tricks my mother had taught me, and he had groaned with pleasure by the end. "Hopefully I'll be pregnant by harvest," I said, touching my stomach. The thought made me feel ill. I turned to the small table where Sapphira usually worked, no longer wishing to speak of Ahab.

"You're out of ink." I waved to the empty pot. "And I wish you to write a letter."

"I'm sorry, Bel," Sapphira said. Her face was drawn. She would have been up late, writing down the events of the past days. "I meant to make more, but I haven't had a moment. I will do it now."

"It's no matter." I put my hand on her shoulder. "Sit. Rest. I will make it myself." I waved away her protestations. "Ink made from Tyrian charcoal shall bring me close to home again," I said, tucking my skirts up so that I could move freely.

It was simple to mix the charcoal and gum together. Sapphira knew her work well, and so she'd already ground the charcoal so that it was as smooth as powder. It smelled sweet, and I knew she must have taken it from the temple of Astarte that was in the palace at home. They always burned the sweetest wood there, cedar and cypress. The gum too was thick and honey-colored, gathered, I was sure, by her own hand. I stirred them with water and left the mixture to thicken, but I still felt a strange energy in my limbs, and my eyes roamed the room until they fell on the jars that contained the ground sea snails that lived only in Tyre. I'd meant to boil down the snails into purple dye to make a robe for Ahab, but he had plenty of fine robes sewn with gold and embedded with precious stones. He did not need one more, even if it was purple. And with the amount of purple needed to dye a whole robe, I could create a fine purple ink that would last me the rest of my life if I was careful. I smiled at the thought of my life being written down with ink the color of kings and set to work. Soon, I had the ground sea snails boiling away in tin vessels, and though my hands were empurpled and cheeks red from the stoked flames, I was content.

"What sorcery is this?" The voice was mild, but I turned quickly, the peace that had filled me dissipating at his words. It would not do for someone, anyone, to accuse the princess of Tyre—*of Israel*, I reminded myself with a weary disappointment—of sorcery.

"Don't be foolish," I said as Elijah entered the room. "I'm only mixing ink for Sapphira."

He nodded, and a smile flickered over his face, which surprised me. He had been teasing me. No one spoke to me like that, and I wasn't sure if his familiarity was a comfort or an imposition. "I don't recognize this," he said, peering into the tin pots, then coughing and wrinkling his nose like a child.

I laughed. The ground sea snails smelled vile when they cooked down, like seaweed drying in the sun. "Sea snails," I said, as Elijah coughed again.

"Charcoal is much cheaper and does not stink like a pig's pen," Elijah said, stepping back so that he could no longer smell the snails.

"It also does not shine purple in the sun." I frowned, beginning to feel foolish at my wish to create purple ink. "Why have you come?"

"The prince has asked that I show you his wedding gift," Elijah said.

"And he sends you?" I raised an eyebrow. "Why not a maid or eunuch?"

"He wishes me to record your . . . delight. When you see the gift," Elijah said.

"Well," I said, looking around for the gift. "Where is it?"

"It is in the city," he said. "But nearby."

I sighed. I was tired and did not want to walk in the city, but I supposed I must show some enthusiasm for a gift from my new husband—and besides, I was curious. Sapphira stood as I did, but I saw the way she swayed, obviously exhausted from the previous days' events.

"Stay here," I said, brushing my hand over her arm. "Sleep. I will tell you about it once we return."

Sapphira nodded reluctantly, and I followed Elijah from the room and out into the city.

I was pleased Elijah didn't slow as we walked, but let me match him gait for gait. The palace was built on an acropolis, and the capital spread out around it, so we walked downhill, our sandals kicking up puffs of dust. We stopped when a large herd of goats crossed our path, and while we waited, I turned to look at the palace. The brown stone looked better in the morning light, the large blocks fitted neatly together by Tyrian craftsmen. When Omri had constructed the palace, he had sent for stonemasons from Tyre. Columns towered against the sky, and though they did not suit my taste, there was no doubt they made the palace look imposing.

The sun was hot, making the air ripple, and for a moment it looked like there was a huge pool just outside the palace. My mouth watered at the sight of the cool water, and just the thought of diving in made me feel refreshed, made my body momentarily relax. I blinked as a shadow crossed the sun, and the image vanished, leaving only a patch of bare land where an oasis had stood. The loss of it made me draw in a breath, and grief rose as strong as bile in my throat. I bit down on the inside of my cheek and inhaled through my nose until the grief cleared. *I am the princess*, I told myself. *If I want a pool to be made, it shall be. I will talk to Ahab about it tonight.*

"My lady?" Elijah said. The goats had gone, and I wondered how long I'd been staring back at the palace like a foolish child.

"Let us continue," I said, striding forward. We walked through a market where merchants shouted out their wares, holding out lengths of linen and baskets of eggs, jugs of wine, and cages full of flapping doves. The air was heady with fig and almond blossoms, but the sweetness made my head swim. I wanted to turn back, but I would not show weakness in front of the king's scribe, so I continued to march on until Elijah pressed a gentle hand to my arm, forcing me to stop. The street was blessedly shadowed from the sun, the stones cool, and I drew in a deep breath as I looked where he pointed.

Before me sat a temple, built, I knew instantly, from Tyrian hands. It was small, but each of the white stones had been carved and fitted with care. The base was etched with symbols I knew well, intricate stars and mountains, Astarte's crescent moon, and even dolphins swimming in a calm sea. The doors stood open, but I could see they were made from fine, light wood, carefully set into the stone. It looked like home. Like Tyre.

"The prince wanted you to have a place to worship your gods," Elijah said. "So he had a temple built for them—for her—Astarte," he said, pronouncing her name clumsily but with an obvious effort to do it properly. I clapped my hands together like a child and laughed. Elijah smiled. "I'm sure the prince will be pleased that you like it," he said.

As we entered the temple my shoulders relaxed. It smelled like home too: like cool, white stone; cedar; and salt. It was larger than it had looked from the outside, set with columns and arches that soared toward the heavens. There was a large statue of Astarte placed in an alcove at the back, but it was to the altar I rushed, to her face carved into ivory. It was plainly done, without precious stones or gold leaf, but it was beautiful. I leaned my forehead against hers and pressed my fingers into the stone. She smiled slightly, the smile of a mother, a friend, and for the first time since arriving in Israel, I felt some sense of belonging.

"Who is she?" Elijah asked tentatively after we had left the temple and were climbing the hill back to the palace. "She's the one on your medallion?"

"She is the queen of heaven," I said. The sun shone hot as we walked up the hill, but it didn't feel as harsh as it had on the way down.

"But what does that mean? What does she do?" Elijah spoke softly, as if he were afraid of being overheard.

"Do you truly know so little of the gods?" I said.

Elijah's face tightened. "It is as I said. There are no 'gods' in Israel. Only Yahweh. We are taught that other gods are false. An . . . abomination." He said the words slowly, as though afraid I would strike him, but I laughed.

"How can they be any more of an abomination than your god? Do not all gods ask for burnt offerings and beautiful temples? Don't all peoples pray and ask the gods for peace and prosperity, for children who are hale and hearty and for rain to fall upon their fields? Why should it matter if I pray to Astarte and you to Yahweh?"

Elijah was quiet for so long that I thought he was angry at my words, but then he said, "Will you tell me a story of Astarte?"

As he spoke, we passed the huge temple of Yahweh. It was many times larger than the temple Ahab had built for me, and I wondered why. Though I was grateful for a place to worship, the size of it suddenly felt like a slight, as much as the almond blossoms engraved on the walls of my room. I knew the stories of the ancient King Solomon building the temple for Yahweh, and I suddenly thirsted for the people of Israel to have the same reverence for the gods of Tyre.

"Long ago the goddess Astarte traveled the world," I said slowly, trying to remember how Shapash used to tell the story. "She swam in the deepest oceans, climbed the highest mountains, slept in deep, dark valleys. Where she trailed her fingers, vines and trees grew. Lotus blossoms fell from her hands and became all the rivers and streams of the world. Women who had been barren came to her, and she touched their bellies and filled them with life. Then, one night, Astarte saw a bright light in the sky. She was the daughter of an ancient sky god, but even she had never seen a star fall from the heavens. She followed the star and caught it just before it hit the earth. She held it in her hands and knew that if she planted it and tended it as one tends a seed, it would become a great city, a great people."

"What did she do with it?" Elijah's voice was that of a wide-eyed child, and I smiled despite myself. There was something compelling about his earnestness, a certain resonance in his voice that made me want to share with him as I did with Sapphira.

"She buried the star and tended it, and from the star grew Tyre. That is why my city always glows, even on the darkest nights."

"A good story," Elijah said, after a long moment.

"It is not just a story," I said as my palm throbbed. "It is the truth."

"A city cannot be made from a star," Elijah said, his voice reproachful.

"And shepherd boys cannot kill giants."

Elijah frowned. "But King David . . . we know that story is true. Yahweh told us—"

"And Astarte told *us*," I said, voice sharp as a piece of glass.

We walked silently until we crested the hill and neared the place where I'd seen the mirage of a pool. *A pool*, I thought. *I will build a pool. Then, once I can swim, I will have a clear mind. I will learn how to teach this man. How to reach the stubborn people of Israel.*

"Come to my rooms this evening," I said to Elijah as we entered the palace. "I wish to make changes to your recording of the fifth day of the wedding. And," I added hesitantly, "if you wish, I will tell you another story of the gods."

CHAPTER 5

There was blood on my sheets. I had felt ill for a few days and had hoped it meant I was with child. But in the six months since we had arrived in Israel, my bleeding returned with each new moon as it always had.

"It will happen when the goddess wills it," Sapphira said, looking up from where she sat at a small table in the corner, marking something down on a sheet of papyrus.

I frowned at her. "Perhaps there is some potion I can take to make a child take root," I said.

Sapphira raised an eyebrow. "There are potions you could take, but I already spoke with the midwife at your request. She said it is too soon to worry."

I sighed and touched my flat stomach. "I hoped to tell Ahab the news today during our meal. I wanted to ask him to put forth my plan for a new temple in Jezreel. After all, if we have our new palace there, I will need a temple to worship."

"I thought the site of the new palace has not been agreed upon?" Sapphira said, looking up at me.

"Not yet." I frowned, throwing my ruined sheets on the floor where I could not see them. "But eventually they will agree that building a palace in Jezreel is better for us. It is less wet there than it is here during the rainy season, and the trade route from the Jordan to the coastal plains runs right through it. It is the perfect place for a second palace. We might be able to build a market even larger than the one here in Samaria. That is, if Enosh will stop whispering in Omri's ear." I fisted my palm. "Enosh has less wit than a camel and the face of an ass, and I do not know why Omri listens to him."

Sapphira groaned as Elijah came into the room. He grinned at her and gave a little bow that made his hair fall into his eyes. "As predicted," he said, "'less wit than a camel and the face of an ass'—I told you she would find a way to insult both his face and his intelligence in the same breath." Elijah sat down opposite Sapphira and held out something. Sapphira made a face but accepted the little glass jar Elijah handed to her.

"What," I said, trying to make my voice angry instead of amused, "are you two doing?"

"Elijah made the first wager, Bel," Sapphira said, looking ashamed. "It's just that you've been complaining about Enosh so much lately, and we realized that you often compare him to . . ."

She trailed away as Elijah said, "To an animal! Sapphira didn't believe you would insult him as harshly as you have, so we made a wager on your next condemnation of Enosh. Whoever lost has to boil the black ink." He gestured to the tin pot that sat in the corner of the room near Sapphira's other supplies. They both hated to boil the ink in the hot months because it required standing over the fire for long stretches of time. "I suppose I just know you better." Elijah eased back in his seat and grinned at me while Sapphira rose and tipped the contents of the bottle into the tin pot, calmly ignoring Elijah's words.

Elijah came to my rooms each night as I requested, and a companionable friendship had formed between the three of us. He and Sapphira often laughed together or consulted each other on their writings. I was happy for their easy closeness, because other than Sapphira, Elijah was my only real companion in Israel.

"How can you know me better?" I said absently, going to sit at the table. "Sapphira and I were born on the same night and shared a cot for years." I looked up, expecting a response from Elijah but caught him staring at me instead. His gaze made me feel uncomfortable. My skin prickled at the weight of it, so I flicked his ear as I might a child. He yelped, and the strange feeling broke. "What do you think Ahab's objections to the temple will be?" I said. "And how can I overcome them?"

Elijah blew out a breath. I often asked him questions about Ahab, and though he did not often give me outright answers, he would at least help me understand Ahab's mind. "You know what his objections will be. He built the temple here as a gift to his new bride, so she would have somewhere to worship her . . . gods," Elijah said, voice dry, and I knew he had been about to say "false gods" but had not wanted me to rebuke him for it. "That does not mean that he wants temples across the country."

"I will visit the new palace as often as he will," I said. "He will surely insist a temple is built for Yahweh; therefore I don't see why one shouldn't be built for Astarte. There can be no harm in one more temple," I said, trying to smile winningly at Elijah as I might at Ahab.

Elijah raised an eyebrow. "You can't trick me, Bel," he said. A part of me wanted to rebuke him for his casual use of my name, but I liked hearing it from him, liked that someone other than Sapphira called me by the name of my childhood. "I know you want to flood this land with your temples."

I wanted to stomp my foot like a child, but instead I just inhaled a quick breath and said through gritted teeth, "I do not understand why Yahweh is so insistent on all the worship of Israel being focused on him. Surely he does not need to be so greedy? Besides, women often want to pray to a goddess, a mother, for . . ."

I trailed away, and Sapphira grasped my hand. She knew how worried I was that I was still not pregnant.

Elijah sighed. "Ahab won't be won over by winning smiles and honeyed words," he said. "Women have lusted after Ahab his whole life, and they're better at sweet smiles than you."

I heard Sapphira groan, but she didn't have time to say anything before I jumped up from the table. "And what *exactly* is wrong with my smile?"

Elijah didn't look impressed. "You're a beautiful woman, Jezebel, you know that. But there's something . . . startling about your smile. Perhaps it is too full of teeth."

I heard Sapphira chuckle behind me. "Her mother has been telling her that her whole life," she said. "Once she made Bel stand beside her for hours and practice smiling into a mirror. Eventually Bel threw the mirror and . . ."

Sapphira trailed away at the look I gave her, and I smiled again at Elijah, more widely than before. "Go on," I said, my voice savage. "You were telling me what I might do to tempt Ahab into helping me."

Elijah didn't even flinch at my smile, just laughed and made a sign to ward off evil. "If you ask him about something that interests him: chariots, horses, how to properly plan an encampment for the army . . . then he'll talk for hours and hours." Elijah yawned. "I have sat through many a discussion of how he revolutionized an encampment simply by moving the stew pot. If you ask him to bring up the planned temple in Jezreel after listening to him . . . he's more likely to be willing. Also," he added, "make sure he doesn't know how you plan to expand the temples."

He looked at me as if expecting me to deny it. I did not. "You want me to lie to him?" I taunted instead. "Doesn't your beloved Yahweh speak against falsehoods?"

Elijah only rolled his eyes at my jab at Yahweh. "I did not say to speak falsely to him. I just said don't tell him the extent of your plans. It will frighten him. It will frighten them all," he said, as he headed out of the room, "if they know of your plans for Israel."

I bent my head back over the book I'd been reading, but before I could focus on it, Sapphira spoke. "You trust him." Her voice was soft. "To tell him your plans for the temples."

"It's only Elijah," I said, only barely listening to her.

Sapphira didn't say anything for a long moment, then said, "Just be careful, Bel."

I laughed. "I'm always careful," I said, ignoring the warning in her voice.

Sapphira nodded. "I know. Just remember that he's an Israelite, Bel. He's not of Tyre."

⊚⊚⊚⊚

As I walked toward Ahab's rooms a month or so later, I realized I had never been there on my own before. Usually he came to my rooms to bed me at least once every few days, but lately he had not come. I had been busy working on the plans for the new temples and had not noticed his absence—had not realized until this moment that I had not even seen Ahab at meals or passed him in the corridors. Even today I was only having a meal with him because my maid Dido had found his favorite eunuch and convinced him to ask Ahab to have a meal with me. On my command, Dido had gotten to know the servants, the other women, and she was a favorite of everyone for her quiet voice and quick smile. It would help if I had other allies in the palace—well, if Dido did, at least. I had long ago learned that my presence rarely cheered or comforted those around me.

Ahab's rooms were sparse for those of a crown prince, with little adornment on the walls or floors. The rooms of a solider, much more than of a king. I walked through the entryway and out to the balcony, where I'd requested our meal be set. Ahab was not there when I sat down, and I tapped my foot against the floor as I waited at a table laid with meats and cheeses, fresh bread and wine. I poured myself a glass of wine and had time to drink half of it before Ahab stumbled out. My eyes widened as I took him in: Ahab did not usually dress in much finery, but he was always well-groomed. The man who stood before me had an unkempt beard and wild hair. He looked wasted as though he had not eaten in days, his once-mighty arms as thin as saplings. He even had dark circles under his eyes, and he needed to shield his eyes from the day, though there were clouds covering most of the sky.

"My lord?" I said, as he staggered to the couch and nearly fell upon it. I wondered if he was drunk, but I had never seen Ahab drink much. He'd told me once in a rare, unguarded moment that he did not like how wine slowed his movements. That a soldier needed to be ready at a moment's notice. Now, though . . . he did not look like a soldier. He looked like a beggar who had been on the streets for years, not the future king of Israel.

"My lord, what is wrong?" I said as he reached a trembling hand toward the large goblet of wine sitting at his side.

Ahab blinked and looked at me with surprise, as if he had not noticed that I was there until that moment. "Jezebel," he said loudly. "Jezebel. My wife."

I looked around, wishing for a eunuch, a maidservant who might explain Ahab's appearance and behavior to me, but we were alone, with only a few birds wheeling in the sky above us. "Yes, my lord?" I asked.

"My wife," he muttered again, before drinking half the wine in his cup in one long swallow.

"Are you well?" I said, putting my hand on his arm.

He flinched and jerked his arm away, spilling the rest of his wine. The liquid flooded the table, ruining the food, but Ahab did not seem to notice. He raised his head, and for a moment I thought he would roar at me like a wild beast, but finally he just lowered his head, as if it were too heavy to hold up. "Yes, wife," he said finally. "*I* am well."

I knew he was lying, but I also did not know him well enough to probe him further. For a moment I wished that I did, that he would speak to me of his problems. I was, as he said, his wife. But then, I looked into his red-rimmed eyes and felt only disgust. He was weak. Perhaps he had lost at dice the night before. Or perhaps one of his soldiers had disobeyed his command. Either way, it did not really concern me. I knew that he had not wanted to marry me. I had not wanted to marry him. But we were wed now, and I would not lose out on my chance to make my mark on Israel just because my husband had drunk too much wine.

"I haven't seen you in many weeks," I said, trying to keep my voice soft. "But I learned that you received a new chariot that is fast as lightning. Perhaps you would tell me of it?"

Ahab did not look at me. "Chariots," he mumbled. "What use are chariots?"

I felt my temper begin to rise. I did not know what was wrong with him. He had not come to my bed in weeks. It was *his* fault I was not with child yet. And now he wouldn't even look at me. How was I supposed to put my plans into place without Ahab's help?

"I have learned that the king is meeting with his advisors today," I said, deciding to just be forthright. "I was hoping you would put forth my temple plans. For the one that is to be built with the new palace." Perhaps he would not remember that he had not yet agreed to the temple.

Ahab sighed. "I am not going to the king's meeting," he said. "I am too weary."

"It is in an hour's time," I said, looking at the bright sun that still shone behind the silvered clouds. "It will not even be dark before it is over."

"I am too weary," Ahab repeated.

My temper grew even hotter. I wanted to throw my wine in his face. Did he care nothing about improving Israel? *Of course he does not*, I realized, looking at the dark circles under his eyes. Ahab would be king eventually. He had no chance of becoming nameless. He did not have to fight to make his mark on the land. From the moment of his birth until the day of his death he would be remembered. His name would be recorded in the book of kings even if he was a drunkard king who did nothing but sleep with his concubines and throw dice. My palm throbbed, but I fisted my hand around it and closed my eyes, trying to pretend I was standing in the cool sea of Tyre, trying to let my anger float away. I had to be strategic, as Sapphira often counseled me. I could no longer howl and throw tantrums. "I am sorry you are unwell," I said quietly. "Perhaps . . . perhaps you could send me in your stead, my lord. Then I can share their plans with you. On a day when you are feeling less . . . weary."

Ahab picked up a piece of soft cheese and held it up to his mouth.

It dripped with the wine he had spilled, and he did not eat it, just held it between his fingers. After a long moment he squashed it between his fingers. "Go, then," he said. "It does not matter to me what you do."

◎◎◎◎

I took Ahab at his word, leaving him to stew alone as I walked quickly back to my rooms. I dressed in fine robes and had my maids put up my hair, then painted my lips red and lined my eyes with kohl. Ahab might not be tempted by honeyed words and soft smiles, but his father was.

I ignored the whispers that filled the room when I entered it and kept my eyes only on the king. I bowed before him and then smiled. "Majesty," I said, taking care not to show too many teeth.

"Ah, daughter," he said, waving at me to stand. "It is always a pleasure to see your beautiful face."

I kissed him on the cheek and smelled something sour but did not let my face change. "I am here at the behest of your son," I said, keeping my voice gentle. "He was weary today and asked that I sit at your side in his stead." I bit my lip and lowered my eyes. "I did not wish to intrude on your private meeting, but I must do as my lord commands." I raised pleading eyes to Omri and ignored the throbbing in my palm.

Omri hesitated a moment, but then smiled. "Of course you must obey your husband," he said. "You are welcome to join our table. Though I am not sure how much you will be able to understand. We mostly spend our time on figures and long reports from different governors of my cities in Israel."

"I will do my best," I said, smiling sweetly and trying not to retch from the scent of his breath. I took a seat beside him and settled in, laughing when he laughed and agreeing with everything he said until talk finally turned toward the new palace.

Enosh immediately began by telling the king his plans, putting forth a city where he wanted the palace to be located, a location that I knew would only fill his own coffers with gold thanks to the increased trade. I smiled pleasantly at him until he finally paused to draw breath. Then I turned to Omri and said, "My lord, didn't you spend your boyhood playing in the valley of Jezreel? Surely the new palace should be built where you are comfortable?" I laid a hand on his arm, and he beamed at me.

"I don't remember telling you that, my dear. It must be my failing memory from growing old," he said with a little chuckle, as if daring anyone to agree. I smiled back at him and did not tell him that he had never told me about spending time in Jezreel, but that I had recently learned about his youth from Dido, who had befriended Omri's favorite concubine. "I agree with the princess," he said. "We are comfortable in Jezreel. The palace will be built there." I saw Enosh's eyes flash, but he did not protest, as he, like all of us, knew of Omri's petulant temper when anyone questioned his decisions.

"Of course you will construct a new temple for Yahweh in Jezreel," I said smoothly. "And I know you will also build one for Astarte too, so that I may worship there as well." Omri looked unsure, so I added, "Just a small temple, my lord. Only big enough for me and a few others to worship as they will." I touched his arm again, smiling sweetly.

"Yahweh will be angry enough that Ahab built that temple for you here in Samaria," Enosh said quickly. "He commands us to have no foreign gods before him."

I saw Omri hesitate at the words. I rushed to say, "Please, my lord. I only ask this small gift. I am so far from home, and I wish to pray to the gods I grew up with. Yahweh would not mind one small temple—Astarte is surely no match for him, not in Israel." The words were bitter on my tongue as I thought of the power in Astarte's temple, how she had created Tyre, created the very people who had begun civilization, but I swallowed down the bitterness of my own words and just continued to smile.

Slowly, Omri nodded. "Yahweh asks us to welcome strangers," he said. "And it is only one more temple, as the princess says." He patted my hand. "Soon you will have your own children and will not have a moment to think of temples. Until then, you may build your temple in Jezreel."

I ignored the sting at his mention of children, ignored the feel of his soft, moist hands against mine, and just smiled again, making sure I showed no teeth.

◎◎◎◎

I was weary as I made my way back to my rooms, so I took the back corridor that was usually used by servants. I should have felt triumphant; I had successfully placed the palace in Jezreel and had permission to build a temple there, but I only felt as though I wanted to sleep. It was hard to constantly fight with these stubborn Israelites. I was trying to build their land into a worthy kingdom. A place that could be said in the same breath as Tyre. Why couldn't they understand?

I thought of Omri's soft hand, his sour breath as he leaned toward me. If Omri had been a man on the streets of Tyre, I would not have stopped to speak with him, and now I had to bow at his feet. I thought of my mother, how she was a queen and yet would never have gone to the king to beg for a second temple. My mother cared only of her own pleasure—parties and gambling, sailing around the harbor and gossiping with the women of court. She never seemed weary, never seemed to doubt herself or her place there. The court loved her: praised her beauty, her effortless charm and smile. But by the time her bones were dust she would be nothing but a nameless wife of a king.

I am more than my mother, I thought, straightening my back. *Long after I am dust, my name will be remembered.* I turned the corner with this thought ringing in my ears, and so I was momentarily confused by what I saw in front of me. The flickering torch illuminated the corridor and shone on the faces of two people locked in an embrace. They were kissing and I almost turned to go back the way I had come until I realized who I was staring at. I gasped, and Elijah and Sapphira broke apart, turning toward me.

"Bel—" Elijah sounded breathless, ashamed. I felt a burning, sharp in my throat, like I had just swallowed seawater, but it was Sapphira I stared at, Sapphira who met my gaze with a fierce look.

"Come with me," I said, grabbing her wrist and pulling her away from Elijah. I did not look back as we left him alone in the corridor, but I could imagine the way his shoulders drooped, the way his hair fell in front of his eyes, how— I cut off my thoughts, focusing instead on the throbbing in my palm, the anger hot as the midday sun in my chest.

Sapphira followed me dutifully to my rooms, but when I slammed the door and turned on her, her face was unrepentant.

"Explain yourself," I said, in a voice I'd never used on her before. It was commanding, more strident than I'd meant to be, but it kept the anger burning through me and did not let me think of anything else.

"What is there to explain, Bel?" Sapphira said, palms fisted by her sides.

"You are unmarried, and you were—you were kissing—that man—" I said, not wanting to say his name.

Sapphira gave a short laugh. "I have kissed men before, Bel. You have never cared."

"You kissed boys in Tyre," I said. "Boys, not men, not—Elijah."

"You are married to the future king of Israel," Sapphira said, a bite in her every word. "Each month you are angry that you are not pregnant with his child. And it *must* be his." She paused, then spoke softly. "Elijah cannot matter to you."

The ache in my throat returned. Because Sapphira was closer than my sister. She knew what she did when she said he *could not* matter.

"I forbid you to—"

Sapphira threw up her hands. "Don't do this to me, Bel. Don't. I have given up my home, my family. My possibility of marriage to come with you."

"But—you don't want to get married," I said, surprised. "You never have."

"Even if I did, I wouldn't have," Sapphira cried. "Because I could never leave you. Do you know what it means to be indebted to you, Jezebel? Do you know what it means that my life has become subsumed in yours? I have no life. Not without you. You are princess of Tyre; you will be queen of Israel. *You* have to fight to be remembered. I am not remembered even by people I have known my whole life. Your father does not know my name, and I grew up sharing a nursery with his daughter."

I stared at her. I had not thought, had never thought, of what her life with me was like. How she had no life without me. I felt . . . ashamed. Terribly ashamed. What would she do if she left me? There was no call for female scribes, and her father had given her dowry to her brothers. She could not marry even if she wished to.

"I have to have something small, something of my own," Sapphira said quietly.

"But Elijah—"

"Don't, Bel," Sapphira said, voice gentle again. "He is your friend. He can only ever be your friend."

"He is your friend too," I said. Then I asked, even though I knew it was a dangerous question, "What was it like? Being with him?"

Sapphira laughed. "It was like . . . like being with a friend." She sighed. "In truth, Bel, I have not cared for any of the boys—or the men—I've kissed. I just wanted to see if something might be different with Elijah. But I don't think he was really any more interested in me than I was in him." She took my hand. "I am too devoted to you to be with anyone else. I don't want to be with anyone else. But I need *something* of my own."

"Do you want to go home?" I asked, and my heart began to beat fast. I could not imagine my life without Sapphira, but I would also not be the cause of her unhappiness. I had been forced to Israel. *I* had no other choice. She still did. "I will give you a large dowry. You could marry any man in Tyre."

"No," Sapphira said, looking out the windows at the city below us. "No, I rather like Israel." I made a face, and she laughed, then turned back to me. "And I won't leave you. Remember what Tanith said? For all our lives we will be together."

Until the end. Neither of us said it, but neither had we forgotten Tanith's words.

"I'm sorry," she said. "For kissing him. Perhaps I did not realize how much . . ." I had to turn because she was looking at me searchingly, and I knew that if she looked for too long, she would see it, see the desire deep inside my chest. I thought of my mother, of the lovers she had, how happy she always looked. But I shook my head, forcing the thought away. "It does not matter to me who you kiss," I said, making my voice light, but turning so she could not see my face. "I was just startled. And you're right, of course. He is just the king's scribe. He does not matter. He does not matter at all."

CHAPTER 6

After that first meeting with Omri and his advisors, I continued to ingratiate myself with Omri, smiling prettily anytime I passed him in the corridors, walking through the gardens with him, dropping my eyes so I always had to look up at him and even slouching when I was near him so that he might feel tall and proud even though I was of a height with him. Soon he began asking that I sit near him at meals and continue to attend the meetings with his advisors. "It is so refreshing to see your young, beautiful face across from mine as those old men speak on and on," he said one day, nearly two years after I'd arrived in Israel. Ahab had remained absent from the meetings and from my bed for some months after our meal together, but eventually he returned to both, though I had not yet fallen pregnant. I had worried that Ahab's return would mean I would be barred from the room, but neither Omri nor Ahab seemed to mind me there. I did not often speak during those meetings, as I'd usually pressed my point with Omri beforehand and he had agreed to whatever I'd requested. I had not grown fond of the king during our time together—often when I left him I felt ill—but in the end, it was worth it. In the past two years I had caused five new granaries to be built across the country and filled them with grain in case of famine or drought. I had encouraged stronger trade with Tyre, and much of the court now wore purple belts or sashes. We had negotiated peace with a band of outlaws on the edge of our borders, which Ahab and I had worked on together. I had thought that as a warrior he would be constantly thirsty for bloodshed, but in truth he preferred to try for peace before drawing his sword. I was proud of all these things, but mostly I was proud of how my gods were flourishing across the land. I had now caused seven temples to be built and was constantly sending for priestesses from Tyre to fill them. When I walked through the city I saw many wearing pendants with Astarte's face on them, and Israel had never had better harvests—a gift, I thought, from my goddess for spreading her name across the land.

I could smell the sweet smoke from the sacrifices at the temple when Sapphira and I stepped outside the palace and into the courtyard. I was strangely nervous as I shaded my eyes and looked across the horizon to the cloud of dust covering what I knew was the latest caravan from Tyre. After years of pleading with my father, he had finally consented to send Tanith, my childhood friend and the diviner from the temple of Astarte, to me in Israel. I had had to send a number of Ahab's new chariots to him for him to agree, but having the diviner at my side was more important than chariots.

I paced as we waited, wondering, as I glanced at Sapphira, how she always managed to be so still and calm, even though I knew she was as excited for Tanith to arrive as I was.

"I practice," she said, glancing at me as though reading my mind.

"I did practice," I said. "As a child, I—"

"You 'practiced' until your mother's back was turned," Sapphira said with a little laugh. "As soon as she left you would start moving again."

"Well." I sighed. "There is too much inside me to be still."

"I know," Sapphira said. "That is why you need me."

However, when the caravan finally arrived, we both cried out Tanith's name and embraced her. The three of us had never been as close as Sapphira and I, but we had spent as much time together during our girlhood as her training had allowed. As we grew older, we had seen her even less as her skill in divination had grown. Her skill had been another reason my father had been loath to lose her, which was why he'd demanded such a hefty price in return, but I'd known it would be worth it to have Tanith at my side.

"Your Highness." She bowed to me, though her mouth quirked up at the edge. "I thought the journey would never end. It is so good to be on ground that does not move," she said, though she patted her horse's side affectionately.

I smiled at her and said, "I am glad you have come. I wasn't sure if you would."

"I considered it for a long time," Tanith said, looking to the horizon as if she could see Tyre from where she stood. "A part of me did not want to leave Tyre, but I was also growing tired of the high priestess who replaced Anath. I did not like how she treated the other priestesses. And when I got Sapphira's latest letter, I felt . . ." She looked to the horizon for a long moment. "I felt the goddess wanted me here. By your side."

Sapphira nodded, but I was made uneasy by Tanith's words. "Why?" I said. "Why did the goddess want you with me?"

"Bel," Sapphira said gently. "Perhaps we should let Tanith rest first? She has come a long way."

Sapphira's goodness, especially at times like these, could needle me. It was important that I knew as much as Tanith could tell me, but then I took in her weary face, the dust caked on her hands and feet, and felt ashamed. Tanith was my friend. She had come to Israel for me. Now that she was here, I could ask her to intercede with the gods for me each day if I wished. I could wait for her counsel one more day. "Would you like to rest?" I said, softening my voice. "You are welcome to stay here at the palace for as long as you wish." I gestured to the building behind me and watched as Tanith's eyes swept over the giant stone blocks, pale gold like the hills, cut and fitted by Tyrian craftsmen, the huge columns and ivory that adorned the doorways.

"No. I would rather go to the temple."

Sapphira and I led her through the city quickly. The closer we got to the temple, the more anxious I became. I wanted Tanith's approval of it, wanted her to see that it was no less than the one she'd worshipped at in Tyre.

We were nearly there when Tanith said, "What is that? A song?" She stopped to listen. "Jezebel?" She smiled. "They sing your name."

I nodded, pleased with Tanith's words. I knew that the people sang the wedding song Elijah had written for me in their temples and at festivals, and I had noticed lately that their eyes followed me when I walked to the temple each morning.

"Bel is loved," Sapphira said. "Her marriage to Ahab has brought much wealth to Israel."

"Since trade has opened up with Tyre, the people of Israel, particularly Samaria"—I gestured to the market we stood in—"have grown prosperous. Several merchants have even started to carry purple silks, like the markets at home—" I cut myself off. "I mean like the markets in Tyre." I kept my voice light as we continued to walk through the market, pointing out a school that I had had built and mentioning the granary that was almost finished in the eastern hills.

We finally arrived at the temple, and Tanith smiled when she saw it. "They did well," she said. She touched one of the cool blocks as we walked in and continued to smile as Sapphira and I showed her the fine marble altar, the neatly kept pens for the animal sacrifices, and the priestesses' rooms.

"There are seven temples across Israel now," I said when we finally sat in the courtyard next to the priestesses' rooms. A small fountain burbled nearby, and I closed my eyes for a moment, letting myself imagine that the water was the tide. "And we plan to build more, especially now that you're here and can help us see better."

"You have been busy," Tanith said.

"It has not gone as quickly as I wanted," I said. "Israelites are stubborn when it comes to their god, Yahweh. Some of them claim that other gods are an abomination." I laughed lightly, but Tanith frowned.

"Has the king or the prince objected to the temples?" she said, rubbing her hand against the indigo-bright cushion she sat on.

"No," I said. "They have given me leave to build whatever temples I wish."

"Not wherever you wish," Sapphira said. "They would not let you build one in Caesarea."

I waved a hand. "It was a small mistake on my part," I said. "I should not have brought it up so soon after building one in Akko."

"Do they come here to worship with you?" Tanith said with another frown.

"No." I shrugged. "But the king's scribe has said he will come soon." Tanith looked confused, and I said, "The scribe is the voice of the king. Once he begins to speak well of the gods, the court will follow. He is the king's cousin and close to the prince as well."

"I'm sure you're right," Tanith said. "But he is just one man, even if he has power." She hesitated for a moment then said, "You don't fear the people's stubbornness? You don't worry that they will blame you for changes they do not like?"

I laughed. "I have made Israel prosperous. Why would they blame me? You heard how they sing my name. And I have never spoken against their god or their worship of him."

"Israelites have a long history of rebelling against foreign gods," Tanith said doubtfully.

"That was many long years ago," I said. "I respect and honor all gods. Why should they not do the same of mine?" I saw that she wanted to discuss it further, but I did not see what there was left to say. I stood, clapping my hands together in dismissal. "I will let you rest. But I will come tomorrow so that we might discuss how to best teach these people about Astarte."

◎◎◎◎

Some weeks had passed since Tanith had arrived, and I was in my rooms, reading Elijah's reports of the day while he sat opposite me, flipping his knife over in his hands. Sapphira was sitting at the table, writing on a sheaf of papyrus. Then, the doors to my room were thrown open, and a maidservant stood there, wide-eyed. "Why do you disturb me?" I said, annoyed at the intrusion.

"My lady." The woman bowed, and a long dark curl bounced in front of her eyes, reminding me of fresh-caught fish flopping on the deck of a ship. I looked away from her and caught Elijah's eye, and his mouth quirked as if he'd read my thoughts.

"Calah is about to give birth," she said slowly.

She looked frightened, but I could not think who she was speaking of or why I should care that she was having a child. I looked back at the papyrus before remembering a small woman with dark hair and startling, pale eyes, green as glass. I'd first noticed her because Ahab had been watching her all night during a festival months before, and his interest in her had irritated me as much as a biting fly.

Still, I did not understand until Sapphira straightened and looked at me. "Calah," she said slowly. "Calah, who is pregnant with Ahab's first child."

My mother had been the one to tell me that my husband would lie with other women. She said it casually when I was still a young girl. "All men do," she said, looking fondly to the harbor where my father and brother were bringing the royal ship in.

"Not Father," I said, thinking of the glances he gave my mother, the way his eyes followed her when she left the room.

She laughed. "Of course your father does. Do you think I'd want him in my bed every night? Besides"—she grew grave—"he is king. Kings might have one queen, but they have many wives and many concubines."

I raised my chin. "Then I will have many men too. As many as my husband has women."

My mother's face grew stern. "You will not," she said. "Not until you have a child from him. Once you give him the heir he needs, then, with discretion . . ." She fluttered her fingers vaguely. "But there must be no question of whether the child is his."

I crushed my fingers into a fist and tore the corner of the papyrus I'd been reading, but kept my head bent over it so I did not have to meet the maid's eyes. Everyone knew that this child was Ahab's. Ahab's, but not mine.

I'd been told Calah was with child by Ahab himself. He'd

flushed when he said the words and cringed, as if expecting my reproach, but at the time, I hadn't been concerned. My father had
many children with women who were not my mother, but only my
brother and I mattered. However, as the months passed and Calah
grew round while I did not conceive a child of my own, I began to
worry. I knew, as all women did, that no matter how many schools
and temples I built, no matter how much gold the alliance between
Tyre and Israel had brought—no matter how my name was sung
in the streets—I was nothing without a child.

"What of it?" I said to the maidservant, who was still standing
in the doorway, eyes wide like a frightened cow.

"It is customary—" The woman swallowed and looked at Sapphira.

"They want you to attend the birth," Sapphira said, voice soft.

"As it is a royal birth—" the maid said.

I snapped my head up. "It is not a royal birth," I said, voice low.
"It is only the birth of the prince's bastard."

The woman cringed at my words, flicked her eyes to Sapphira,
who nodded. Then she fled from the room.

"Bel," Sapphira said. "Ahab has specifically asked that you attend this birth."

I inhaled sharply and turned away from her so that she could not
see my face. I looked back to Elijah, who had stopped flipping the
knife and reached his hand across the table. His fingers were long,
the tips of them stained dark as always. The hair below his knuckles was much lighter than the hair on his head, catching the falling
sunlight and shining like bronze. I did not know if the hand was offered in succor or in pity, but I did not touch it. I could not touch it.
I refused to look at either of them as I stood, raising my chin. I
walked into the other room, slowly putting on my royal robes,
clasping gold around my throat. Sapphira was standing beside the

door when I returned, and Elijah was still sitting at the table. It looked as though he was carving something into the wood, but he put down the knife when he saw me.

I did not look at him again, just walked stiffly toward Sapphira, who followed me out of the room. We walked down the long hallway until we reached the concubines' quarters, which were at the far end of the women's rooms.

I paused a moment before walking in the door, taking a deep breath.

Calah was sitting on a birthing stool, holding on to a rope and lowing, face red. A midwife stood nearby, and other women of the court were clustered around the room. They all looked at me when I entered the room, and even Calah lifted her head and stared at me. She was panting, and I was glad to see that the pain had turned her young face old. My palm was throbbing as I stared at the woman who had spread her legs for my husband. I wanted to slap her face, but I just smiled widely. "I pray the gods bring you safely through your pain." I knew Calah was a devout follower of Yahweh, and it pleased me to see her face pale at the mention of my gods, but before she could object to my words, she grunted and began to scream.

The women fluttered around her. One of the women put rags in her mouth so that she would not disrupt the sleep of the king, then the midwife began murmuring instructions in her ear. I moved to the corner of the room and tapped my hand against my thigh, wondering if Ahab had made me attend Calah's birth as punishment for not having my own child. I did not know him well enough to determine if he was capable of such cruelty.

I stood in the corner for hours, Sapphira by my side, until finally, with one last scream, Calah's child was born. The midwife cut the cord still pulsing with lifeblood, then washed the child and rubbed it with salt. She was about to hand it to Calah when I stepped forward and put my arms out. The women in the room whispered, but all I could feel was the fast beating of my palm. The midwife hesitated for only a moment before handing me the baby. The child's lips were pressed together, and its skin was red as clay. "Is it a boy or girl?" I said to the midwife.

"A girl," the woman said, wiping her blood-slicked hands on her robes.

I nodded, pleased. A girl could never rise above her status as a bastard. "Call her Delilah," I said as I handed the baby to Calah. Calah's eyes were wide with fright, but I saw a dark anger spark in their depths as I held her child, as I named her.

"It means delicate, does it not?" I said, smiling widely again, as though I did not know the story of the woman who had seduced and murdered their beloved hero, Samson. I smiled until Calah finally bowed under the weight of my gaze. "It is an honor to have you attend me," she said. "The child shall be named as you wish."

Sapphira followed me as I left the room, putting a hand to my arm. "Bel—you did not need to curse the child. She's only a girl. She is blameless."

"Enough," I said, voice suddenly cold. "I will not have this child usurp me, Sapphira. Even if it is a girl." She frowned and made to speak, but I raised a hand, weary. "No, Sapphira, no more."

Sapphira set her teeth. "I shall stay with Calah tonight. I will help her with the babe," she said, turning from me.

I walked back to my room alone, my ears still ringing from Calah's screams. I kept smiling pleasantly, though I did not know why. I could not seem to drop the smile from my lips until I finally reached my room and slumped against the wall, rubbing my ruined palm. The throbbing had finally stopped, but I felt unwell as I remembered the look on Calah's face when I held her child before she did. Fear rose in my belly as I wondered if I would ever hold my own child in my arms. I wondered what Ahab would do if I did not. Would he simply replace me with one of the women he bedded? Calah, perhaps? I wondered what she might do to me if I became only a barren, nameless concubine, but couldn't picture anything but the girl's sweet-lipped smile, her piercing eyes shining like jewels. No matter what, she was no threat to me. But there were plenty of other women in the court who would be happy to take my place, happy to turn on me like vipers.

Something shuffled in the darkness of my room, and I stiffened until a lamp was lit and I realized it was only Elijah. His hair was unruly, and his eyes were dazed. "I'm sorry," he said, standing. "I only thought to wait for you. I must have fallen asleep."

I nodded and moved toward him even though I knew we would both be in a great deal of trouble if anyone found him alone in my rooms this late. "It was a girl," I said, stopping a few paces away from him.

The lamp cast golden light on his face and made his eyes shine. He nodded. "Did Calah live?" His voice was quiet.

I laughed shortly. "Calah is fine. She and the babe are healthy." I gestured to the sheets of papyrus that sat on the small table. They looked liquid in the flickering light. "You will write the announcement of her birth," I said. "The prince's first child."

Elijah nodded slowly. "It is my duty," he said.

I wondered suddenly what my father's other children were called. I had never asked. I pictured Sapphira saying that not even my own father knew her name, and I felt a wave of sickness sweep over me. I thought of how she had looked at me in the corridor after I had named the baby. "You will put her name down," I said. My fingers trembled, and I quickly dropped my hands. "It is Delilah."

"I don't usually include the names of girls—"

"Write it down," I hissed through clenched teeth. "She shall have the honor of her name, at least, written down in the book of kings."

◎◎◎◎

After Delilah's birth, I spent even less time in the women's quarters. I had not gone there often, but there might have been one or two women I might have befriended with enough time. I knew now that until I was with child, it would be dangerous to become close to any of them, dangerous to share secrets that might be used against me one day. So, I stayed away from them, preferring the company of Sapphira and Elijah.

Elijah was easy with me in a way few other people were. He did not seem to fear my anger, and one night, he even laughed after I shouted at him over a word in a song that he refused to change.

My palm throbbed, and I took a step toward him, body coiled like a snake about to strike, but he did not move back.

"Bel," Sapphira said pleadingly from across the room, but I ignored her.

"I cannot change it," Elijah said, laughter still in his voice. "It would ruin the song, and I would have to begin again."

"Then begin again," I said.

"No," he said, and he did not even flinch when I slammed my hands down on the table.

"You would disobey me?"

He sighed and grabbed my wrist, pulling me toward the table. His hand on mine surprised me so much that I did not stop him. "Look." He pointed to the line below the one I'd wanted changed. "It will ruin the ending." I realized he was right at the same time that I realized he was still holding my wrist. He let me go, stepping back.

I dipped my head, cheeks flushed. "On the day of my birth, my own mother was afraid of my anger. Most people are."

Elijah did not look surprised. "Your anger is not the first I have faced." His mouth tightened. "You know my father was nephew to the king," he said. "He was the bastard-born son of Omri's brother." He looked at me, and I wondered if he was thinking of Delilah, but I merely nodded at him to continue. "My father felt he had been cheated, cheated at birth because he was not seen as a true son."

I opened my hand and looked down at my palm, touching the mounded skin there. I understood what it was to be cheated of a birthright.

"When Omri took the throne, it only became worse. My father was the son of his elder brother, but Omri was the one who became king, and though my father benefited from being the king's nephew, he was not given a position in court." Elijah's hands, usually always busy with a pen or knife, stilled. "He married my mother soon after. He beat her. And when I was born, he beat me too." Elijah's hands flexed as if he wanted to wrap them around his father's throat. His face was smooth as sand, but his voice rumbled like a boulder about to cause a rockslide.

"Why did he beat you?" Sapphira said quietly. Women were used to being beaten, of course, but men usually beat their wives and daughters, rarely their sons.

Elijah shrugged. "Because he was angry. Because I could not always remember each of his commands. Because I once questioned a law of Yahweh. He was very devout," Elijah said. "He called me a fool, often, for questioning. He thought Israel was being led to damnation and ruin because of our foreign trade, because Omri tolerated the religions of the lands he conquered and did not wipe out those who chose to follow other gods."

I shook my head. "Omri is right," I said. "Think how Israel has prospered since my marriage to Ahab. There are temples to Astarte all over Israel, but the followers of Yahweh are not being harassed for their beliefs. Why should all gods not be honored?"

Elijah gave a short laugh. "My father would not agree. And he would not see your marriage to Ahab as good. The only time I ever remember his happiness was when I became the king's scribe. He was pleased I had a place in court. He wanted to make sure that his name would be remembered, even if he was only a bastard."

I shifted in my seat, uncomfortable that my own wishes so closely mirrored those of such a man.

"Were you pleased with your place at court?" I asked, not wanting to discuss his father anymore.

Elijah shrugged. "I found my schooling to be . . . difficult, at least at first. I would have rather my hands hold a shepherd's crook than a pen."

"You would rather spend your days with sheep than writing?" I frowned, thinking of how as a child, I had only wished to hold a pen properly.

"I prefer goats." Elijah smiled. "But no, I do not wish I was a shepherd. Not anymore," he said, holding my gaze for a long moment before dropping his eyes.

◉ ◉ ◉ ◉

After he told us about his father, Elijah asked me for stories of the gods. It was as if, after admitting his father's devotion to Yahweh, he had freed himself somehow.

He liked the stories of Astarte best and hated those of Anat just like Sapphira, which only made me tell them more. I would grin in delight at the grimace on their faces when I spoke of Anat ripping out the entrails of her enemies.

"Sapphira has always hated how direct Anat is," I said. "She thinks she could have used subtlety to get what she wanted. But why do *you* hate Anat?" I asked Elijah.

"The . . . blood," he said, face pale. "I do not like it." He looked ashamed for a moment, then said quietly, "I do not even like seeing myself bleed after a scrape. It makes me feel ill and faint."

I felt a sudden tenderness toward him at the thought of his turning pale at blood, but instead of giving in to it, I said, rather harshly, "You cannot be so weak as to object to bloodshed. Yahweh has demanded as much—more. Didn't your own King David bring the foreskins of two hundred Philistines to Saul as a bride price? Why shouldn't Anat do worse to her enemies?"

"At least David was a man. For a woman—even a goddess—to see so much blood . . ."

"Women do not fear blood," I said, even though that was a lie. Fear had filled my chest only this morning when I once again saw the red spots on my bed. I had to have a child soon or Ahab would replace me, turn me into a nameless concubine.

Elijah moved to rest his hand on mine in comfort, but I flinched away. "Don't touch me," I said, and his face grew pained before falling back into its usual lines of implacability.

"The way of the woman is on her," Sapphira said from the corner, as if hoping to soften the blow of my words. "The goddess has not yet blessed—" She stopped at the stricken look on my face.

Elijah's eyes flicked to me, and his mouth, which had been rigid, grew gentle, tender at the mention of another month without a child. He stood and gave me a small bow. "I will leave you now, my lady," he said, closing my door softly so that just Sapphira and I were left in the room.

I did not want to dwell on his face, on how he had tried to touch me, so instead I turned abruptly toward Sapphira and the stack of scrolls before her. I picked one up, expecting to find her recordings of the week, or those from Elijah, but they were in a hand I did not recognize. I frowned but then realized they were archives of the history and customs of Israel, things I had not bothered familiarizing myself with.

"I have been reading some of the old scrolls that were left in the scribes' school," she said, avoiding my gaze. "You did the same when we were in Tyre."

"But I was reading the stories of Tyre—"

"And I am reading the stories of Israel." Sapphira's voice was flat, as though she was angry.

"But why would you—"

"We live in Israel, Jezebel," Sapphira said. "I want to know the history of this place we live. And . . . I like it. I like Israel."

"What is there to like?" I gave a long sigh. "It is hot and dusty and—"

"And this is our home," Sapphira said, finally looking up at me. "I have grown to enjoy the heat. It is good to feel the sun on my face without having to shield it from sea spray."

I looked down at my hands. I had lived in Israel for two long years, but they were still as dry and cracked as they'd been the day I'd arrived. Sometimes they bled, leaving drops of blood across the papers that held my plans for Israel. No matter what plans I made or how my name was whispered in the streets, I would never live by the sea again. Tears suddenly filled my eyes, and for a moment I thought I might fall to my knees and howl as I used to when I was a child, but then my doors were thrown open and Elijah ran back into the room, face flushed like a child.

"The pool is ready!" he said, coming toward me with his arms out. For a moment I thought he would lift me up, dance me across the room, but then he turned toward Sapphira, who had jumped off her stool at his entrance. They did dance then, one quick spin across the room, and I laughed, clapping my hands.

"We must go see it," I said, forcing my sadness away. The pool had taken years to plan and complete. I had wanted, more than anything, to swim once more, but I had also wanted it done properly and had sent for craftsmen from Tyre who had built it to my exacting standards.

"I can't, Bel. I said I would help . . ." Sapphira trailed away for a moment, then sighed, as if in defeat, and said, "Help Calah with Delilah tonight. She hasn't been sleeping well."

I gave her a tight smile. "Of course." I had been trying to keep my promise of letting Sapphira build her own life in Israel. I knew she liked helping with the children, and I would not allow myself to interfere with her just because of my pettiness. It was not her fault I did not have a child yet.

"I will go with you," Elijah said slowly, and Sapphira stiffened as we stared at each other. The air had gone still, heavy. Elijah and I were rarely alone together; Sapphira was almost always with us, and her presence brought a lightness to all our interactions, a sensibility, like the gentle pressure of a hand that prevented a step off a cliff.

I should not go with him. I knew that. But I had to see my pool, so I merely nodded and left the room before I could see the warning on Sapphira's face.

I walked through the halls quickly until I had reached the entrance that led outdoors to the pool. When I finally saw it, I did not take off my sandals or my robe or act in the way befitting a princess. I merely dove into it. The water caught me, held me like a mother's tender arms, and I began to weep, weep as I had not since leaving Tyre.

Suddenly, there was a huge splash, and bubbles erupted all around me. Someone shouted, grabbing my hand. I stood, for the pool was not deep, and saw Elijah floundering like a newborn calf in the water.

"Bel!" he shouted. "Bel!" His voice was panicked, eyes wide. "Are you hurt?"

I laughed. "Why would I be hurt? I grew up swimming in the sea around Tyre, with currents strong enough to wreck ships on the rocks. I am not afraid of a small pool." I looked around. "Isn't it marvelous?" It was inlaid with blue and white tiles, each hand-crafted by Tyrian artisans to show a different god. The steps leading into the pool were inlaid with precious stones and in the middle a white marble fountain shaped like a dolphin rose, burbling water from its mouth. Towering plants and fig and lemon trees grew around it, scenting the air with their perfume and covering the pool with so much greenery that those who swam here had total privacy.

"It's . . ." Elijah wrang water out of his hair. He looked younger with the wet clothes plastered to him, water running from his dark hair. "I don't like water. Swimming."

"Do you even know how?" I said flippantly before diving under the water and pulling him under.

"No!" he said when he came up again, sputtering. He even looked a little angry, which was rare for him.

"But you jumped in after me," I said, floating on my back and staring at the setting sun, which was turning the fields golden and glossy. "Why did you jump in if you can't . . ." I trailed away as I realized the answer to my question. Elijah's face still held the panic that it had when he jumped in, and I reached out, touched his face before I could stop myself. He swallowed and closed his eyes, leaning into my touch. His beard was soft under my hand, and I trailed a single finger over it.

"Bel—" he said, voice hoarse. He moved closer to me, his robes billowing in the water, and for a moment I felt the pressure of his body against mine. I could feel the weight of his eyes on me, heavy as stones, and I wanted his arms, which were still pressed at his sides, around mine, holding me close against his chest.

I heard a sudden noise and jerked back, swinging my head around, but saw only a small mouse that had disturbed a stone. I swallowed hard. My mother's laughing face suddenly appeared before me. I pictured the sideways glances she gave to men who weren't my father. I wondered suddenly what had happened to those men. My mother had had one particular favorite, a man with hair golden as the sun, who had disappeared one day and was never seen again.

"No—" I said, backing even further away from him. "It is not safe. And Ahab is your cousin." I saw the guilt in Elijah's eyes, saw the safety it would provide us, and I pushed hard against it as though it were a bruise. "Surely your god has commands—some sort of command about—" Elijah's eyes flicked from my face to my gown, which clung to me, heavy with water. "Ahab is my husband," I said. After her lover had disappeared, my mother had despaired for weeks. I could not afford to fall into such despair.

I raised my chin. "I will be queen of a great nation. I cannot risk—I cannot risk my name being . . ." I faltered at the look on his face, the tears I saw before he climbed out of the pool, strode up the path, and left me alone.

CHAPTER 7

Elijah and I did not talk about that moment in the pool. I sent Sapphira for his reports, and he no longer came to my rooms in the evening, asking for stories of the gods. I missed him. I missed him more than I wanted to admit, but I tried to focus on my role in the kingdom, tried to be a good wife to Ahab. I spoke to him about his time as a soldier, asked for his war stories, and tried my best to fascinate him. Eventually he took to following me to bed every night, and when I lay with him, I thought only of the baby I needed. I did not think of Elijah, did not imagine him in Ahab's place.

I did not even notice at first when I fell pregnant. It was Sapphira who came to my room with linen sheets in her arms. I had often remonstrated her for acting as my maid, but she said she enjoyed working with the other women, enjoyed knowing each room of the palace, especially the ones the rest of the court had never seen. "Bel," she said slowly, putting the sheets down on a low couch. I was in bed, though it was not yet dark, and she crawled in beside me as she had done when we were children. "Bel," she said again. "Did you bleed last month?"

I blinked at her blearily. I had never felt wearier, and since Elijah had stopped coming to my rooms, the days had seemed to blur together. "I'm trying to sleep," I said, putting my hand across her mouth as if we were young children again.

But she would not leave me alone. She shook my shoulder until I finally sat up. "Sapphira—" I said, annoyed, "I want to—"

"Jezebel," she said, turning my face so I looked in her eyes. "Have you bled in the past two months?"

The look in her eyes made my heart beat faster, and I thought back, trying to remember the last time I had seen blood on my sheets. I could not remember it since the night Elijah had jumped into the pool after me.

Sapphira's eyes widened, and she took my hand. "I think you are with child, Bel."

Sapphira's voice was strange—almost awed—and it made my skin prickle. I moved so that my back leaned against the wall and said, "No, it must be wrong. I must have just forgotten . . ." I counted back again, knowing, even as I did, that I had not forgotten. I knew I should feel pleased—ecstatic. This was all I had hoped for in the past years, but the thought of being with child made me feel ill. Made me feel afraid.

"How did you know?" I said, trying to distract myself. "How did you know I haven't bled?"

Sapphira blushed. "Don't be angry, Bel, but . . . well, you know how everyone is . . . anxious for you to have a child. So the maids . . . the maids always check your sheets. And they . . . they told me, just now," she said, cringing slightly, as though waiting for my anger, but instead I just closed my eyes. It was humiliating to learn that each month the maids checked my sheets for blood.

"Send for Tanith," I said, drawing my legs to my chest. "I must speak to her."

Sapphira squeezed my hand. "I'll ask someone to bring her to the palace immediately."

It seemed to take hours, but Tanith finally arrived. She took one look at my face and immediately began drawing things out of her bag.

"When did you learn of it?" she said quietly. She took my hand and drew me out onto the balcony, with Sapphira hovering at my shoulder as if afraid I would collapse.

"Just before we called you," I said, not asking how she had known about the child.

Tanith glanced up and gave a sharp nod. "For this, we must look to the skies," she said. "There is much to learn from the paths of birds." She gestured, and I saw that the sky was full of birds, dark ones that circled over the palace. I shivered, but Tanith shook her head briskly. "It is not their coloring that matters, but how they move." She placed a hand on my still-flat stomach, and I flinched, but she did not move it. She looked back up at the sky while keeping a hand on me and said, "What is it you want to know?"

My mind, which had been full of questions only moments before, went still and quiet, and I knew that I really had only one question that mattered. "Will this child . . . will they . . . will they subsume me?" I asked. Sapphira glanced at me, but I did not care how selfish it sounded—how selfish it was. I would not become my mother. I would not become a nameless bearer of sons.

Tanith did not close her eyes, did not shake with some mystical force as I imagined she might. Instead, she just watched the sky for several long, breathless moments. Finally, she removed her hand from me and brought her eyes to my face. "No," she said. "No, Jezebel. You will not become consumed by your children." She frowned, then said, "None of your children will be greater than you."

Tanith's words should have calmed me, but I still felt strange. I took a deep, gasping breath and turned from the balcony, crawling into my bed. Sapphira and Tanith sat beside me, each grasping one of my hands.

"You *want* this, Bel," Sapphira said softly. "Ahab will praise you—you will give him an heir. And you can teach the child of Tyre, of the true gods."

I took another deep breath as my heart began to beat slower. I turned back to Tanith. "Do you see anything else?"

A frown still marred her forehead. "There is something . . . some darkness here," she said finally. "I cannot see any more. Perhaps another god is blocking my sight. Perhaps Yahweh does not wish me to see."

A wave of nausea swept over me. I could not tell if it was real or imagined, but I gritted my teeth and thought, *No*. I would not fear Yahweh. Yahweh could do nothing to me. "If you cannot see it, it is probably a girl," I said with a forced laugh. "No matter. I know more than any how girls can strengthen a kingdom."

◎◎◎◎

It was soon known that I was with child. Courtiers I had never spoken to stopped me in the halls, and the women spoke gently to me; a few even gave me suggestions to help with the nausea and aching breasts.

Elijah knew, of course. But he did not return to my rooms, and I did not ask for him.

I began to have strange dreams. When I told Sapphira of them, she smiled. "It's a good sign," she said. "Nikkal said that she had dreams with the boys."

"What did she dream of?" I tried to keep my voice cool, disinterested. I was standing on the balcony, trying to catch a glimpse of the sea, but the day was hazy and all I could see was ripples of heat.

"She dreamed of the babe, of course," Sapphira said, dipping her pen into a bottle of ink but letting it drip back into the pot as she spoke. "She dreamed of feasts, she said. She wanted figs more than anything, but it was the rainy season, and she couldn't get any. So she said the feasts in her dreams were full of figs: lamb stuffed with them, sweet figs spread on bread, she even dreamed of wine made from them." Sapphira made a face. "That didn't sound at all pleasant, but she said it tasted like nectar of the gods."

"She didn't dream of . . . of anything else?" I looked down at my stomach, which had just started to round, the swell like that of a melon.

Sapphira blushed and set down her pen, then turned around and looked at me. "If you mean . . . if you're asking if she dreamed of . . . of men. Of what happens in a marital bed, then yes, she did. She said that all women do. Don't let it worry you."

"That was all?"

"That was all she told me," Sapphira said. Her face creased. "Why, Bel? Are you having strange dreams?" I didn't say anything, but she rose and placed a gentle hand on my stomach. "Why don't you ask one of the palace women?" she said. "I've never been with child; I only know what Nikkal told me. I'm sure they could better answer your questions. Huldah or Judith have both had many children."

I nodded and left the room, but did not go to the women's quarters. Instead, I went to my pool. It was surrounded by a thick grove of trees, and no one was allowed to swim in it except at my invitation, so I stripped off my clothes and waded in naked, the way I used to swim in the sea. I was cold but did not put my arms around myself, because I did not want to touch my belly. I had been having dreams, but nothing like the ones Sapphira spoke of. Nothing I could ask the women of. I did not dream of the child or food or men.

I dreamed of blood.

I dreamed of peeling the skin off my brother, Baal Eser, until nothing remained but his bones, white as the walls of Tyre.

I dreamed of slitting Ahab's throat with my knife, letting the blood run down my hands, warm as the sea in high summer.

I dreamed of bathing in a red pool, washing my hair with it, letting the blood fill my eyes, my ears, my mouth, until I was swallowed by it.

The dreams had started a week before, and I had woken from them gasping, clawing at my face. I had washed my hands over and over, but even now in my pool I could still feel the wet, warm blood clinging to them, could still taste the metallic tang of it at the back of my throat.

I shivered and tried to dive under the water, but my stomach made me buoyant. My ears were ringing, and for a moment I wanted to rip the thing out of my stomach, to stop the dreams of blood and be nothing more than myself, swimming in cool water.

But when I turned and saw the red streak in the water, I hoped I was dreaming again. I dunked my head under the water with my eyes shut tight, praying to Astarte that when I surfaced the water would be clean, but when I opened them, all I saw were tendrils of red swirling around me. I climbed out of the pool, dripping blood and water onto the tiles, staring down at my thighs. I reached a finger out and swirled it in the blood, then brought it to my lips and tasted it, hoping for some miracle, but the taste was just as it was in my dream: salty, metallic, warm as the sea before harvest.

I went to my rooms as quickly as I could, calling for Sapphira, for my maids. Sapphira arrived first, to find me sitting in bed, still naked. Her eyes flicked from mine to the sheets already speckled with blood, and her mouth crooked open but she didn't say anything. Instead she brought me a robe and laid it over me gently.

"I dreamed of blood," I said softly. "I dreamed of peeling the skin from my brother . . ." I recited my dreams to her over and over, but she did not flinch or move away. She just held my hand as I spoke. She held my hand as the midwife arrived and told me that the child was washing out of me, receding like a tide.

"Sometimes the gods will it," the midwife said, and I blinked, trying to understand her words. She thought Astarte had willed this? I looked at the dark spots on my sheets. Could Astarte have done this? But Astarte was the Mother. Why would she take a child from me? I remembered what Tanith had said, how she thought a god was blocking her sight. *Yahweh*, I thought. Yahweh was the only one who would not want me to produce an heir for Ahab; Yahweh was the only one who could still be angry that Ahab had married a foreign princess, against his commands. Perhaps he was even jealous of me, jealous of the prosperity my gods and I had brought to Israel.

Sapphira still held my hand in hers, squeezing it so tightly it was almost painful, but as soon as the midwife left the room, I released her grip. Slowly I reached for where the blood was thick as ink and dipped my finger into the pooling red. *YAHWEH*, I wrote out, the letters uneven. I heard Sapphira's sharp intake of breath beside me, but I did not care. I wrote the god's name as a curse and a promise— that I would not forget what he had done.

⊚⊚⊚⊚

Ahab came to my rooms later that day, but he stood in the doorway, as if afraid to come any nearer.

"The child is gone," I said slowly. I knew I should blame myself, knew I should beg his forgiveness, but I could not. It was me whose position was precarious again, more so than ever before. Ahab had other children. They were bastards, but he had still held them in his arms, seen his likeness in their faces. He would grieve for this child, of course. But he would grieve it as the loss of his heir. He could always get another wife, one who could give him another child. If I could not conceive again—if I could not give him a child . . . I would be hidden away in the women's rooms. I would become a faceless, nameless concubine, not even allowed to return home. The thought frightened me more than any other. He nodded. His face was stern, but I noticed him twisting his robe in his hand. "You may come in," I said tiredly.

Ahab hesitated before slowly walking across the room toward me. I did not know what I expected, but when he reached his hand toward me, I recoiled. He paused as though I were a wild dog. Then he touched my arm, raising a hand gently to my cheek. I closed my eyes, refusing to weep, refusing to give him the satisfaction of comforting me. I turned sharply away, and his hand fell foolishly at his side. "Thank you for coming, my lord," I said as I walked out toward the balcony.

I heard him still in the room, heard him draw in breath as if about to say something, but he didn't, and eventually the door closed softly, leaving me alone.

◎◎◎◎

I bled for days.

The midwife gave me potions to drink, maids brought me rich meat and wine, but the bleeding wouldn't stop. It was just like my dreams. Except now, when I woke, the blood still surrounded me.

I was standing on the balcony looking to the just-visible sea a few days after I had begun to bleed. I had insisted that Sapphira go back to her room and sleep, as she'd been up with me most nights, and so I was alone when Elijah entered the room. His face was sorrowful, but his body glowed with life. He walked toward me and stood beside me on the balcony, resting against it. His arms were brown and shining in the sun. His beard was trimmed, and his hair had grown so long a curl brushed my face. He smelled good, sweet, like he had taken a bath and come away clean. And for a moment, I felt my dreams take hold of me. I wished for a sword, a knife, a sharp piece of glass that I could thrust into him over and over and over until blood ran from him as it ran from me. Until he knew what it was like to bleed like a woman. The thought was so visceral that it made my stomach turn. My palm throbbed, but I ignored it. He had done nothing to me. It was only Elijah.

I jumped when his fingers touched my cheek. His fingers came away wet, and at the tenderness in his eyes a sob rose in my throat. He enfolded me in his arms, and I howled into his chest, soaking him with water and salt like the sea. And as soon as he held me to him, I knew that I had been right to be afraid. Because now that I knew what it was to be held so tenderly, I did not want to give it up.

◎◎◎◎

I have learned that wars are not created by large things. Not at first. At first, a shepherd is only thinking of his thirsty sheep when he lets them drink water from an enemy's well. A man thinks only of his children when he does not share their bread with a hungry stranger. A woman yearns for solace when she wakes up in her bed, afraid.

That was how it began.

Elijah stayed as the child bled out of me. He sat beside me and stroked my hair, and Sapphira lay beside me and held my hand. Even Topaz could tell something was wrong, because she curled up on the foot of the bed, licking me when I stiffened from pain.

Then one day, about two weeks after the bleeding had started, it stopped. The light of dawn fell on the coverlet, making it look like spun gold, and there was no red stain around me. Sapphira was not with us, she must have gone to fetch the potions she kept forcing me to drink, but Elijah had fallen asleep in the chair beside me. He was bent so that his head rested on my bed, his hair like a dark river on the white sheets. I reached out a hand and gently twirled one of his curls around my finger. It was as soft as newly combed wool. He did not wake, and I considered what had begun. What could continue if I allowed it. I thought of my mother, my need to have Ahab's child. I thought of waking in the dark, the taste of blood in my mouth.

I ruffled my hand through Elijah's hair, and he sat up slowly, eyes drowsy from sleep. I pulled the linens away from the bed and looked at him. He did not hesitate. He just crawled in beside me, wrapping his arms around my body.

It did not begin, as so many think, with my breasts, with the space between my legs. I did not line my eyes with black and coil gold in my hair. I did not weave a dark spell into the air and offer sacrifices so that he might desire me. All I did was make space for him in my bed.

If they knew the story now, they would say I had planned it to be so. That from the moment I had seen him I had wanted him. They would say I was wily as a serpent, a wolf in sheep's clothing.

If I had been a good woman, I would not have wanted. Not have taken. A good woman stuffed rags in her mouth so that when she screamed as she birthed her husband's child he could continue to rest, without being woken from his sweet sleep.

But I remember the truth of that time. I remember a woman, barely more than a girl, who took the comfort she needed.

CHAPTER 8

In the year since I'd lost the child, I had not become pregnant again. I knew the court was whispering, wondering what the prince would do, but I knew too that as long as Omri was alive, it would be difficult for Ahab to cast me aside. They were growing too rich from their trade with Tyre to so anger my father now. But once Omri—who was old and sickly—died and Ahab was made king, he would need a queen who produced heirs.

So with Sapphira I began to create plans for how to strengthen Israel's alliance with Tyre. Since I could not give a child to Ahab, I decided to give him the next best thing: wealth.

Growing up in Tyre, I had met kings and rulers from all over the world. Many of them needed wives. For years, Israelites had not been willing to marry their women off to other nations because Yahweh forbade it, but since my marriage to Ahab and the expansion of the temples of Astarte across the land, the people of Israel could see the advantage of prosperous allies. So I began to pair the women of the court with Tyrian nobles who needed wives.

And at night, when I retired to my bed, Elijah was waiting for me.

It had been Sapphira who had forced us to make a more concrete plan of what to do now that Elijah was my lover. That first morning after Elijah had spent the night in my bed, she had come into the room early as she always did. She flung open the doors to the balcony to let the light in and before I'd had time to raise my head, I heard her stop halfway across the room. "Oh—Bel—" Her voice was choked. She ran to the door, turned the key that always sat in it, and slipped it into her pocket. Elijah had woken and sat up, the morning light flooding his bare chest. I had thought that her voice had been sad, tender, even, but I realized now, as she marched over to Elijah and yanked him, fully naked, from the bed, that she was furious. Elijah was a tall man, larger than her, but he had been barely awake and entirely unprepared for the viciousness of Sapphira's actions, so he went sprawling to the floor.

"Sapphira!" I shouted, not even bothering to wrap a sheet around my own naked body as I leapt from the bed too.

"No—" Sapphira's voice was shaking, but the finger that she pointed at me was not. I was so startled by the command in her voice that I cringed back. I had never, *never* heard Sapphira speak in such a way. She looked . . . like some type of avenging goddess. Like Anat. I glanced at Elijah and felt a terrible desire to laugh, thinking wildly that I hoped Sapphira would not do to him what Anat usually did to the men who opposed her.

Elijah had climbed stiffly to his feet, trying to shield his groin as he did, but Sapphira just glanced at him then gave a snort, turning to me. "*That* is why you have chosen to do this?" she hissed at me. "Because Ahab could not satisfy you?"

This surprised me even more than anything else. Sapphira knew—she knew the nightmares I'd been having. She had offered to sleep beside me, but I had not let her, because I had needed at least one of us to sleep, needed one of us to be able to continue our carefully made plans. She looked between both of us now, and I wondered if she was jealous. If she thought I had picked Elijah over her.

"I love you as much as ever," I said, trying to placate her. "It was not like that, you know."

Sapphira laughed bitterly. "I am not *jealous*, Jezebel. I am angry. Furious that you would put yourself in danger in this way without a thought of your safety. Of mine."

"I would never put her in danger—" Elijah began, but when Sapphira turned on him, his words trailed away.

"If someone else had come into the room this morning, what do you think would have happened? You both would have been dragged in front of the king. Bel would have been stoned. *I* would have been stoned."

"No," I said, confused. "Omri would send you back to Tyre. He would not stone you too . . ." I trailed away as I saw tears glistening in her eyes. I realized suddenly what she meant. She would choose to die at my side rather than leave me.

She took a deep breath and turned away from us, but we both saw how she wiped her eyes on her sleeve. "Will this be continuing?" she said, turning back toward us, voice suddenly practical.

I hesitated, but Elijah didn't. "Yes," he said, standing beside me and wrapping an arm around my waist. I leaned into him without thinking, but I saw Sapphira's eyes track the movement.

"Then we need to make a plan to keep you from being found out."

Sapphira quickly decided what we would do. The court was used to Elijah spending his evenings in my room, and no one, not even Ahab, had ever questioned it, but we'd had nothing to hide before. I knew that Sapphira wanted me to say that I would send him away at some time during the night, but I did not want to promise that. I wanted to wake up from my nightmares with his arms wrapped around me. I wanted to listen to his heart beat and know that I was safe.

I had always slept with my doors closed, and now I locked them too, with only Sapphira, Elijah, and me having keys. Sapphira, who always woke early, agreed to wake us each morning so Elijah could slip out the servants' corridors before my maids arrived. I also promised her that I would never go to Elijah's room, never sleep with him there. This Sapphira did make me swear, and I did without much reluctance. I had never even been to his room before; I had no reason to go there when Elijah was already used to coming to my rooms at night.

"Sapphira," I said, once Elijah had left that morning. "Sapphira, I'm—"

"Don't tell me that you're sorry, Bel," she said, not turning toward me but continuing to write on a sheaf of papyrus she'd pulled from her robes. "I told you he would be dangerous."

"He's not—"

"He is." She turned toward me. "He makes you lose all sense. You always have a plan. Always. But this morning . . . you didn't. You slept in with your lover for all the world to see."

"I need him," I said, trying not to choke on the words but not managing to keep my voice steady.

Sapphira's pen stilled. "I know. That is why I have agreed to help you," she said. "But I don't have to be pleased about it. I do not have to be happy that you have found comfort in his arms."

Sapphira and I did not talk about Elijah and me anymore, and our days mostly went back to the way they had been. Elijah and Sapphira still worked on their reports together, borrowed knives, and discussed lines of songs, but I did notice that Sapphira simply refused to boil the black ink anymore, leaving the pungent task to Elijah's hands, not even thanking him when he filled her bottles.

Elijah being my lover did not mean that I did not still read his day's writings each night, making him change a word here or there, arguing with him for the inclusion of my name on alliances I had helped forge, on schools I had caused to be built. "The king's name is already on it," he would say, shaking his head.

"And it would be no thing to add in the name of his daughter-in-law," I said. "In Tyre—"

"They would not have included it in Tyre either," Elijah said. "So you have no argument."

I stared at him. "I still want my name to appear beside the king's," I said. "If it is here, perhaps it will eventually be the same in Tyre."

After arguing, often long into the night, we got into bed. We made love, but it was almost as much a pleasure to me that Elijah would stay in my bed after and talk with me. He would tell me the gossip of the court, and I would tell him my plans and strategies for Israel. Some nights, I would tell him stories of the gods until he fell asleep, his mouth open, face soft as a child's.

After months with Elijah beside me, my dreams of blood finally stopped, and I was able to sleep peacefully beside him until one night, I woke to find Elijah thrashing about in bed, arms over his face as if he were trying to protect himself. Elijah always slept deeply and so still he could wake up in the same position he'd fallen asleep in, so I was surprised to see him writhing beside me. He muttered something, but I could not make out his words. I shook him, but he did not wake, and unease crawled through my skin. "Elijah," I said, keeping my voice quiet. I could not risk someone hearing me, even though the walls were thick, and my rooms were set apart from the women's quarters. I shook him again, and still he did not wake, but this time I heard him say "Yahweh." He sounded afraid. His face was flushed, and the single torch flickering in the room illuminated a bead of sweat rolling down his face, making it glimmer like a pearl. He began to shake, and his lips moved noiselessly. Then, he stopped moving, seemed to stop breathing, and I gasped. "Elijah!" I said, terribly afraid and suddenly uncaring if we were overheard, splaying my fingers against his bare chest and placing my head near his lips.

"Bel?" Elijah's eyes snapped open.

"You were shaking," I said, trying to keep my voice steady. "And then you were so still. I thought for a moment—" I took a deep breath and leaned my head into his chest. He wrapped his arms around me, and neither of us spoke for a moment.

"It was just a dream," Elijah said, voice rough and breathless.

"What were you dreaming of?" I said, wondering what horrors he'd seen. "I thought I heard you say 'Yahweh.'"

Elijah shook his head and held me tighter. "It was nothing. Go back to sleep, Bel," he said, voice muffled in my hair. But after his breaths had evened, I lay awake wondering whether he had been calling out Yahweh's name in supplication or fear.

◎◎◎◎

I went down to the temple early, but even then, it was hot, and my hair, which had been wet and cool from my morning swim, dried too quickly. I'd hoped the swim would invigorate me after another troubled sleep. Elijah had been having nightmares for months now but would not tell me what they were about. Most nights I had to wake him as he flailed, muttering, but I could never hear more than the name of his god. The dreams had changed Elijah too; he was more taciturn and had taken to staring off into the distance as if he saw something the rest of us could not. I wondered, sometimes, if the dreams were a punishment for the adultery we committed, but I would not be apart from him, so I prayed that they would pass as mine had.

I shook my head as if I could dispel my fears about Elijah's dreams like a fly and forced myself to look around the market. It was larger than it had been before, with more stalls, and it was beginning to show the changes I had wrought in Israel over the past three years. The pinched look that came from men and food being funneled into an always-hungry army had faded, and the merchants I passed sold luxuries like blue and red silks, spices from Egypt, and ivory figurines shaped like little animals. Plump-faced women haggled with merchants and held up bags heavy with coins, while their children laughed and ran underfoot, begging for sweets. I was proud of the market, proud that instead of old, tough meat rotting in the sun, there were grapes, purple and plump; figs; and melons that sweated with juices that all but the poorest could afford.

I was thinking of this with satisfaction when I stumbled over something in the street. I bent, thinking a dog must have been caught in a sack, but then I saw a pair of bright eyes, pale as the sky above us. For a moment I wondered if I'd come upon a god in disguise, but when I looked closer, I saw not a god but a child. A girl, perhaps four or five. She shrank away from me like a dog expecting a kick, and the fear in her eyes made me flinch.

It was not as though I'd never seen a street urchin before—no matter how prosperous a nation was, they were always around— but as I looked at the starving child, I felt a deep sadness instead of the anger that was usually so readily at hand. I thought of myself at this girl's age, how I had lived in a palace of white stone, been petted and spoiled and given everything my heart desired. I had not once wondered if I would eat that day.

I bent to lift the child but was driven back by hands that had arched into claws. She jumped at me like an animal, hissing and screeching, trying to scratch at my eyes but only managing to cut my wrists. Still, for such a little thing, she left deep red marks that began to bleed. I should have backed away from her then, but her anger did not scare me, so I lifted her from the ground and heaved her over my shoulder as though she were a sack of grain. She screeched and hissed and beat at my back with her fists, but I managed to get to the temple after only a few minutes of struggle.

I could not manage to open the side entrance, so I marched through the open temple doors, even as worshippers turned and stared. The girl's screams filled the space, bouncing off the stone and echoing like a strange song. I walked as quickly as I could to the rooms of the priestesses, calling out for Tanith's help and commanding several others to bring food and a bath. Tanith arrived quickly and came to stand beside me, her face sorrowful as she took in the girl's wasted body.

"We're not going to hurt you," I said, voice raised over the girl's din. "You are safe here." The girl did not believe me, especially once she saw the bath the priestesses began to fill with water, steam curling off it. As Tanith and I tried to lower her into it, she howled and tried to claw at my eyes again. It took three of us to get her into the bath and scrub her clean while she screamed. Tanith and I were panting and soaking wet by the time we let her scamper out of the tub. We had managed to get her into a robe one of the priestesses brought, but it was much too large and puddled around her, reminding me of foam at the base of a waterfall. She crouched in the corner, whimpering. "No one else should come near," I said, and Tanith and the other women nodded, taking a step back. I approached her carefully, holding out a large platter of food. Her eyes widened and she fell on it like a dog, suddenly uncaring that I was close. After she finished the food, she scampered back to the corner, and I sat next to her carefully. Her eyes were still wide, darting around the room, but she did not seem as frightened or angry, though I was sure she would attack me again at the least provocation. After a long moment, she looked directly at me, then pointed at the medallion that had come loose from my robes in the struggle. Her eyes were bright, but, I thought, this time with interest, not anger. "The goddess Astarte," I said, letting her touch it. "Mother of all."

The girl's eyes widened, and she leaned toward me, crooning a song, a lullaby, perhaps the only legacy from her own mother. Her hair was very fine and red in the light that poured in from the window high above us. I wanted to reach out and touch it, but I did not want to frighten her, so I merely sat with her until she finally fell asleep, exhausted. I smiled when I saw her eyes flutter closed. I knew what it was to have an anger so fierce it was like a fire that consumed everything. *That anger probably saved her life on the streets*, I thought as I touched the red lines on my arm. "What are we to do with her?" I heard one of the priestesses mutter to another.

I raised my head sharply. "She shall live here," I said, voice hard.

Tanith nodded. She looked at her for a long moment, then said quietly, "Perhaps she would make a good diviner. I will look out for her, Bel."

I nodded gratefully as I watched the girl's eyelids flutter.

"What should we call her?" Tanith said. We'd asked the girl her name, but she'd only shrugged, which had made a shiver of unease crawl down my back. What could it be like to be unnamed? And, worse, to not care about the lack?

"Call her Minta," I said. I'd heard the name long ago from a Greek trader and had always liked it, the click of the tongue that made it sound determined, strong, like the final word in a poem. "Make sure she's well cared for. I will check on her often." I bent toward the sleeping girl, and her eyes snapped open as she bared her teeth. "It is good for a priestess to have a fire in her belly. I think you will like the stories of Anat best," I said, thinking that this girl would stand up to death without flinching, just as the goddess had.

◎◎◎◎

I told Elijah the story when he came to my room that night. I'd already had Sapphira add it to her daily report of my day, but I wanted Elijah to add it to his too, wanted to talk about a new plan that had begun to sharpen in my mind, where the children on the streets were taken in by the temples and taught of the gods. After all, it would be easier to teach children of gods other than Yahweh, rather than trying to change the minds of stiff-necked adults. We'd some success, the temples filling with worshippers and the gods being given offerings, but many still shied away from them, still declared that Yahweh's was the only voice that they would listen to. And while I didn't care which god they worshipped, I did care when they wouldn't marry their sons and daughters to foreigners because of Yahweh's commands.

"She is small," I said, rubbing salve into the cuts the girl had made on my wrist. "But I have never seen or felt such anger, except perhaps my own. And she was so hungry." My voice cracked as I remembered how she had fallen on the food. I turned to Elijah but saw that his eyes were closed.

"Why aren't you listening to me?" I said, irritated.

He turned toward me, and the evening light caught his eyes and made them glow like a brazier. "Did it ever occur to you that I have my own troubles?" His voice was strange—angry, I finally realized. I hadn't ever heard him angry before, not truly, but now his fists were clenched, and his eyes were tight as a sail about to break in the wind. "You go into wearying detail of your day every evening, and some nights I do not wish to listen."

"You are my scribe," I said. "It is for you to record the events of my day."

"I am the king's scribe," Elijah said. "Why not tell your own scribe about the girl?" He mentioned Sapphira carelessly, as if he did not know her, as if she were *only* a scribe.

"I did tell Sapphira about her," I said. "But I also wanted to tell you. I want to be sure it is written down."

"What is there to write down?" Elijah flicked his hand in annoyance. "You brought a wild street child to your temple."

My palm began to throb with anger. "She has been beaten and starved on the streets of Samaria," I said. "She will be taken care of in the temple of Astarte. She would not be so lucky, I think, in the temple of Yahweh."

Elijah's eyes widened. "Yahweh is not what you suppose him to be," he said stiffly. "Even so, it does not matter. I will not write it down."

"Who are you to decide what you will and won't record?" I demanded. "It matters to the king what happens to the orphans in his own capital city."

Elijah slammed his hands down on the table. "No," he said. "No, it does not. I record your days because you ask it, but that does not mean it matters. Everything you do will be attributed to Omri, to Ahab. Why can't you understand the place of women in Israel?"

I rose and looked down on Elijah, voice hard. "I understand the place of women in Israel. I am no fool. But I am Jezebel, Crown Princess of Tyre, future queen of Israel. And I will not be nameless."

"You will—" Elijah said, teeth gritted. "Why don't you understand? Your name will *never* be written down in the book of kings."

I felt as though he had slapped me. "How dare you speak to your princess in such a way?" I wanted to fall upon him as Minta had fallen upon me, cut him until he bled.

Elijah stood, and I noticed dark circles under his eyes, hollows in his cheeks. "I'm your lover, Jezebel. I have the right—"

My head was buzzing like it was filled with a swarm of locusts. "You forget yourself," I said. "Leave." I turned away from him.

"Bel—" he said. "You can't just command me from your presence like I'm some—"

I turned back to face him. "*You* are a scribe. I can command you to leave, can command you into exile. I can command your death with a wave of my hand." The words tumbled out of me like a swift current, and Elijah's face slackened. As I watched it change, I felt horror crawl in my throat because I *could* force him to leave, to be exiled—killed—and then go to dinner without a drop of blood on my robes. The knowledge of it ran through me like quicksilver. I'd never considered how little control he had, how little power.

It was terrible to realize, but some part of me, the part of me that had been angry from the moment I drew breath, relished the knowledge because when it came to Elijah, *I* was ruler—king.

Even as I thought it, he went from the room as I'd commanded, and I was left alone.

I ran out to my pool and jumped in. I screamed under the water, but not with anger—with shame. I had once again not considered the position of one of the people closest to me, like I hadn't considered Sapphira when we'd first moved to Israel.

The powerlessness of Elijah's position suddenly, truly struck me. He risked the wrath not only of the king, the prince—but mine as well. Everyone knew how swift my anger could be. Any one of us could have him killed at any moment. I thought then of Ahab's concubines, of how they vied for Ahab's favor, knowing that the more children they had from him, the less likely he would be to desert them or send them away. Even I needed children from Ahab, which was why I had not flinched from him when he'd begun returning to my bed a month after the babe had died.

Elijah did not even have children to placate me with. *And any child we had together would never know him as their father*, I thought, knowing that all my children would be claimed as Ahab's. Elijah was as powerless as a woman in our relationship. His children would be taken from him. He might be a man, but his name would never be written down in the book of kings. He would never be remembered as his father had wanted. And the more time he spent with me instead of at the king's side, the less power he had. He used to spend his days with Ahab, hunting, playing dice, racing their horses around the hills, but I couldn't think of the last time I had seen them together. He had given up everything, for me. And I had treated him as a plaything I could discard at a moment's anger.

I did not even bother to dry myself, but walked back to my rooms, leaving wet footsteps shining on the cold floors. When I reached Sapphira's door, I hesitated before knocking on it. "Is something wrong?" she said when she opened it to see me dripping in front of her.

"Did I wake you?" I said, wondering if I had ever asked, or even cared when I had woken her before.

Sapphira raised an eyebrow and nodded slowly.

"I'm sorry." I sat on her bed and rubbed my palm. I wished it would throb, wished for the anger that made me feel clean and bright and scrubbed everything else away. "Did you truly wish to come with me?" I said, thinking of the tears in her eyes when we'd left Tyre.

Sapphira blinked, then sat down on the stool opposite me. She put her hand on my knee. "What is wrong, Bel?"

I sniffed and was suddenly afraid I would begin to weep like a child. I pinched the bridge of my nose and said, "Elijah left. He wasn't listening to me, and I got angry and . . ." I looked down at my hands. "How did my father treat his concubines?" I said, not looking up.

Sapphira shrugged. "I'm sure he treated them well," she said. "He was known for his kindness to everyone."

"He was not always kind," I said, thinking of how he'd slapped me when I'd objected to going to Israel, how he'd killed the previous king's family.

Sapphira said nothing for a long time. "He was a king," she said finally, voice soft. "Kings cannot always afford kindness. Not if they are to rule well." She sighed, then said, "But I do think he was kind to his concubines. None of the women I knew complained."

"What about Melita?" I said, thinking of the concubine I'd watched leave court, face streaked with tears.

Sapphira shrugged again. "I was too young then," she said. "All I know is that she displeased him, and so he sent her back to her father. I never asked why."

"I never did either," I said, running a finger down a long red slash Minta had given me. "She would never be able to marry again," I said. "Never have children or leave her father's house. Not once people knew she'd been with the king and been spurned by him."

Sapphira nodded slowly. "It is the way of things," she said quietly.

It does not seem right, I wanted to say, *that one person should be able to control another's life. Their very existence.* I did not say it, though. I just sat with Sapphira until finally she said, "I wanted to come with you, Bel." She squeezed my hand. "I wanted to see a place other than Tyre. And I knew that being with you would always be . . . interesting," she said, a little smile on her lips. "And you did not force Elijah into your bed. He wanted to be with you."

"But what is it, to be with me?" I said.

Sapphira didn't say anything, merely held my hand until I rose to go.

I left my rooms with my head bent. I hesitated on my threshold. I had sworn to Sapphira that I would never go to Elijah's room. But . . . but I needed to speak with him. I swallowed down the guilt at the betrayal, then made my way quickly to his rooms, keeping my head bowed and veiled so that no one would know who I was.

When Elijah opened the door at my knock, his eyes widened in fear. He quickly drew me into the room and bolted the door behind me.

His room was small and sparse. A bed stood against one wall, and there was a small window with a view of a courtyard and a large table full of his writing tools: pens and knives, skins and papyrus. The room smelled sharply of ink and the musk of animal hides.

"You can't be here," Elijah said, fingers still knotted in my robes from where he'd pulled me into the room. "If anyone finds out—"

"The king will have me stoned," I said. I had once seen a man stoned in Tyre. He had been alive through it all, and I'd watched the panic rise in his eyes as he drowned under the weight of the rocks. I would jump from my balcony and be dashed on the ground below before I would allow myself to be killed in such a manner.

Elijah flinched. "He wouldn't—"

"He would." I stared at him, feeling shame so hot and sharp it almost felt like anger. How could I show him how sorry I was? "I want to stay," I said finally. "Here with you."

I saw the happiness in Elijah's face before it creased with fear again. "What if Ahab comes tonight?"

"He came last week. He rarely comes again so soon." Rare, but not unheard of. We stared at each other, the silence in the room thick as honey.

"Do you know how I feel when I see him go to your room?" Elijah said suddenly. His face was as calm as still water, but his eyes burned, holding mine like I was a snake and he a charmer. "Sometimes I pass him in the corridors or see him get up from dinner and look toward your rooms, and I know—*I know*—he's going to you. To your bed. Where he will touch you: your face, your hair, your hands." He traced a finger over the mound in my palm that hid the star. "And I know you'll touch him back. And you'll . . ." He touched my throat with one finger. "And when I think of it, I want to smash his head in with a rock. Even though he is my cousin and has always been kind to me. Even though he has the right to you, and I have nothing."

I'd never heard him speak so. The passion—the violence—in his voice was so vivid I could picture him standing over Ahab with the rock still raised, my husband's face bloody, blank-eyed. I did not know what to say, so I buried my head in his chest, then lifted his hand and kissed his knuckles until he let me lead him to bed.

Our lovemaking that night was different than it had ever been before. There was a violence to it. He bit my shoulder so hard I thought I would bleed, pressed his fingers with such force they bruised me. It was as though he wanted to consume me—as though he could keep me safe, keep me with him, if only he returned my vicious anger with his own.

Afterward we were both wrung out and laid on the bed, panting. He began to drift off as he usually did, and I realized that I didn't want him to, didn't want him to begin dreaming again.

"Tell me about your dreams," I said, trying to keep him awake and wondering if by speaking them aloud, he would finally be rid of them.

He did not say anything for a long time, and I was wondering if he'd fallen asleep when finally he said, "They're more like visions—than dreams." His chest grew taut. "I keep hearing someone calling my name."

"Who?" I said, even though I thought I knew the answer.

He hesitated. "It sounds mad . . . and if I say it . . . that might make it true." It was the reasoning of a child, but I kept quiet until he spoke again. "I hear the voice of Yahweh." His voice was a whisper. "I am wandering alone in a desert and Yahweh appears before me. When I wake, I can never remember his face, but I know it is . . . terrible to behold. It is not meant for mortal eyes." He traced a finger around my lips. "Then he speaks." He was silent for a long moment before he continued. "He says that he has chosen me for something important. That I will save Israel from ruin."

I wondered what ruin Yahweh foresaw. Famine, drought, plague? My chest tightened at the thought. Israel was just becoming prosperous. Any one of those things could destroy all I'd built. "Gods have spoken to mortals before," I said. "Didn't Yahweh speak to Moses? To David? Perhaps you will help make Israel into a great kingdom as they did."

Elijah sighed. "It is what my father always wanted," he said quietly. "He prayed every day that Yahweh would speak directly to him like he did to the prophets of old."

"Perhaps his prayers have been answered in the form of his son," I said gently, but Elijah stiffened and moved away from me so there was space between us.

"I have no desire to be like my father," he said. "He was a cruel man."

"Do you not want to save Israel?" I said, beginning to think of what disaster might befall us, how Elijah might help me save the country.

"Of course," he said. "But in my dreams when I looked down, I saw that I was standing in a river running red. Red with the blood of those I'd killed. It was terrible. As terrible as looking at Yahweh's face."

"It was just a dream," I said. "Gods often speak to us through our dreams. That does not mean they will come true."

"I do not want to hear the voice of Yahweh." He shifted so that we were face-to-face, and I could see only a glimmer of his white teeth. "We could leave. Leave Israel," he said suddenly. "Go back to Tyre. You could swim in the sea every day, and I could be a scribe for a prosperous merchant."

I laid back on the pillow. It was a foolish dream. Not even a dream. It was not possible. Surely Elijah knew that? Knew that I would not be able to move back to Tyre, to become a scribe's wife and nothing more? I wanted to protest and felt my palm begin to throb, but I remembered my earlier anger, how ashamed I was of it, and instead of telling him how impossible his words were, I just kissed him and said, "Tell me more."

His words were fevered as he spoke, as he drew a picture so vivid I could see it. An olive tree outside the door of a little house carved out of white stone. A bench where he could sit and write and look out over the city. A goat that would give warm, sweet milk every day. He described what I would do, how I would have hands dusted white with flour as I made his bread, how he would teach me to bank a fire, to gut a fish. How we would be alone together, forever. He did not say it, but I knew he wanted the dream to last until our bodies turned to dust, until no one knew either of our names.

I let him speak until yellow light filled the room and I finally had to go. I had a hollow feeling in my stomach as I walked to my room, thinking of how he'd pictured me. Could he actually see me with white-floured hands? Was that what I was to him, even after all this time? A woman who would shape dough instead of a nation? I had just climbed back into my bed, was about to ring the bell for my maid and pretend I'd been here all night, when the doors flew open and Sapphira ran to me. Her eyes were wide, her robe askew. "Bel—" she said. "I only just thought to look in Elijah's room. He said you'd just returned. How could you? You know how dangerous it is, what would have happened if—" She cut herself off and shook her head. "It does not matter now." She took a deep breath, and I knew suddenly what she was about to say. I wanted to run away from her, from the words that I knew were about to tear Elijah and me apart forever, but I felt frozen, empty—a bird falling out of a bright sky.

"The king is dead," Sapphira said. "Ahab is king. And you are . . ."

"Queen," I said softly, thinking of the dark circles under Elijah's eyes when I'd kissed him goodbye.

"I love you," I had said, for the first time. The last time.

PART II

⊙ ⊙ ⊙ ⊙ ⊙ ⊙ ⊙ ⊙ ⊙ ⊙ ⊙ ⊙ ⊙ ⊙

There was never anyone like Ahab, who sold
himself to do evil in the eyes of the Lord,
urged on by Jezebel his wife.

—I KINGS

CHAPTER 9

Every moment I was with child I hated it. I hated the way my arms and face grew soft and pliant, like overripe fruit. I hated the way men averted their gazes as my stomach swelled. The women who had avoided me since I had arrived in Israel five years before—a foreign princess with foreign gods—no longer averted their eyes. Instead, they approached me without fear, touching my arms and my stomach, cooing at me like birds coo at their young. They seemed to think the softness of my face was an invitation.

I had thought it would be the Mother, Astarte, who would be with me as I birthed the child, and it was to her I prayed and her whose altar I filled with the choicest morsels from the kitchens. But it was Anat who filled my thoughts as my blood darkened the sheets and dripped wetly on the floor.

Sapphira held my hand as the long hours passed, until finally, the child was born. When they put him in my arms, I felt disappointment. I wanted—deserved—a crown of bone like Anat. One that would speak to the way my bones had cracked and broken to bring this child into the world. Instead, I had nothing but this soft thing in my arms, soft lips that were crawling like a spider, trying to get at my milk-swollen breasts.

"He's hungry," I said, holding him out to the wet nurse, who immediately let him suckle her. I laid back on my pillows, exhausted, wanting only to sleep. I woke some hours later when I heard whispering in the corner of the room. I wearily opened an eye, too tired even to jump at the face bending over mine. "He's very wrinkled," Minta said, pointing to the baby asleep beside me. I tried to prop myself up on my elbow but could not manage it for the pain.

Sapphira appeared behind Minta. "I'm sorry for waking you, Bel," she said. "But Tanith just arrived with Minta; they are here to look into his future," she said, rubbing a finger lightly over the baby's cheek.

"I am teaching Minta about divination," Tanith said, her voice vibrant as always, "and she begged to accompany me today."

I nodded and smiled wanly. It was common in Tyre for royal children's futures to be divined. I tried to sit up again, and with Sapphira's help, I managed it. I was exhausted but happy to see Tanith and Minta. I had inexplicably wanted my mother during the long hours of labor, had even called out for her, and though these three women were not my family by blood, they were the closest thing I had to the women who would have surrounded me had I given birth in Tyre. Minta's brow was furrowed as she continued to poke and prod the baby, who woke up with a grunt but did not begin to cry. He stared at her with dark eyes, and Minta stared back, seemingly entranced. "Do I need to stand?" I said, wondering if I had the strength, but Tanith shook her head.

"We can sit with you," she said. Minta scooted in closer to me, Sapphira beside her, and Tanith on her other side. Tanith picked up the baby and cradled him in her arms. For a long moment we all crowded together, looking at him, and then Tanith began to sing quietly. Her voice was high and clear as she sang, praying that Astarte would care for him as her own, that he would be blessed. After some time her song ended, and she pressed her fingers lightly against the baby's forehead. He frowned, and his lips began to pucker as though he would cry, but Tanith ignored his whimpers and closed her eyes. It was unsettling to see her eyelids flutter, and she was quiet for so long that I began to feel anxious. Finally, she opened her eyes and smiled at me. "He will be a good man," she said. "Kind and generous."

I frowned. Perhaps another woman would have been happy with such a pronouncement, but goodness, kindness—these were qualities that could get a king killed. I looked down at my tiny son, whose fingers were curled around mine.

"Will he be a good king?" I asked.

Tanith hesitated for a moment. "I could not see as far as I usually can." I frowned. "Not all children have clear futures," Tanith said. "Some paths twist more than others. It is not unusual, especially not for a child who will be king one day. But he will be a good man. Surely that will make him a good king." She glanced away for a moment before looking back at me. "Come now!" she said, climbing off the bed. "Let us have some wine and celebrate the prince's birth. After all, he will not be king for many long years."

◎◎◎◎

I looked for Elijah in his face. Skimming my thumb down his nose, I thought it might have a bump at the bridge like his. The baby didn't cry much, but neither did he seem happy. Mostly, he seemed confused by the world he'd been brought into. His brow reminded me of a sea-ruffled sandspit. Elijah had looked like that when he was writing, so focused on his work that he looked angry.

I thought suddenly of Elijah trying to pronounce Anat's name, how his brow had furrowed and his tongue had tripped. I lifted my son and held him to me. He was only seven days old, but he would not be as Elijah had been, unknowing of the gods, unable even to say their names.

"Once there was a goddess called Astarte . . ." I was nearly through the story of Astarte planting the star that would become Tyre when the doors to my room were thrown open. Ahab rushed in, yellow robe streaming behind him, and I started. I had only ever seen my husband take short, measured steps, but here he was, breathing heavily as if he'd run to us the moment the seven days of impurity had elapsed. He'd been told of the birth, of course, and the celebration throughout the city had been loud, keeping both the baby and me awake, but I had not expected him to arrive the moment I returned from purifying myself with water, a palace tradition that I actually liked. It felt good to scrub myself clean after the grime of birth.

I held the child toward him. "A son, my lord."

Ahab reached for the babe and I willingly put him into my husband's arms. I'd been holding him for hours, and my shoulders ached with the weight of his body. "I would like to be alone with my wife," he said, surprising both me and Sapphira, who had been sitting beside me on the bed. She raised an eyebrow but didn't object, merely bowing to the king before retreating to her own rooms. It was strange to be with him during the day, and I shifted, wondering why he wanted to be alone.

Ahab bent over his son, and I felt a sharp pain in my chest. For a moment, I wondered if my ribs, which had broken during birth, had broken again. But no, I realized, it was simpler than that. With Ahab in the room, I could no longer pretend that the child was Elijah's. I could no longer imagine a different future in his face.

⊚⊚⊚⊚

The last time I'd seen Elijah had been two years ago, just before I was crowned queen. I'd been able to hear the murmurs of the gathered crowd from the small room I stood in and was just waiting to make an impressive entrance when Elijah walked in. My eyes had widened when I saw him dressed in rough traveling clothes, a staff in his hand. "Where are you going?" I said. "Ahab and I are about to be crowned king and queen."

"Come with me," Elijah said, catching my hand in his. His fingertips were still stained black.

"I cannot go anywhere right now," I said with a little laugh, looking down at my purple and gold robes.

"Please, Bel." He lifted my chin gently, so I was forced to look him in the face. "Come with me now. We'll go back to Tyre. We'll get that little house by the sea. You can swim every day."

"It was only your dream," I said slowly. "We could never actually—"

"We could," he said, holding up his hands. "I will write. We can easily find a town that needs a scribe."

"And what will I do?" I said, looking down at my ruined palm. I wondered if he was teasing me. He could not believe that I would leave with him.

"We will be together," he said. "You will do anything. Anything you want." But even as he said it, a horn blared and the light in his eyes dimmed as he looked toward the throne room.

I gave him an incredulous smile. "Do you truly think I will be happy? In a small house by the sea? Herding goats?"

"Yes," he said, twining his hands around my waist. "You will be with me."

I pulled back. "Elijah—you can't possibly believe . . ." I stared at him. "They will replace me," I said. "From all writings. From all the songs. It will be as if I never came here. Never did anything."

"They could replace you now," Elijah said. "For not having a child."

My hand began to throb. "They can try," I said, gritting my teeth. "But they will not succeed." I lifted my chin. "I will not be forgotten. I won't leave."

Elijah bent his head as though I'd kicked him in the belly. He took in a deep breath that sounded like a broken cry, but when he lifted his head, his eyes were clear. He put his hand on the side of my face for one long moment, then bowed. "My queen."

"Don't leave," I said as he made his way to the door. "We can continue as we have."

Elijah shook his head. "I can't. I can't, Bel. I need to be with you. To have you, just you. I can't share you with Ahab—with Israel— any longer."

"Why are you acting so foolishly? What has changed?"

"I will not be your concubine, Bel, not anymore," Elijah said. "I would be your husband." His voice was choked. "I do not *want* you to have a child with Ahab. I want you to have my child. Our child. Entirely apart from this court, from this world."

"It is not possible," I said. "You know that. Ahab is my husband. He is the king of Israel now. Think of what I can accomplish at his side, as queen."

"Queen," Elijah said bitterly. "You would be queen over being my wife?"

"Yes," I said, my palm throbbing with anger. Why would he ask me such a question? How did he not know the answer already? "But, Elijah—" Trumpets began to blare, and the doors swung

open. The court of Israel—my court—stood before me, and when
I turned to look back, Elijah was gone.

⊚⊚⊚⊚

Ahab held the child up, and he began to squirm, which startled
me from the long-ago memory. With his face to the light, I
could see that the babe looked like Ahab, my husband. Not Elijah,
my lover, who I had not seen in two years.

"He's beautiful," Ahab said. He held the child to his chest, then
sat on the bed with me. I moved slowly to make room for him, my
body still aching from bringing his child into the world, though I
knew my discomfort was not something a king would notice.

"You must be in pain still," Ahab said. "Here." He moved closer.
"Lean against me." His voice was gentle, and he wrapped an arm
around me while holding the baby in his other.

I stiffened for a moment, surprised that he thought of me. But
eventually I let my aching body soften and leaned into him, though
hesitantly. Ahab had been in my bed many times, but after he always left and returned to his rooms. He was not the type of man to
sit and talk to in the dark, nothing like Elijah. His arm was hard
with muscle, and the hairs on it were fine and reddish. The arm of
a warrior was different from the arm of a scribe, but I still felt comforted by his touch.

Ahaziah had seemed large and weighty when I held him, but he
fit in Ahab's large hands like a doll. Ahab bent his face toward him
just as the baby opened his eyes. He blinked slowly when he saw
his father's face, and his face twitched like he was trying to smile.
"Did you see that?" Ahab said, turning toward me with a smile
very like his son's.

"He knows his father is here," I said, with a catch in my voice. I looked at the little table across the room where I had spent so much time with Elijah and then looked away.

Ahab leaned back against the pillows. "I wish my father could have seen him and known that we have an heir. That Israel is safe."

"I wish my father could see him too." I surprised myself with the admission. "I sent him word, of course," I said, knowing this child was the bridge that would connect Tyre and Israel for generations, but also knowing that as a foreign queen, I was not able to return home. The moment I had married Ahab, I was supposed to forsake my father's house forever. I looked through the open doors out to the horizon, but the far-distant sea was covered in clouds. "In Tyre we bring the babe and mother to the sea, to commit the child to the goddess."

"You're always looking to the horizon," Ahab said, setting Ahaziah down gently on the bed between us and turning to me. "What do you hope to find there?"

Any other time I wouldn't have answered him or would have laughed off his question, but ever since the baby had been born, I'd felt different. The world seemed . . . dimmer, somehow. I felt as though I were an empty melon rind, with all the sweetness scooped out. I wanted, as I had not let myself want in years. I wanted Tyre: the cool breezes off the harbor, the sails turning pink and red in the dawn, the skim of salt always on my lips. I wanted Elijah to be holding *our* son and wondering at his face. So, I turned to Ahab and told the truth. "I look for the sea. When I was first brought to Israel as a bride, I was told that you could sometimes see the sea on a clear day. So, I began to look for it. I suppose I never stopped."

"It was a part of your life, then, in Tyre?" Ahab said.

I frowned, thinking he was mocking me, but then I saw that his face was curious. "Of course it was. It's everything to Tyre, you must know that."

Color rose in his cheeks. "My father arranged the marriage, you know. I've never been to Tyre. I know why our marriage was good for Israel, but I know little about the place itself."

"It's an island city," I said. "I could see the sea from every window, every balcony. There are two harbors in the north and south, and so every day I would see ships come in, sails aloft. Sometimes my father would take my mother and brother and me out in the royal ship." I said, thinking of the time a line had slipped from my brother's hand and I'd grabbed it. The strength of it had bloodied my hand, but I'd held it steady until my father had steered us back to harbor.

As I told Ahab the story, his eyes widened. "Your father was not afraid of one of you falling into the harbor?"

"I did once," I said. "Father turned sharply into the wind and caught me off balance."

"You fell?" Ahab asked, shocked.

I laughed at his look. "I was fine. I'd been swimming all my life. I just floated on my back, and when I saw that my father wasn't coming back for me, I swam to shore. A dolphin swam with me most of the way," I said, remembering the fish's skin, wet, but smooth as silk.

Ahab's eyes widened. "Why didn't your father come back for you?"

"He had a meeting he couldn't miss," I said. "He knew I would be fine. Several dolphins live around Tyre. They used to play with us. Sometimes they would help injured sailors back to shore. Sailors who weren't from Tyre," I added. "They tried to come into harbor as our sailors did, but they often wrecked on the rocks because they didn't understand the wind."

Ahab shivered. "I can't imagine being alone in the sea like that. Carried back to shore by a beast."

"Do you not know how to swim?" I said with a laugh, but when I saw his face was pale, the smile dropped from my face. One did not laugh at a king. I shifted away from him, hoping that I might escape the brunt of his slap, but Ahab only chuckled.

"Where would I learn to swim in Israel?" He swept his hand toward the hills, crisp and brown in the sun. "The Jordan is dark as the earth, and though my friends swam there, I did not wish to swim where I could not see my own toes." Ahab wiggled his brown toes, and I was so startled I laughed. I realized I had never had so long a conversation with my own husband.

"I could teach you," I said tentatively. "To swim, I mean."

Ahab put a gentle finger on Ahaziah's stomach, watching it rise and fall for a moment. "I would like that," he said. "Is that why you built the pool? So you could have somewhere to swim? Your own bit of sea here in Israel?"

I nodded. "When I first arrived, everything seemed so . . . dry. The water is even different here. It tasted flat and stale. It was years before I realized it was the difference between water from a well and the water that we had at the palace in Tyre, brought from the nearby stream every day."

Ahaziah began to whimper, but before I could call for his nurse, Ahab picked him up and began to joggle him on his knees. "Nothing to fear, little one," he said tenderly.

I remembered suddenly the first time I'd met Ahab. He'd frowned when he saw me, and I remembered thinking that he did not want me for his bride. "You were not pleased with me when we first met," I said as he continued to bounce the child.

"I was pleased," Ahab said, voice suddenly stiff and formal. "It was a great day for Israel when our two houses were joined."

"You were not pleased," I said, remembering how disinterested he'd been, remembering too how Elijah's eyes had roved over me with such intensity I thought he was the man I was about to marry.

Ahab sighed. "I knew I had to marry. But I did not want to marry a woman who was not of Israel. And when you came in that day you looked so foreign. You were taller than me and wearing that purple robe covered with depictions of Astarte." I remembered that he did not stumble over her name, he pronounced it properly, as Elijah had not been able to do. "You were weighted down by as much gold as I was, and while I wished to be in my armor with my men, you held your chin up and your back straight. You looked like . . . a goddess. And I did not want a goddess. I wanted a wife."

His voice caught on "wife," and when I looked at him, I saw a flash of pain on his face. "There was another woman," I said, wondering how I had not realized it before, though in truth I had not thought of Ahab when he was not in my sight. In those early days, I had been consumed with my plans for Israel, by Elijah.

Ahab's face twisted, and I thought he would leave without answering, but he looked down at Ahaziah and his face softened. "I was taught to never speak about other women to you. That it would be disrespectful . . . but since you asked, yes, there was a woman. There have always been women." His voice was defensive, but I just nodded. I knew there would always be other women. "But Ahuvah . . . I loved her. She was the daughter of one of the courtiers. We grew up together. She had long brown hair that curled up at the bottom. She was small and delicate; she didn't even come up to my chest." I looked at my long legs, stretching out further than Ahab's on the bed. "I knew—we both knew she could never be my wife, could only hope to be my concubine. But when you came . . ." He looked at me and blew out a breath, but his eyes were soft. "She was with child. My first child," he said, looking down at Ahaziah and touching the soft dark curls on his head. "So no, I was not pleased when you came. You were installed here, where she had once been—" I frowned, looking around the room. I should have known that another woman had lived in these rooms before me, should have seen her touch in the delicate flowers that adorned the walls. "She died," Ahab said quietly. "The babe with her."

I remembered suddenly that long-ago day on his balcony when he'd acted so strangely. "That day I came to your rooms, and you looked . . . She had just died?"

Ahab nodded. "A few weeks before. I was not . . . not well. I had been drinking for days, and seeing you . . . it made me so angry. That you were alive, and she was not." He was shamefaced as he said it, but I understood. It had made me angry as well to stand by his side as we were crowned, to sit beside him at feasts instead of Elijah. The thought of that connection made me feel a tenderness toward him I never had before. Elijah had not died, but he was gone too. Ahab and I were together, and always would be. "I'm sorry," I said, putting my hand in his. He squeezed my hand, and we looked at the child on the bed.

"May I stay tonight?" Ahab said. "With you and the babe?"

I could have said no, could have returned to my thoughts of Elijah, my wishes for what might have been, but instead I nodded and made room for him in my bed.

CHAPTER 10

H e's such an easy babe," the wet nurse said when she handed me Ahaziah after his latest feeding. The baby's eyes were closed, but his eyelids fluttered as if in a gentle breeze.

"He is," I agreed, holding him to my chest until the woman smiled and left the room. Once she was gone, I put Ahaziah down in his cradle.

There was something . . . strange about the child. He only cried when he was hungry, and even then, the cry was soft, whiny. His lip would quiver and quiver, but he never really screamed, only whimpered softly until his wet nurse returned. Recently he'd begun to watch me as I went about the room, and he'd smile whenever I approached. I knew this should please me, but it only made me warier of him. I'd done nothing to gain his affection. And he was not a child who would grow to be a shepherd or merchant. He was a child who would grow to be king of a great nation. His affection should not be so easily won. When I brought this up to Ahab, he laughed and chucked the baby under his chin. "He has time to learn such things," he said. "Besides, kings need not be stern and unforgiving all the time. They are allowed small things too, like the pleasure of sun on their faces and the sweetness of figs in their mouths." I thought of my father, who laughed often but who I'd also seen beat a man until he bled. Kings needed to be ready for blood as quickly as laughter. It was the only way they could survive.

It had been a month since Ahaziah had been born, but I still did not feel myself. Sapphira said I needed to give myself time, but my body, which had once been so sure and strong, felt strange to me. For days after the birth I bled, and my stomach was still rounded and puffy, like bloated seaweed. My face had turned angular once more, but the softness in my arms and legs would not go away. Even my thoughts were slow and stupid. I tried to read a letter that had been sent to me about a school I was building on the coast, but I could not focus on it. I heard Ahaziah's whimper no matter where I was, and the figures seemed to float in the air like a mirage. I thought of how I used to work with Elijah and Sapphira for hours, reading their reports, discussing and arguing about my plans for the country. So much had changed since then. Elijah had disappeared after that day in the throne room, and I had not heard from him since. I wondered if he was still angry that I had not left with him. If he still thought of me.

There was a new scribe now, and while I read his reports, he did not come to my room. Instead I had Sapphira gather them. We went over them together, then she would return to the man and tell him the changes I had requested. At first it had been because I could not bear another man in my rooms as Elijah had been, but as the years had passed and I had more duties as queen, I simply did not have the time anymore.

The midwife had told me to stay in bed for several more weeks, but I woke one morning to a room that was hot and stuffy. Sapphira had thrown open the balcony doors, but there was no breeze, only a land rippling with heat. Sapphira laid beside me on the bed, fanning herself and slowly sipping a cup of wine, but I did not want to join her. It was too hot even to swim, and I paced the balcony for a moment as I thought longingly of the temple. Its marble walls and floors made it always cool, and as I looked back at Topaz, who was panting on the floor, I decided it was time to leave my rooms. As my duties had expanded, I had found it difficult to walk all the way to the temple and had not worshipped there in some time. It had prompted me to begin building a small temple in the palace, but it would not be complete for some time yet.

"I cannot stay here a moment longer," I said to Sapphira, pulling on a gauzy white robe and veil that I had not worn since I'd come from Tyre. I belted it around my waist and was pleased to see that my waist was beginning to shrink again. "I am going to pray at the temple."

"Shall I come with you?" Sapphira said, beginning to rise from the bed, but I shook my head.

"I would rather be alone today," I said. "It has been so long . . ." I couldn't remember the last time I had been alone, even before the baby; my duties as queen meant I was always surrounded by courtiers and advisors during the day, and in the evening Sapphira was with me as always.

I looked at the baby, who was asleep in his basket nearby, and Sapphira nodded. "I understand," she said. "Perhaps it will be good to thank the goddess for the babe."

I nodded, though I intended to think of anything *but* him.

I had not realized it was a market day, but I was glad for it because when I entered the city no one looked at me, too busy waving cinnamon in the air, holding up lengths of white linen, leading goats for sacrifice. Sweat beaded my brow, and I was pleased to finally reach the shadow of the temple. I was about to enter, but I was stopped at the side door by a guard.

"Halt," he said. "No one but the priestesses may enter this way."

I laughed. "I can enter anywhere I please," I said, wondering if he was making some kind of foolish jest. I swept my veil away from my face as I straightened my back and glared at the man.

"Your Majesty," the guard said when he saw my face, giving me an obsequious bow. "I did not know—the high priestess ordered that all who come this way be inspected—I did not realize—" He continued to babble even as I moved past him into the shadowed corridor. Once he was out of sight I stopped and leaned against the wall with a little sigh. The stone was crisp and cool against my back, and for a moment I leaned my whole body into it as though it might embrace me. At least he had recognized me.

I stopped in a shaded alcove to watch the supplicants and priestesses. I recognized many of them from Tyre, but others were from the streets. The children we had rescued often stayed with the temple even after they were grown. It made me feel better to watch them, their cheeks full, faces happy as they performed their duties. Perhaps I would talk with Ahab about building more temples throughout Israel so that we could house and train even more orphans. They would be fed and clothed and taught of the gods as Minta had been. I flushed when I thought of Ahab, which made me chide myself. *You're not a virgin bride heartsick over a sailor. He's your husband. You have been together dozens of times.* But I had begun to think of him in ways I never had before, about the strength in his arms, the smell of him, sweet and musky, so different from Elijah. I was not ashamed of my time with Elijah, but I did wonder sometimes what Ahab would do if he found out. Would he have me stoned to death? Would he care not at all? I wondered too which reaction I might prefer. I thought of how angry Elijah had been when he talked of Ahab in my bed, but somehow I did not think Ahab would have the same reaction. It bothered me, bothered my vanity, perhaps, that Ahab might not care if I bedded another man, so I'd begun to dress more carefully when I knew Ahab was coming, had trailed my fingers across his chest once or twice in a way that made him stiffen and reach for me before he remembered that we could not be together until I healed from the birth.

I was so lost in my thoughts of Ahab that I didn't notice the commotion until I heard raised voices. A man with a richly embroidered robe was holding the wrist of a young priestess. I could not at first tell who the girl was until I heard her voice: Minta.

"I gave my sacrifice," the man said, voice rough. "And now you'll lie with me as the goddess demands."

I was about to interfere when Minta whipped a small silver knife from her belt and held it against the man's neck. "Astarte does not demand that her priestesses whore themselves out to every man with a white goat," she said.

The man let go of Minta's wrist, and Minta lowered the knife enough that the man could scamper back, but he did not run far. "I know who Astarte is," the man said. "We all do. The whore queen bewitches Ahab with the wicked arts of Astarte and turns Israel to ruin. You're no better than her, girl. You'll show me what you learned now or when I find you later in a dark alley."

No one moved for a moment. Then Minta lifted her knife, slitting the man's throat as neatly as a butcher cutting the throat of a heifer. His face was angry even as he died, spurting blood over Minta and the white marble floor. "It is treason to speak of the queen in such a way," Minta said casually, wiping her knife on her robes.

The temple was absolutely silent, all eyes looking at the dead man. Then the guards began to approach Minta, but the other priestesses converged around her, blocking their advance.

"Leave her," I said, walking out of the shadows and throwing off my veil. It fluttered to the floor and landed in the pool of blood, turning crimson. "I said, leave her," I repeated when one of the guards began to advance again. He muttered something, color high on his cheeks, but another guard, the captain, perhaps, bowed to me and placed a restraining hand on the man's shoulder. I put my arms around Minta. "Clean that up," I said to the guard who had tried to disobey me as I led Minta away, keeping my voice steady even though my heart was racing.

Minta was shaking too, not with fear, but anger. Her cheeks were flushed with color, with the man's blood, and her eyes gleamed. "It was treason," she said. "To speak of you in such a way. To blaspheme Astarte."

"It was," I said, keeping my arm around her and leading her to the priestesses' rooms. "Elissa," I said when I saw another young priestess. "Fill a tub with cold water. And fetch Diviner Tanith for me. Quickly." I clapped my hands together, and the girl ran off. As we stood there, I thought of the man's words and felt fury rise within me. Minta had been right to kill such a man. One who would threaten her. His words about me came into my head again, and I mouthed the word "whore," feeling angry and sick, my head swirling. *It is just one man*, I told myself firmly. *One man who hates you for coming from Tyre, for changing his stubborn country.*

Tanith came hurrying toward us, her robes flapping in her haste, and her eyes widened when she saw the blood that covered Minta. "She needs a bath, in cold water," I said to Tanith, shaking my head so that she would not question me in front of the girl.

Tanith blinked for a moment then nodded. "Elissa is bringing the water," she said. We stood in a circle and watched as Elissa filled a tub. "Get in," I said, leading Minta to the tub. Her eyes still shone, but when she got in the water she began to shake, and the color left her cheeks. I gently loosened her hair from its braid and cleaned it, while Tanith wiped the blood off her face and hands. When she was finally clean, she looked as young as she had when I first brought her to the temple. Her eyes were wide as she looked up at me. "It was treason," she repeated. "I killed him." She looked down at her shaking hands then back up at me, eyes pleading. "Did I do right?"

"You were protecting your queen," I said, stroking her hair. "You did right."

Tanith and I stood outside her room after we put Minta to bed, and I told Tanith what had happened. Her mouth screwed up when she heard what the man had said. "I'm glad Minta had her knife," she said shortly. "But what will the king say?"

"Leave the king to me," I said. "The man committed treason. He would have been hanged anyway. This way was . . ." *Not* better, I thought. But some part of me had rejoiced to see a man like him dead at my feet.

Tanith put her hands over her face, and when she looked back at me, she was troubled. "Something is happening, Bel," she said, twining a finger through her hair.

I noticed suddenly that her hair, which had once been thick and red, was streaked with grey. Had it been grey the last time I saw her? It couldn't have been, it wasn't so long ago.

"He was not the first man this month to demand a priestess bed him," she said. "Someone is spreading these foul lies, but I don't know who. It seems to come from visitors to the city more than anything. As if someone far off hates us. Hates Astarte." *Hates you*, her eyes said, though she didn't speak the words aloud.

"Have you seen something?" I said, leaning toward her. "Something that might explain what is . . . why this is happening?"

Tanith sighed. "My vision is clouded, Bel," she said. "I thought when I looked into Ahaziah's future it was dark because he is a prince. But now . . . I cannot see almost anything. It is as if there is some dark mist before my eyes. When I look at entrails or the sky or the flight of an arrow . . . I am blind." There was fear, true fear, in her eyes, and for a moment that fear washed over me like a wave. "I am worried that this darkness is some . . . curse," she said.

"Who would curse us?" I said. "Israel has been at peace for years now."

Tanith bit her lip. "Since moving to Israel I have spent time learning about Yahweh," she said. "I thought that if I wanted to bring other gods to Israel, I would need to learn about him too. He is not like our gods, Bel." She fluttered her fingers nervously on her knee. "We worship our gods, bring them sacrifices, pray to them, and occasionally they might grant us a blessing, but mostly . . . mostly they do not care about us. They are too busy with their own troubles to look down on us, to give us commands and rules to follow." I nodded. Everyone knew that gods were mercurial and strange. As different from us as a bee to a lion. "But Yahweh is not like our gods," Tanith said, frowning. "Yahweh is always watching, always giving commands from on high to Israel. He brought the Israelites out of captivity in Egypt, he gave stone commandments to Moses, he helped a boy slay a giant . . . he is intimately involved in the lives of Israelites. And he does not like interference."

"But we are not interfering," I said. "We have not forced the people to turn from him. We have brought prosperity to his people. We have—"

"We brought them other gods to worship."

"What of it?" I said, my palm beginning to pound. "Since the day I arrived in Israel I have heard nothing except complaints that I brought my gods with me. I am entitled to worship as I always have. Why should Yahweh care if some Israelites follow my gods too?"

"Yahweh is a jealous god," Tanith said quietly.

I shook my head. "No. I have brought prosperity to this land. I have turned it into a place worthy of respect. I will not stop just because of one god." I stood. "The people are agitated because it is so hot. Once the rains come everything will settle down. That is where these rumors are coming from. And besides, the people love Ahab. Love me. Love does not so quickly turn to hatred," I said, trying to believe my own words as I stood up to leave, to flee the temple, flee the darkness that had overtaken Tanith's visions and led to a man, dead, on the white steps of my temple.

◎◎◎◎

I had not yet told Ahab about Minta killing the man in the temple, and when I was shaken awake in the early hours before the sun rose, I was momentarily afraid. Had Ahab sent someone to make me account for what had happened? But when I opened my eyes, I saw Ahab bending over me, smiling. "Get up," he said, flicking the covers off me like a child. I hissed and tried to grab them, but he merely laughed again and crossed the room so I would have to get up to reach him. It was terribly hot, so I was sleeping naked, and I saw him still as he watched me stand and stretch. I prolonged the stretch purposely, rising to my toes and arching my back. It was pleasant to be an object of desire again. Ahab swallowed then said, "Put on traveling clothes. We're going to be out all day." His voice was hoarse, and I took my time getting dressed while he watched.

"But where are we going? Should I wake my maid to dress my hair?"

"There's no point to that," Ahab said. "Can't you just—" He flung his hands out, and I finally realized he was gesturing for me to braid my hair away from my face.

"I could, but I want to know where we're going."

"I can't tell you," Ahab said. "It's a surprise."

"Tell me," I said, so close my body rubbed against his. "I don't like surprises."

Ahab swallowed again, and I was sure he was about to answer me, but he only smiled again and said, "No." He held out a hand. "Come."

I followed him out, surprised that he hadn't told me. It pleased me to be so thwarted. I was used to being obeyed; only Elijah had ever really told me no, and it was unexpectedly stirring coming from Ahab.

He led me through the still-dark palace to the stables, where a chariot stood. It was Ahab's chariot, made to be fast and light in battle, but even still, it glinted with gold. It was small, with room for two people who stood close: a driver and a soldier holding a spear or bow. Horses were already hitched to it, and a single servant stood by their heads. The animals were large, with short necks and feathered hooves, and though it was still dark, I thought their coloring was pale gold. Ahab nodded to the servant at their head, took the reins from him, and motioned for me to get in. I hadn't ever traveled by chariot, preferring a camel or my own small horse. I almost asked again where we were going, but I could tell by the slight smile on Ahab's face that he expected it of me, so I just flicked my scarf over my shoulder and climbed into the chariot. Ahab got up behind me, and I was held in his arms as he flicked the reins.

We wove slowly through the city streets until we came out the west gate and into the valley. Then Ahab flicked the reins again and the horses took off running. I laughed as the wind whipped at my face; for a moment it felt like we were riding a ship out of the harbor in Tyre, the horses' flying manes cracking like a taut sail. They ran as the sun came up, gilding their pale coats until we might

have been riding the sun itself. The land around us was beautiful in
the early sunlight, the groves of olive trees dark and green, and
even the dusty path we rode on seemed transformed by the light, as
though we rode on a swift-moving river of red and yellow earth. I
leaned back against Ahab, and he tightened his arms around me,
and I realized that I enjoyed the feeling of him nearby. I did not
love him as I had loved Elijah, but perhaps I did care for him, in
some way.

"This chariot was designed for speed," Ahab said in my ear.
"Usually that means it is a rough ride, but these horses pull it as
though it were made of air. They're the best I've ever had. They've
never been in battle, and my stablemaster didn't want me to buy
them, wanted me to get more experienced warhorses, but I want to
show the world that Israel is ready for peace. What better way to
do that than by the king's horses?"

"Will that be a problem if you do have to go into battle?" I asked.
"Won't you be more vulnerable?"

"They're still trained as warhorses," Ahab said, raising his voice
over the wind. "But they have . . . an innocence about them that
horses who've seen battle don't. It's probably foolish, but they
seemed more at peace than the other horses I've had. I liked that."

It was strange that my husband, the king of Israel, preferred
peace over war. I knew no other king who would have picked
horses because they were peaceful. My own father had ridden a
stallion so vicious it regularly bit its groom. Even my horse was
ready to rear and kick at any provocation. I thought of Ahaziah
then and gave a little sigh. The child had inherited his father's gentleness. They would both need me if war came to Israel. Ahab
might hope for constant peace, but I knew that the more prosperous Israel grew, the more others would want to take it from us.

Ahab continued to talk as we rode, pointing out the various

mechanisms of the chariot, his voice as excited as a child's. I fell asleep to the sound of his voice and woke only when the chariot finally stopped. When I opened my eyes, I was blinded by something that shone like a polished mirror in the sun. I shaded my eyes and, once they adjusted, realized what I was looking at: the sea.

I stumbled out of the chariot and ran, throwing off my sandals as I went before plunging into the water. I laughed as I was tumbled by the waves, as the salt caused my eyes to stream and the sand scratched my skin. Eventually, though, I surfaced and looked onto a perfect expanse of bright sky and bright sea.

Ahab stood by a large palm tree at the edge of the water, and I smiled and gestured to him, then, remembering that he couldn't swim, waded back to shore. I stood dripping in front of him for a moment then wrapped my arms around him. When I pulled back, he was as soaked as I was, and I felt suddenly shy, like a young girl. "Thank you," I said, taking a step back from him.

"I know you miss Tyre, the sea," Ahab said. "Since we can't go there . . . I thought it might be pleasant to have a day here." He pointed to the rug he'd laid in the sand, a basket with food and wine beside it. "And . . ." Color rose in his cheeks before he finally said, "Perhaps you can teach me how to swim?"

We spent the whole day swimming, eating, and lying on the sand in the hot sun. The water was lovely and cool, and though Ahab didn't take to it easily, he was determined, and by the end of the day he could follow me around like a very slow fish. He liked most to float on his back and look up at the sky, and for a long time, we looked up together and talked of our plans for Israel.

"We need to build more temples," I said. "It is good for Israel to learn of gods other than Yahweh. And they can take in even more orphans."

"I'd like to build a school for scribes right here in Samaria,"

Ahab said. "My new scribe is acceptable . . . but he's nothing like Elijah."

My stomach twisted at Elijah's name on Ahab's lips, and I purposely turned my thoughts toward Ahab's new scribe. He was a small man, with a pale face and pale hair, who reminded me of a mouse. I did not even know his name.

"I wish Elijah had not left just when my father died," Ahab said. "I needed him."

I needed him too, I thought, but knew it would be a betrayal of both Elijah and Ahab if I said it aloud.

"We spent many long days together when we were boys," Ahab said. "For a time, we were as close as brothers. But once I got married, he seemed to drift away. You probably knew him more than I, by the time he left."

I'd long schooled my face to betray nothing, but my heart began to race. What did he mean by that? Had Ahab found out that Elijah had been my lover?

"He was always in your rooms, so you could read his reports," Ahab said. "At the time, I thought it was foolish; why would you want to listen to the events of the day, again?" He frowned. "You don't do that anymore, though."

I was surprised Ahab had noticed. I shifted, hoping that he would not notice my discomfort. "I became too busy, once I became queen."

Ahab nodded. "Yes," he said. "Much of the pleasures of life are now subsumed in reports and courtiers. Still, perhaps if I had done the same, if I had spoken to Elijah each night, we might have stayed close. He might not have left." He sighed. "He did not even tell me he wanted to leave court. I wish I knew why."

"A man was killed in the temple of Astarte yesterday," I said suddenly, wanting to stop Ahab's musings on Elijah.

Ahab frowned and stood up. "Killed? In an accident?"

"No," I said. "Minta, the priestess I brought to the temple when she was a child, slit his throat."

Ahab's frown deepened. "Why would she—"

"He wanted her to lie with him," I said. "She refused, and he threatened to take her by force."

"Even so, killing is against the command of Yahweh. She must be hanged for it."

"She will not be hanged," I said, leaving the water and wringing my wet hair. The feel of the sand beneath my toes was suddenly irritating.

"It is the law," Ahab said, following me out of the water. A cloud had covered the sun, and the sudden darkness made the sea dull and flat.

"I have said she will not be hanged," I said, voice flat.

"I am the king," Ahab said, voice rising. "My will is law."

He sounded so much like my father, I almost believed him. But then I looked at him. His robe was dripping wet, his face red from the sun. He did not look like a king. He looked like a boy playing at being a ruler.

"I thought *Yahweh's* will was law," I said, twisting my hair back into a braid, wondering if I was foolishly baiting Ahab. He might be a gentle king, but surely he had some tipping point, some moment when his dominance would subsume him, make him angry.

"Of course it is," Ahab said, "but don't be ridiculous, Bel. You cannot protect a murderer just because you are fond of her."

He never called me Bel. The use of the name softened me, and I finally said, "The man said other things too. About me." I lifted my chin. "He called me a whore. He said I had bewitched you with wicked . . . arts. And turned the kingdom of Israel to ruin."

Ahab's face went still. Not calm, but hard, like stone. The face of the famed warrior who had killed many, many men. "To say such things is treason," he said. He came toward me and put a gentle hand on my face. "I would have killed him myself. Perhaps your girl—the priestess—did right." He shook his head. "The people have sung your name in the streets since you came here. You have brought prosperity to Israel. Do not listen to the ravings of one man."

We spent the night by the sea, and we laid together for the first time since I'd birthed Ahaziah. Ahab was sweet and gentle, but all through the night, no matter how he touched me, I could not stop thinking about what the man in the temple had said. I hoped that Ahab was right, that the man's words meant nothing. After all, he had been only one man. One man's words could not change an entire nation.

CHAPTER 11

After teaching Ahab to swim, something changed between us. He spent more time with me in my rooms, talking over the future of Israel. We planned schools, temples, and huge silos for grain storage. We discussed how we might avoid war, how we might show our strength without the fighting and bloodshed Israel was so accustomed to. Athaliah was born soon after her brother, and Ahab was enamored of her. After her birth, both she and I were sick for many long weeks, and when I was finally well enough to get up from my couch, the baby was a stranger whose thin, reedy cry was as irritating as the whine of a fly. She was small and delicate and looked nothing like me, but Ahab loved her, and I was glad to have provided him another child. Still, it was really Sapphira who seemed happiest with Athaliah. She always had the baby in her arms, crooning to her, rocking her as she slept, and rushing to her when she cried.

"Why did you bring her in here again?" I said one evening about two months after Athaliah's birth, when I was trying to read a new song Sapphira had written. The baby wasn't crying, but she was making little mewling sounds like a kitten and Sapphira was bouncing her on her hip and speaking to her in a high-pitched voice I found annoying. "She was perfectly happy in the nursery with Dido."

"She missed us," Sapphira said absently, holding the baby up to the sky and pointing at the perfectly normal sun setting behind the clouds.

I sighed. "But I want you to change this line, and now you can't because you're holding the baby."

Sapphira turned slowly, my daughter held tight in her arms. "It doesn't have to be done tonight, Bel," she said. "I can fix it as easily tomorrow, or the next day, or next month, and nothing will be different, except for her," she said, bending down so her cheek brushed Athaliah's.

"It will be forgotten if it is not corrected today," I said.

"It doesn't matter," Sapphira said, voice unusually loud.

"It matters to me," I said, feeling my palm begin to throb. "I want this line changed so it properly reflects what I've done—"

"Your children reflect you," Sapphira cut me off. "Or they would, if you paid any attention to them."

I stared at her. Sapphira had never spoken to me like this before. There was anger in her voice, but also . . . derision.

"I am just telling you the truth," Sapphira said, cheeks red. "Ahaziah hides behind me or his nurse when he sees you because you are a stranger to him. And I don't think you've spent more than a few hours holding Athaliah since she was born."

"They have the best of everything. Skilled nurses and a nursery that is gilded in gold. Athaliah is just two months old, and she wears royal colors." I pointed to the purple blanket Athaliah was wrapped in. "I am a queen," I said. "I cannot spend my time closeted up in nurseries with my children even if I wish to."

"You do *not* wish to!" Sapphira shouted. "You do not *have* to spend your days planning and scheming. You could read a few less of the daily reports that are supposed to be for the king's eyes only and spend time with the children you birthed."

I had never seen Sapphira look at me with such dislike before, and it made me feel odd: defensive and wrong-footed instead of angry, as I wanted to be. "I did not ask for children—" I began, but Sapphira cut me off again.

"You prayed for children for years," she said. "Do you not remember how you wept when you found blood on your sheets? You were so distraught when you lost your first child that Elijah and I slept by your bed . . ." She trailed away and looked down at the baby still sleeping in her arms. We did not speak of Elijah anymore.

I ignored her mention of Elijah and said instead, "I prayed for an heir. I needed an *heir*, Sapphira, you know that. Without an heir Ahab could have put me away, could have made me a concubine and gotten himself another wife. A new queen. You know the precarity of my situation."

"Your situation is not precarious anymore, Bel," she said, voice softer. "You don't have to fight as you did." She held Athaliah out as though I would suddenly look at her and feel . . . whatever it was Sapphira felt for my daughter.

"What do you want from me?" I said, suddenly weary. "My mother did not pay any more attention to me than I do to my children. She spent all her time on her own pleasure. If I did that, Israel would not be half of what it is. And it can be more. It can be better than it is even now. If only I keep fighting for it."

"But what will you leave your children with, if not your love?" Sapphira said softly.

I laughed bitterly. "What will love do for my children? It will not feed them or clothe them. It will not end wars or establish trade with other countries. Athaliah will not marry a man she loves. She will marry a man her father selects for her because that is what women do. Women leave their home and their family and all they love for a strange land where they do not know a soul." I knew that if I closed my eyes, I would see myself as a child, running along the docks, outracing the ships in the place I loved best because I had known I could fly. But I did not close my eyes. "And if they find love there . . ." I sucked in a breath as I pictured Elijah's face. "If they seek love, find it in the arms of another, they become dull and witless vessels of pleasure. But they can become more than a mother. More than a queen. They can become a name. A name with power." I looked at my daughter, at her tiny lips sucking in the air, the brightness of her hair. "I will do more than love my children. I will give them my name. *Jezebel*. A name that they will be proud of. One they and their children and their children's children will remember." I reached out and touched the softness of Athaliah's cheek, then looked at Sapphira. "I did not realize you cared for children," I said.

"I did not want to get married," she said shortly. "That does not mean I never wanted children."

"But when we were girls and Nikkal mentioned you having children, you were distraught."

"I was twelve, Bel," Sapphira said, shaking her head. "Most children do not know their true wishes when they are young. Most children are not like you," she said with a little sigh, dropping a kiss on Athaliah's forehead.

"I am giving my children what I can," I said, voice pleading. "You can give them love. I will give them a secure future. Rule of a kingdom that is at peace, not war. A place where their people will love them."

Sapphira nodded, reaching out her hand, though she did not smile and did not ask forgiveness for her words, as she once would have, and I felt all at once that the girls we had once been were well and truly gone, leaving only tired women in their place.

◎◎◎◎

One night, about four years after Elijah left, and a year after Athaliah's birth, Ahab and I planned a huge festival for the whole city of Samaria. Our trade with Tyre had been even more profitable than usual, and the city overflowed with wealth. The people's cheeks and waists were plump, and most nights, song could be heard on the wind. That night, we were going to throw our gates open to the people and thank the gods for the prosperity showered upon us.

The palace had been adorned with olive branches and flowers from our gardens. White tents had been erected, and our kitchens had filled the air with scents of fresh bread and roasted goat and lamb. The children of the court had driven everyone mad begging for the sweet cakes that the cooks had made, and more than one small hand had been burned by a cake snatched too hastily. Huge casks of wine stood at the ready, and entertainers had been brought in from all over the country. I'd also instructed that a special altar to the gods be erected in the courtyard and had asked it to be made of marble, inlaid with precious stones and gold filigree.

I had decided that I would preside as priestess for the night, and instead of wearing a sumptuous gown like the rest of the court, I dressed simply in a pure white robe, my medallion of Astarte my only adornment. I did not even let my maids paint my face, leaving it clean and unpainted.

By the time I left my rooms and walked out to the crowds that had gathered in the courtyard, the festival had already started. I had sent Sapphira out ahead of me, and I saw her in a corner with some of the other women of the court. Musicians were playing flutes and drums, wine was spurting from casks, and a group of women were dancing. Ahab and I entered together, and the sounds of festivity fell away. Everyone's eyes were on us, but it was my name I heard whispered through the crowd, not Ahab's. The robe I wore was thin and showed the curves of my body, but it was not my body they stared at. It was me, my whole person, as if they were seeing a goddess come to life. I was happy with their attention, but even as I smiled, a spike of unease pricked me. Some said my name joyfully, gratefully, but others sounded angry—resentful.

"Israel has enjoyed peace and prosperity for several years now." Ahab raised a hand. He wore gilded robes and was weighted down by gold. The difference between us could not have been more visible. "In no small part because of the union between our house and Tyre," he said, taking my hand. I smiled at the crowd again but wanted to frown. The people did not listen to Ahab as they should. Some in the back still spoke, and a crowd of merchants were playing dice in the corner and had not stopped even to listen to their king.

"We are pleased with the prosperity Tyre has brought to Israel," I said, raising my voice so that it cracked across the courtyard like a whip. The men stopped playing their dice, and the youths in the back stopped speaking. It was a long silence for so large a crowd, and I made it stretch for several moments until I said, "We will now give our thanks to the gods for this prosperity." There was a whisper then, a breeze of voices, but I ignored them and picked up the white lamb that had been brought out to me. All eyes were on me as I approached the altar and knelt before it. I slipped my silver knife from my belt and brought it down on the lamb. There was a spurt of warm blood on my hands, and I drew in a quiet breath, as I remembered the dreams of blood that had made me wake screaming. Elijah had been with me then, had wrapped me in his arms until I fell back to sleep.

You have brought prosperity to Israel, I reminded myself. *You have shed no blood other than what was necessary*. I thought of the man Minta had killed as I lifted the lamb and put the pieces of it on the fire, offering it to the gods. I filled a bowl with wine, then carefully spilled it on the altar, the engraved prayers that filled the bowl shining dark as the sea. "Let the gods continue to favor Israel," I said softly. I was still kneeling when I looked up and saw a pair of dark eyes watching me.

Elijah.

I stood quickly, but by then, the man who'd been staring at me had gone. Ahab waved at the musicians to begin playing, and noise filled the courtyard as I searched the crowd for his familiar face, but there were too many people, too many dark eyes on mine. I must have been imagining him, the memory of my nightmares conjuring him like a spirit.

"That was well done," Tanith said, appearing at my elbow and startling me. She'd been the one to teach me what to do, and I nodded at her, grateful for her approval. "Astarte will be pleased," she said.

I smiled and shook my head, trying to shake off the remembrances of Elijah. "One can only hope their god will be as pleased," I said, nodding to a group of priests who stood in the corner.

Tanith nodded. "They have seemed more . . . strident lately," she said. "They've been troubling my priestesses."

"Troubling them?" I said, thinking of the man who had tried to assault Minta.

"Not like Minta," Tanith said. "But they've been denouncing

Astarte in the market, preaching against the people who enter our temple, and speaking harshly to any priestess they meet."

I felt anger roil in my belly. "Astarte has brought prosperity to their land. More prosperity than Yahweh ever did. We have not made the people forsake Yahweh. Besides, why should they care if the people worship Astarte as well as Yahweh? If the people find Astarte to be a more forgiving god than Yahweh, then it is up to them to make their god appeal more." I turned to Tanith. "The next time you hear of a priest of Yahweh doing such a thing, come and tell me. My priestesses are not to be molested in any way."

"Will you dance, my lady?" Ahab said, appearing at my shoulder and holding two goblets of wine. His face was flushed as if he'd already had several, and he looked like a happy boy rather than a king. "I even brought you an almond cake," he said, holding up the sweet he knew was my favorite.

"We need to talk about the priestesses," I said to Ahab, though I took the cake from him. It was covered in honey, and if I had been in private, I would have licked it off my fingers, but as it was, I broke it apart, watching the delicate almond flakes fall to the ground.

"We will talk tomorrow," Ahab said, grabbing my sticky hand. "Come and dance with me!" He pulled me to him as the musicians struck a wild tune. Everyone in the courtyard began to dance, from the youngest babes to the oldest grandfathers, and I tried to relax in Ahab's arms as he spun me around and around. Soon, there was only the blur of torchlight, bright colors from the robes around me, and my husband's close face, but as he pulled me in for a deep kiss and I closed my eyes, all I saw were those dark eyes again.

The festival went on long into the night, and by the time the musicians put down their weary heads, most of the people were asleep in the courtyard, under cloaks and blankets or on the softest bit of straw they could find. The night had gotten wild as the wine had flowed and music played, and I'd seen more than one couple sneak off into the darkness together. Ahab had tried to pull me into a dark corner himself, his eyes wild, body full of wine, but I had gently pushed his hands away and directed one of the servants to take him to bed. I could feel eyes on my back, making it prickle with unease; it would not do for the people to see their king so lacking in decorum.

I retired to my rooms and stepped on the balcony as dawn began to break. For a long moment I watched people trickle out of the courtyard in twos and threes, children screaming and merchants hurrying to their shops before their wives found out that they had been out all night. The sun finally rose over the hills, and I was just turning to finally seek my bed when I saw a man leaving the courtyard and walking toward the throne room. I wondered if he was still drunk from the festival and if I'd need to send guards to turn him out of the palace, but then he turned and looked up at me. He wasn't close enough for me to be able to call out to him, but I knew suddenly who it was. I knew his dark eyes as well as I knew my own. Elijah had come home.

CHAPTER 12

My face and lips were painted when I left for the throne room, wanting him to see me as the fresh-faced maiden I'd been when we first met. I heard raised voices as I came closer and hesitated. Had Ahab been caught up with another contingent of his foolish advisors? I'd begged him for years to find new ones, replace the men his father had trusted, specifically Enosh, but he'd resisted, saying he could not dishonor the men who had done so much for his father and Israel.

I rushed inside, and Elijah turned from where he stood near the doorway. I had forgotten he was of my height. I'd grown so used to looking down on both men and women that it was a delight to simply match gazes with him. I was stepping toward him when he said, "Here she is."

His tone made me stop and look at him more closely. Could I have mistaken him? Could it be someone else? But no, of course not. It was Elijah, with his dark hair, a beard now spotted with grey, and wild eyebrows. I wanted again to embrace him but kept myself a pace apart as he stared at me with a strange look in his eyes. For a moment, I thought it was the burning of a long-lost lover, but then his mouth twisted and I realized that it was with anger that he looked at me. Hatred. My stomach tightened, and for a moment I wanted to cringe back like a dog that had been kicked.

"Look at her. Even now she wears a medallion with the image of her goddess between her breasts."

I touched a finger to the medallion, which had slipped out of robes in my eagerness to get to the room. Astarte's image had nearly been worn away by my fingers. He had touched it himself when we'd laid in bed, naked except for the image of the goddess between us. "You look like her," he'd said once. "So proud. A true queen."

He looked at me now like I was an aberration—a stain upon his sight.

"Elijah—you—you—" I'd never lost my voice to him before, and it made me feel hollow, like a mussel whose insides had been scraped clean by an eager fisherman.

"Don't be foolish," Ahab said, voice mildly annoyed. "It is a piece of jewelry. It means nothing."

"It means nothing," Elijah said slowly, "that your foreign queen leads Israel to ruin and damnation?"

Confusion flooded me at his words. He knew more than any what I had done for Israel, the schools I'd erected, the orphans housed, the poverty erased. What had happened to him in the years since he had been gone? "Cousin," I said, trying to keep my voice even. "Perhaps you would rather have a meal, a bath, and retire to your rooms for a time. We can continue to talk in private."

Elijah's eyes glittered. "You hold no sway over me. I am the prophet of Yahweh, and I see you for what you are."

I did not know what to do. What to say. What did it mean when he called himself the prophet of Yahweh? He had never wanted to be a prophet. He had only wanted . . . he had only ever wanted me.

He turned toward Ahab. "I began to have dreams. Dreams of Yahweh calling my name. I left so I could answer those dreams." His eyes did not even flick toward me at the lie. "Once I left, Yahweh instructed me, gave me the wisdom to see Israel for what it is. Filthy. A cesspool. Because of *her*. Because of your queen. Jezebel." He grimaced as he said my name, as if it were poison on his lips. In all the years we had been together he had only used my full name when he wanted my attention, when he wanted me to listen to him. Otherwise, he had just called me Bel. *Bel*, he had said, when we lay in bed together, a smile on his lips.

"You forget yourself," Ahab said, his voice a growl. I was relieved that he was going to defend me, but then he said, "Israel is not a cesspool. I will not have such words spoken against it."

My palm throbbed at how he ignored Elijah's slight to me, but I still went to stand by Ahab. "I am your queen," I said to Elijah. "I have brought prosperity to Israel. I will not hear a word spoken against it. And you will give me proper respect, or you will find yourself in chains." Even as I said it, my eyes were roving his face, his body. What could have happened to him since he'd been gone to make him say such things? He was leaner than he'd been when last I saw him, but there was something else about him, something strange and fervent in his movements, as if he were an instrument in the hands of another. *Yahweh*, I recognized. Even now he was in the grip of his god.

He looked straight at me. "You have turned the people of Yahweh into whores of Astarte."

I recoiled with a sickening thud in my stomach. It had been him all along. Elijah—*Elijah*—was the one who was spreading rumors about me. Elijah was the one who was making the people angry, who was saying that I was bewitching Ahab. Elijah was the one calling me a harlot. A wicked queen bringing Israel to ruin. I took a step toward him and said, "What do you know of such things? When your people were still scrabbling in the dirt like beetles, mine were creating the letters that would wing across the world like birds."

"What of the priestesses and temples that lead Israel to false gods?" Elijah said. "They teach only idolatry, harlotry. The people follow their example. As they follow the example of Jezebel." He turned to Ahab. "And you. You are no king. You look at her and grow weak. Her breasts granted her the temple of Astarte. Her long, shining hair gives her the priestesses she needs to spread her wicked lies across the land. And what is between her legs gives her dominion over you, Ahab. Over Israel."

Ahab stood, but before he could speak, I struck Elijah across the face. He was a tall man, but he still fell at my feet.

"You address your queen on your knees or not at all," I said, grinding my nails into my palms so that I did not place my foot on his neck until it cracked. The prophet crawled away from me, and I shuddered. This man could not be Elijah.

He stood, spitting blood on the floor before wiping his mouth and turning toward Ahab. "The sins you commit are greater even than the evil your father committed. As the Lord, the God of Israel, lives, whom I serve, there will be neither dew nor rain in this land except at my word."

⊚⊚⊚⊚

When I woke the next morning, I felt moisture on my skin and was satisfied that the rains would come. The prophet might say what he liked, but he could not control the rains. No god had such power.

Only it did not rain that day. Or the one after. The sky was dark, but not one drop fell. Instead, gold and purple lightning streaked across the sky as thunder crashed. I could hear children all over the city crying at each *crack*, and I wondered if my gods were trying to release the rain but were being stopped by Yahweh.

On the third night after the prophet's curse, I rose from my bed and went out to my pool. The hairs on my arm stood on end as lightning broke across the sky, but no rain fell. I slipped off my robe and dove into the pool, hoping it would soothe me, but my worries did not dissipate as they usually did in the water. Israel was always on the edge of drought, even during good years of rain. In the past years, Ahab and I had built enough grain silos that the country could survive famine and drought for a time, but not forever. I thought of the look in the prophet's eyes when he'd made the curse, and though Ahab said that it would be over soon, that we had done nothing wrong, I'd heard his voice waver, his face weaken.

I'd been too weak when Elijah had made his proclamation, too shocked to act like the ruler I was supposed to be. My father would have arrested any prophet who'd cursed the king. He would have forced him to repent of his words or he would have had him ripped into pieces. My father would have done it himself and not even blinked at the blood on his hands. But Ahab was too gentle for such tactics. Too devoted to Yahweh, even after all this time. And now I could do nothing, since Elijah had disappeared after his pronouncement, as though Yahweh had spirited him away. Why would he do this to me? Why would he try to ruin everything I had wrought? I dove under the water and screamed, screamed until I was gasping for air and had to break the surface. Lightning flashed, outlining a man standing by the edge of my pool.

He took off his sandals and put his feet in the pool, and for a moment, it was as though nothing had changed, as if we were talking as we used to, him sitting while I swam. I could have pretended, if I wished, that he had not just cursed me. Cursed Israel.

But I was not so foolish. I screamed for a guard, but the thunder stole my screams and Elijah laughed. His laugh, of everything, made me most furious. It sounded . . . so *like* him. I wanted to howl as I had on the night I'd been born, but instead, I reached for the dagger I kept at my side, before realizing I was naked in the pool, having discarded my robe before jumping in. He must have known what I was reaching for because he held it up. There was no light except the occasional flashes of lightning, and it made my dagger look strange, like something a witch might use, rather than what I used to cut meat and clean my nails.

"You've threatened me with this enough," he said dryly. "You think I don't know you keep it on you always except when you're swimming?"

"Since you have cursed Israel with a drought, I doubt I will be swimming much longer," I said, voice hard, even though the thought made me want to sink to the bottom of the pool and stay there.

"I didn't curse the land," Elijah said, sounding weary. "You did."

I stared at him. "I did nothing to this land except bless it. I brought prosperity to Israel. Schools, grain, temples."

"Temples that teach of the Baals. Foreign gods."

"You *know* her name," I said, voice rising. "Don't call her a Baal. Say it."

"Astarte," Elijah said finally, looking me in the eyes. For a moment I could see our previous selves so clearly: me a young bride, him a young scribe, as I taught him about the gods.

"You begged me to tell you her story," I said. "All their stories. You know there is no evil in them."

Elijah raised an eyebrow. "Anat bathes in the blood of her enemies."

"Yahweh had killed thousands before this," I said. "And if Yahweh truly *does* stop the rain, then thousands more will die. Thousands of innocents, your people. Children who have never known the bite of hunger will know it now if you do not renounce your words."

"They are not *my* words or *my* curse," Elijah said. "Yahweh has pronounced your deeds evil."

"What evil have I done?" I said with a little laugh. "Made the land flow with milk and honey? Fed orphans and enriched the land?"

"The temples of Astarte are throughout the land," Elijah said. "Your priestesses practice harlotry. Prostitution."

"They do not," I said. "And if you believe such rumors, then you are a fool." Elijah's jaw tightened. I knew the words would hurt him, knew that it was what his father had called him. But I was not sorry for them. I wished only that they were full of poison that would puncture his tender flesh.

"One of your priestesses *killed* a man, a wealthy merchant. She was not hanged and works even now in your temple. And you talk about innocents?" Elijah did not raise his voice, but in the flashes of light I could see that he was growing angry, and I was glad. The angrier he grew, the longer he would stay, and someone might notice he was here.

"He threatened her," I said.

"She broke the sixth commandment."

"Astarte does not have such commandments," I said. "He called me a whore and said I had bewitched Ahab."

Elijah's face was still hard, but I thought I saw his eyes flicker, saw his fists clench at my words. "You were the one who told me to listen to Yahweh," he said. His voice was almost flat, but there was a strange timbre in it, a note that rang off. Like he was pleading. "You were the one who told me that Yahweh would use me to make Israel into a great kingdom."

I stared at him. "I said Yahweh might use you to make Israel better. Greater. More like—"

"More like Tyre?" Elijah said.

"Tyre is a great kingdom," I said. "It has prosperity, trade, culture."

"It has foreign gods that demand blood as sacrifice."

"Those are false rumors, as you know well," I said. "When did I tell you stories of blood sacrifices?"

"You would do it, Jezebel." I shivered at the sound of my name in his mouth. I wanted to tell him not to speak it aloud, even as I wanted him to whisper it in the dark. "If Astarte asked you to give a human sacrifice to make your name greater, you would do it."

"Would you do less for your god?" I said. "Did your god not ask Abraham to sacrifice his son?" Elijah's eyes flashed in annoyance. "Yes," I said. "I have read the stories; I have listened to prophets greater than you."

"I am the greatest prophet of all," Elijah said, voice heavy as a stone. "I hold back the rain."

"You glory now in death? You glory in the harsh commands of your god? How very like your father you are," I spat out, wanting to hurt him, wanting to watch his face crumple.

"You made me like him!" Elijah howled, grabbing at his own hair and looking well and truly mad. "Before you came to Israel, I was merely a scribe. A man. Then you came and you . . . you enchanted me with your face and your voice and the stories of your gods. If I had not taken to your bed, if I had not held you in my arms, perhaps I would not have become . . . perhaps if I had been alone in my own cold bed, I would not have heard Yahweh. Perhaps I would have ignored the voice, dispelled it as a dream if I had not been full of the stories of false gods."

He heaved out a gasping breath, and the wind ruffled his face, making his hair fall into his eyes. I almost reached out and moved the dark curls away, but instead I forced my hand to my side. "You cannot truly blame me for this." I waved my hand at the dry sky. "You left."

"I asked you to come with me, Bel. You said no."

I flinched when he called me by the name that only my close friends—my family—used. I had not heard it from his lips since he left, and hearing it now was like having my hand held over hot coals. "How could I have gone with you?" I said, trying to keep my voice from trembling. "I am queen of Israel. Princess of Tyre. Where could we have gone that they wouldn't have known me?"

"You were a coward," Elijah said, voice rough. "You were afraid to leave. Afraid to be nothing. To be with me."

"I was not *afraid*," I hissed. "I did not *want* it. I did not want that life, that dream of yours. When did I ever pretend to be different than I am? When did I ever tell you that I would be satisfied with such a small life? How could you have believed that I could have gone with you, could have baked your bread and rubbed your feet and had your children? I never pretended to be different than what I was. I never told you that I wanted—"

"You should have wanted *me*," he said, voice strained. "You should have wanted me as I wanted you. More than anything. More than my very life. We could have been happy together if only you had tried."

I stared at him. How could he think that I could have been happy with him, living alone in obscurity? Had he truly never known me? Never seen me as I was?

"And besides." Elijah broke into my thoughts. "It seems as though you relish your wifely duties now. I saw you dancing with Ahab during your festival," he said, words quick as a tumbling stream. "I saw how you looked at him. And I saw him pull you into a corner to fuck you."

The words were so outrageous I could only laugh. "He is my husband," I said. "You have been gone for *four* years. In all that time you didn't write me one word. You might have been dead. Lost. You were *gone*."

"Did you think I would? After you refused to leave with me?"

"I loved you—"

"Not enough. So, I did what you said. I devoted myself to Yahweh. I studied and learned and listened. And Yahweh has said that your foreign gods are an abomination in Israel. They must be destroyed."

At that moment I would have gladly dragged him into the pool and held his head under the water. Not for cursing Israel, but because I understood the truth now. He had never loved me. How could you love that which you did not know?

I knew he was too strong for me to handle on my own, so instead I stood tall so that all of me was on display. "You may be devoted to Yahweh now, but that doesn't mean you are no longer a man. Aren't you afraid I'll enchant you again, standing here, like this?" My voice was soft as silk. I moved closer to him, so he could see the water running off my breasts. If I could get close enough, I could wrest my knife from him, hold it against his throat until guards came.

Elijah swallowed, and I could see the yearning in his face, the desire. I made my face mirror his and was angry at how easy it was. How easy it would be to be with him again and forget his curses. I stared into his dark eyes and took another step toward him, trying to imagine taking my knife and plunging it into his chest, trying to imagine what his blood would feel like on my hands, but I could not. In my heart I did not truly believe that Elijah had changed so much.

He leaned toward me for a moment, and I saw the same fight in his face before he scrambled up, moving several paces away. "You should clothe yourself," he said, face creased with disgust. "So as not to bring further shame upon your house."

CHAPTER 13

My throat was dry, my lips were cracked, and the skin around my knuckles was bleeding, but I was utterly still upon my throne, as though I were at my ease. I knew my stillness unsettled the men in front of me, knew they wished that the king was beside me, to stop the harlot queen. But the king was not here. And I would not be stopped.

Two years had passed since Elijah's curse upon the land, and since then, not one drop of rain had fallen from the sky. The kingdom had survived the drought only because of the great grain silos Ahab and I had made, but the grain was almost gone, and the country was beginning to feel the lack. When I walked through the market, the merchants' eyes were sunken, their skin papery and hot. They no longer spoke my name when I went by, and as the days passed, I could feel their anger begin to cure into hatred. I used to feel comfortable walking through the city on my own, but now when I went to the temple I had to be surrounded by guards.

Ahab was searching the land with his army for any unknown springs or valleys, hoping they could find enough grass to keep their horses alive, but I knew that it would come to nothing. I knew that Yahweh would not relent. Not unless called upon by one of his own. That was why I'd demanded the men come before me today. They were not prophets like Elijah, they did not claim to speak to Yahweh, but they were priests in his temple. They could ask for the drought to end.

When Elijah had left after that night by my pool, we had searched the entire country for him, but he'd disappeared once again. Finally, I got word that he was traveling around Tyre and its surrounding lands. Ahab had remarked on this, had thought it strange, but it made sense to me. When I thought of him watching the ships coming into the harbor, perhaps even swimming in the sweet, clean sea, I wanted to scream. He'd known I would hear of him in Tyre. He had known that this would punish me. I turned my attention back to the priests in front of me, forcing myself to not scratch at the dry skin on my hands. "You have the ear of Yahweh," I said. "I need you to intercede for us. Ask him to let rain fall on Israel once again."

A priest on the end shifted, and I saw him lick his lips as he looked at the moisture beading on the glass of wine beside me. He was young, younger than I was, and had probably never endured such hardship. He opened his mouth to speak, but then another priest stepped forward, an older man with grey in his beard. "The prophet of Yahweh has spoken," he said. "He cursed Israel for turning to foreign gods." His face was grim.

"You and your families will be rewarded for interceding on the king's behalf," I said.

"And where is the king?" Another priest stepped forward. His eyes were pale and piercing, and he looked at me with disgust. "I see no king here."

"I am the queen," I said, trying to swallow my anger. "I speak for the king."

"You are not a true queen of Israel," the man said. "The prophet Elijah already pronounced you for what you are. A harlot. Leading Israel to damnation."

A courtier gasped, and whispers ran through the room until I raised my hand. "The king commands that you ask Yahweh for rain. The punishment for disobeying the will of the king is death."

"You cannot put priests of Yahweh to death," the man with grey in his beard said. "It is impossible."

I smiled my too-wide smile. "Nothing is impossible," I said. "Not for Queen Jezebel. Now, I ask you again, who will ask Yahweh to relent and let rain fall on Israel?"

I admired the men in front of me for not trembling. But I'd pronounced their sentence already, and so when none of them answered, I nodded to my guards. "You will be hanged for disobeying the will of the king," I said. I saw shocked faces around the room, but I looked back, stone-faced. I had no sympathy for men who would not ask their god to spare the innocents who would die without rain.

Once the granaries ran out, I asked my father for help. He sent what he could, enough to get us through a few more months, but Tyre's own trade had been affected by the drought, and he did not have anything more to spare.

I had finished building the temple inside the palace a few months before the drought, and I was glad that I had completed it. The city had grown dangerous, and so I moved Tanith and Minta there so that they would be safer. I saw them most days, although only for a few moments, only long enough to pray together or squeeze their hands, but it was relieving that I did not have to worry about their safety out in the city.

Tanith looked exhausted when I saw her in the temple that day, and though she offered me a cup of water I refused and made her drink it instead. She was thin, and I knew she must be giving most of her portion to the children, but I did not chide her for it. We had more at the palace, but I'd seen Ahab give most of his dinner to Athaliah the night before, just as I'd turned from giving my bread to Ahaziah. We'd smiled grimly at each other, and I wondered how much gaunter we and our children would grow before the end. "The people still come," Tanith said, "but quietly. At dusk and dawn, when it won't be noticed that they're missing."

"Are the priests of Yahweh harassing them still?"

Tanith gave me a strange look. "No. They don't bother the priestesses anymore. I don't know if there's a priest left in the city," she said hesitantly.

"Why?" I placed my hands around the pitcher of wine in front of us. Moisture was trickling down its sides, and I lifted the drops gratefully to my face. "Where have they gone?"

"They're in hiding." Tanith looked down at her hands for a long moment, then looked up. "From you."

"From me?" I said. "What have I done to the priests of Israel? It's the prophet I'm after, not them."

"Ever since you had those priests hanged . . . well, there are rumors that you're after all priests of Yahweh. That you want them destroyed because of the drought."

I laughed. "If they are foolish enough to believe such things, perhaps it is good that they are no longer in the city."

Tanith reached forward and placed her hand on mine, looking at me directly. "They're afraid of you, Bel," she said softly. "And you know more than any how quickly fear can turn to violence."

I frowned but did not shout or slam my fist on the table as I might have done before. My anger over the past years had changed, growing sullen in my chest like a great anchor that would drag me down. "I know," I said finally.

"You could make a proclamation?" Tanith said. "Tell the people the whole story, how those priests disobeyed the order of the king."

I shook my head. "The rumors have spread. Which tale would you rather tell? One of the murderous queen, or one where criminals are punished for their crimes? The truth doesn't matter. None of it will matter until we can find Elijah."

"I've heard rumors of what he's doing in Tyre," Tanith said. "No one will tell me where he lives, but I've heard he's performing miracles. They say he's staying with a widow and that her flour and oil don't run dry, no matter how far she dips her cup."

"So he has enough, even as Israel starves." I pulled out my dagger and flipped it over and over in my hand. I couldn't see my reflection in it, but I knew that my face had become angular and sharp with the lack of food.

"I've even heard that he's . . . raising the dead," Tanith said, voice awed.

"Don't be foolish," I said. "No one can raise the dead. They are the domain of Mot."

"I trust the man who brought me the news," Tanith said, face strangely alight. "He said the son of the widow became ill and had no more breath in him. Elijah stretched out across him three times and said, 'Yahweh, let this child live again,' and after the third time the child sat up and asked for the sweet cakes he loves."

I stared at Tanith. She was the chief diviner of Astarte in Israel, and yet she believed the prophet could raise the dead? How had Elijah made such a story spread? I thought of the way Elijah spoke, how every word he said was shaped like truth, and I realized he was even more devious than I thought. If he was telling tales about raising the dead, any who lost a loved one would flock to him. Even—I thought, looking at Tanith—those who did not pray to

Yahweh. Why did everyone accede to Yahweh in such a way? Even kings did not get all they wanted.

I rubbed a finger over a leaf inscribed in the white marble wall and leaned my head against it. I closed my eyes, overwhelmed with sudden exhaustion. Tanith rubbed a finger over my hand. "Here." She pulled a honeyed bun from her pocket. "A worshipper brought some flour," she said. "I made almond buns for the children but saved you one. I know you love them."

The gesture made tears flood my eyes, and I took the bun from her. "Thank you," I said quietly. Tanith nodded, clasping my hands in hers. We sat, silent in each other's company, until I had to go. Holding the bun in my hand tenderly, I began to walk back to my rooms.

I was so involved in my thoughts of Elijah that I did not notice the dog before I stumbled over it. I didn't know where it had come from—perhaps it had crept in from the servants' rooms—but it was thin as a reed, and though I had stepped on it, it barely stirred. I bent down to get a closer look and saw that its eyes were closed, its chest hardly moving. I laid a gentle hand on its cheek, and it tried to lift its head to lick me but didn't have the strength. A sob rose in my chest, and I found myself weeping at the side of a street dog I had never seen until that moment. She reminded me of my old hound, Topaz, who had died with her head in my lap years before, after a long and happy life.

Elijah is raising children in Tyre from the dead, I thought, *while forsaking the people he claims as his own. Israel dies because of him and his god.*

I stood, wiping my face on my sleeve, even though I knew it would streak the black kohl lined around my eyes, and lifted the dog tenderly, holding it to my chest like a child. I had meetings to attend, but instead I retreated to my rooms, where Sapphira sat on the floor, playing with my children. "I found it on the street," I said quietly to Sapphira, who looked up when I entered. I went to the silver pitcher by my bed, which had barely a cup of water left in it. I had been saving it to drink after my day was over, but instead I poured the cool water into a bowl and placed it in front of the dog, who began to lap it up greedily. I looked down at the bun still clutched in my hand. It had been years since I'd had a bun with such soft, white flour, and my mouth watered at the sight of it, but I set it down in front of the dog too, thankful that I could give it one good meal at least.

The children had clustered around the dog and were tentatively giving it pats. I sat on the floor with them and Sapphira, leaning my shoulder against her head as Athaliah offered the dog her favorite toy, a wooden cluster of painted grapes. The purple paint had faded, but as I looked at it, I wondered how long it had been since I'd last eaten grapes. We did not have delicacies anymore, not even at the palace. "I am so tired," I said to Sapphira. Sapphira didn't reply, but Athaliah turned toward me and patted my face gently, holding out her grapes to me. "For you, Mama," she said shyly.

"Come here," I said to Athaliah, holding out my arms to her. She hesitated, but after a moment she moved into my lap. I held her to me, feeling the boniness in her back.

"Look, Mama!" Ahaziah held something tightly. He held my conch shell out to me, the one I had brought from Tyre. It had rested on the low table since I had come to Israel, and I still rubbed its smooth interior when I was especially homesick. I felt a fierce love as I stared at the shell. "Come here." I pulled Ahaziah close. "I found this with your grandfather on the beach one day," I said, showing my children the smooth, pink interior. They traced the inside gently, and I felt something crack in my chest. I had to do something. Something to keep them safe. I put my daughter aside and climbed wearily to my feet. I would do it. What I had been dreading.

I filled my basket with two other treasured items and placed the shell on top gently. I covered my head with a dark scarf before taking the long road back down to the city. I was not wearing my royal robes and did not bring my guard with me, so no one paid me any attention as I wended my way through the city. I used to love walking through Samaria, speaking with the merchants in the market, getting to know their names and wares, but the market no longer held pretty trinkets or baubles. The few merchants who still came to Israel brought only food that was vastly overpriced and that still had to be lined up for at dawn because it was all sold within the hour. The women I passed did not look at me but kept their faces to the ground, silent, hungry babies on their hips. I ground my teeth with each step I took into the city. The city that I had built up—that I had brought joy and prosperity to—looked worse than it had when I first arrived in Israel more than ten years before.

I had thought over the past years, in dark moments when my own belly ached with hunger, of trying to find Elijah myself. Of appealing to him because of the love we had once shared, but each time I thought of it, I remembered his face when he had accused me of leading him to Yahweh. He had looked mad. Been mad. I did not think that sweet smiles and talk of love would change his mind. I did not think it would change the mind of the god he was in thrall to. My palm began to throb with anger, with fury toward Elijah and his god, who had brought this devastation upon Israel. Not only had he taken rain and food away from the people, but he had taken my triumph away from me. He had taken the love of the people. They blamed me, saying it was me and my foreign gods who brought drought and famine on the land. I knew that there was no way to change their minds until the drought lifted. When the children began starving, no one cared who truly caused the problem, they just wanted someone to bleed.

As I looked over the desperate city, the withered hills, I knew that Yahweh still held the power here. And perhaps he needed me to acknowledge him, to offer him sacrifice.

I turned away from the city and back to the great temple of Yahweh I stood before. It was much larger than the temple of Astarte, looming over me as I stood in front of it, and seemed grotesque to my eyes. I had never been inside it, but now I walked in the open doors and bowed my head as a supplicant.

As I'd assumed, the temple was ornate, full of white marble, gold, and cedar. I stood in an antechamber, but even from where I stood, I could smell the sweet smoke of burnt sacrifices. I held my basket tighter to my side, took a deep breath, and walked further into the building, feeling as though I were entering the maw of a giant beast.

I had entered a second chamber when a priest appeared in front of me. He had hollows in his cheeks, and the body beneath his long robe was thin, his eyes suspicious.

"Women are not allowed any further into the temple," he said.

"I am here to make a sacrifice," I said, holding up my basket.

He frowned. "You must go to the court of the women," he said, pointing at a corridor to my left. "You will be able to see from the balcony, and I can make your sacrifice for you."

I wanted to shout at him, wanted to tell him that I was queen of Israel, that Yahweh was not my god and I could enter any part of his temple that I wanted, but I forced myself to grit my teeth, to lower my eyes. I was here to humble myself. To sacrifice what was precious so that Yahweh would end the drought. I handed the basket to the priest. "It is wrapped. Do not look at it. Just place it on the altar and burn it."

He frowned again, giving me another suspicious glance. I pulled my scarf tighter around my head. I did not want him to know who I was. "I must see that it is an appropriate sacrifice," he said, before quickly pulling the cloth from the top of the basket, making the items in it fall to the ground.

I had placed my most valued possessions in the basket. A purple robe Sapphira had made for me, a gold bangle Ahab had gifted me, and the shell. The robe and bangle fell to the floor without harm, but when the conch hit the cold stone floor, it shattered into pieces. Tears filled my eyes as I saw it broken upon the floor, and I bent to gather up the pieces of it. My hands were trembling when I lifted them to my chest and looked at the priest. It had been a rumor that I had wanted all the priests of Yahweh killed, but at that moment I would have burned this temple and priest alive and smiled.

"Don't be foolish, woman," the priest said. "It is only a shell." He sighed and took the pieces from my hands, throwing them back in the basket with the robe and bangle. "It is a silly sacrifice, but such are the sacrifices of women. Since you brought it, I will place it on the altar for Yahweh, but it would have been better to bring a bird or calf, something that would smell sweet in his nostrils."

The priest left, and I was still frozen in place. I did not know how to be if I was pretending not to be queen. If I was not queen, I was nothing. Just a woman far from home.

I clenched my hands into fists and breathed in and out for a few moments. *I am humble before you, Yahweh*, I thought as I slowly climbed the stairs to the court of the women. I had done nothing when the man had spoken to me with such derision, I had not killed him when he had carelessly broken my conch shell, I would *not* kill him, even after I left the temple that night. I made it to the balcony and saw the priest approaching the altar. I went to my knees as he lit the fire and dumped my possessions into it. I clasped my hands together as the fire slowly consumed the silk, turned the gold soft, and made the pieces of the shell bright and hot as stars. "I am on my knees before you, Yahweh," I whispered, glad that the balcony was empty. "I have humbled myself before you. I have sacrificed my most valuable, precious possessions. The last remnants of my life in Tyre. I am only an Israelite woman before you, begging you to end this drought, this famine. They are dying. Your people are dying. Save them," I said, voice hoarse. "Save us."

I left the temple that night with the smell of my burnt offerings filling my nose, my hair, clinging to my robes. I looked up at the dark sky as I walked slowly back to the palace, but it did not rain that night. Or the next. Or the next.

CHAPTER 14

More than three years into the drought and Ahab had stopped going out into the city because he could not bear to see them: Young men and women walking slowly, like they were grandfathers, without the energy to lift their heads. Dead piling on the roads with no one to move them. Street children with puffy bellies and dull eyes, too weak to even beg. Much of the trade had dried up, as no one had money, and the few merchants who did come to the market were from far away, fat, with bright eyes, selling food for such prices that even the palace couldn't afford them. One such man had set up his stall in the square a few months before. I'd not been there to see it, but Sapphira had been and had told me what had happened.

"He was wearing rich robes, blue and red, and his cheeks were fat and red like a melon." My mouth had watered at Sapphira's description. It had been years since we'd had melon. "He had jars of flour and oil, figs, olives, dried fish, even grapes. I don't know how he transported them so far . . . but they were still purple and shiny." Sapphira's eyes took on a dreamy quality. "It was the grapes that got him in trouble. He was waving them around like a prize. A merchant tried to buy them, a man who had been wealthy before . . ." Sapphira licked her lips. "He offered the man gold earrings, even a purple belt, but the man laughed in his face. He said he wanted the man's daughter for the grapes. He might have been jesting, but the man's face went dark. His daughter, a little girl, died last year. The man kept laughing at him, and the merchant picked up a rock . . ." Sapphira's face was hard.

The watching crowd had joined the man and torn the merchant apart, taking the contents of his stall and disappearing. The man who'd attacked the traveler had been jailed then hanged, and the few merchants who came to Israel were now heavily armed and surrounded by guards.

Our grain supply had ended long ago, it had not rained, and we could not find the prophet. We had searched all of Israel and the surrounding lands, but no matter how quick we were, he was faster. I asked my father for help, and he sent his soldiers throughout Tyre, but he could not find the man either. Ahab had begun to despair, but I refused to give up. Each day I walked to the temple of Astarte and begged for rain, kneeling before the goddess, but she and my other gods were quiet, and I knew why. Israel was the land of Yahweh, and my gods couldn't or wouldn't interfere. My own prayers and sacrifice to Yahweh had not worked. The only one who could change anything was Elijah. The one man who could not be found.

"Bel?" Sapphira came running into the room, gasping, shouting my name.

I was in the room that we used for meetings. I had just had an hours-long discussion with the king's advisors, trying to determine what to do. I had decided that we had to ask for help from the women I had married off to our neighbors. I hated to beg, but if it would keep us alive for a little longer, it was worth it. It had taken a long time for me to convince the other courtiers, who had not liked the thought of asking for help from neighbors who had been enemies only a generation before, but I had insisted. Now I just needed Sapphira to write them letters asking for their assistance and hope that they had food to spare.

"Is something wrong?" I leapt to my feet.

"I was playing with the children and Ahab in the courtyard when a man came. He whispered something into Ahab's ear and Ahab rushed away, calling for his chariot."

"Where did he go?" I asked as I rushed to the courtyard with her.

"I don't know, Bel."

I paced back and forth as I waited, desperate to know what had called Ahab away with such haste. Finally, I saw clouds of dust coming from the north, and a few moments later Ahab's chariot stopped in front of us. He was covered in dust from the road, but he looked triumphant. He picked me up and swung me around like a child while whooping.

"What happened?" I said, looking up, hoping to see dark clouds there, but I only saw the wide, pale sky stretching toward the horizon without a cloud in sight. "Why did you leave?"

"He was there," Ahab said. "He was sitting under a fig tree, and when I saw him—"

"Who was?" I said, though I already knew the answer.

"Elijah. Obadiah came to me while I was sitting here in the courtyard with the children to say Elijah had a message for me." I frowned, annoyed that Ahab hadn't called me to go with him, but I motioned for him to go on. Ahab's face darkened, hand going to the sword belted at his side. "I wanted to run him through with my sword. Instead, I said, 'Is that you, troubler of Israel?' "

I would have called him much worse.

"He said that he had not made trouble for Israel, but that I and my father's family had." Ahab wiped sweat out of his eyes and patted one of his horses, and I realized he didn't want to tell me the rest of what Elijah had said.

"How could he call me worse than what he has?" I said. "I am not afraid of his words."

Ahab's shoulders were tense. "He said we have abandoned Yahweh's commands by following your gods."

I kicked at a stone in the ground. "I cannot abandon Yahweh's commands if I do not follow him," I said. "He's trying to justify what he's done." Gore rose in my throat as I thought of the last three years, the people the prophet had killed.

Ahab inclined his head but said nothing. He had tried all his life to make Israel prosperous and peaceful, and hearing the prophet—a man who had once been family—say such things wounded him. "The rain," I said, hoping to change his thoughts. "What about the rain?"

Ahab's eyes glinted. "He said to gather the people from all over Israel and meet him on Mount Carmel. He specifically said we had to bring all the priestesses of Astarte 'that eat at Jezebel's table,'" Ahab said. "On the mountain we shall find the one true god, and that god will bring rain."

I had never seen the mountain, but I knew of it, of course. It marked the boundary between Israel and Tyre, rising out of the sea. Both Israelites and Tyrians considered the mountain a holy place and had never settled it, leaving it pure and unspoiled, the domain of the gods.

"The gods will not be pleased," I said, looking up into the still-empty sky. "They are not toys to be made to do our will. And it will take weeks to assemble everyone on Mount Carmel. More will die on the way there. Why is he doing this?"

I knew, though. The prophet was trying to humiliate the king, humiliate me. He knew that we would have no choice but to listen. *The man you once knew is gone*, I thought, clenching my hands into fists. *There is no kindness or love left in the prophet.*

"We have to go, Bel," Ahab said, taking my hand and forcing me to unclench my fist. "It is the only way."

⊚ ⊚ ⊚ ⊚

After speaking with Ahab, I rushed to the temple to find Tanith, but when I saw her, I frowned. She was wasted from the famine, and her hair had gone entirely white, though she was only a few years older than me, and I had just reached my thirtieth year. Her back was bent slightly, and as she walked slowly toward me, she coughed. I wondered if it was because she could not see. If the darkness in front of her eyes also took her health. I didn't say anything to her about her condition, though. I just clasped her hand in my own and told her what we had to do.

She arched an eyebrow, and for a moment I saw her youth showing again as she said, "That prophet certainly knows how to make a good story." She looked at the tapestry on the wall that showed Baal Shamem with his hand spread over the land, rain dripping from his fingertips. "He insults the gods," she said quietly. "Yahweh might speak directly to his people, but our gods care little for the woes of man. It is unlikely they will oppose Yahweh in such a way."

"I know," I said. "But if it will bring rain back to Israel . . ." I looked at Tanith's wasted face. "We have to beg the gods and hope they hear us."

Tanith nodded. "I will tell the priestesses. We will begin packing tonight."

"I want you to stay here," I said, taking a sip of wine so she

could not see the worry on my face. "I need someone I trust in Samaria." It was true, but I also wasn't sure that Tanith would survive the journey to Mount Carmel.

Minta ran suddenly into the room, face flushed. She was as thin
as she'd ever been, but her face wasn't wasted like Tanith's. She'd
told me she still had more food now, living in the palace, than she
had when she lived on the streets, and her young body was full of
strength and life. "I heard of the prophet's challenge to the gods,"
she said, eyes bright. "We cannot let it go unanswered. Your Majesty." She bowed to me, even though she knew such formalities
were not needed between us. She did such things only when she
wanted something from me, and when she raised her head, I knew
what she would ask. "Please let me go to Mount Carmel," she said
to me, even though it was Tanith who needed to give her approval.
"I've heard the prophet wants all the priestesses of Astarte. And
I'm nearly full trained."

Tanith sighed. "It is a long journey, child. And I need someone
here with me."

"No!" Minta said, turning back to me. "Please, Bel. I need to go.
I must answer this insult to Astarte."

I looked at Tanith, who shrugged, and I knew she would not
truly object if I said Minta could go. I looked at the young girl,
fierce and bold, and finally, I nodded. "It will be good for the
prophet to see that the priestesses of Astarte have fire in them," I
said. Minta whooped and threw her arms around me, nearly
squeezing the breath out of me. For a moment she pressed her
cheek against mine, and holding her was like holding my younger
self, a girl who did not have the weight of a country on her shoulders and had no thought for any but herself; a girl who *wanted*.

"Pack your things," I said. "Proclamations are going out as we
speak; we leave soon for the mountain."

CHAPTER 15

The journey to Mount Carmel was long and arduous. Every village we passed through was full of hungry, desperate people who joined our march as we moved on, and soon our ranks had swelled to encompass any in Israel who was well enough to go. We had decided to travel along the coast, as we had a better chance of finding water that way, and it was relieving to be near the sea again. I was surprised to realize I had grown fond of Israel, fond of the way the sun filled the valleys, of the way the hills rose and fell, making the path ahead of us seem mysterious, as though anything could be around the next bend.

We traveled through Caesarea, a large coastal city I had never been in. Parts of it reminded me of Tyre: it had the same white-washed houses clustering on cliffs that led down to a harbor, the same blue shadows and sea-tinged air. I wished I had come before, and I promised myself that once the drought was over, I would return.

The court still traveled together and set up camp apart from the rest of the country, but each day when I woke, I could feel the eyes of the country on me. It was strange to travel with so many. It had the look of a parade, but no one sang or played a flute or drum. Even the children didn't cry much but looked at us with dull, empty eyes. There was also a strange feeling in the air, a simmering, hungry anger that revealed itself in constant dark muttering and fist-fights.

We finally arrived at the mountain after weeks on the road, the moon rising behind it outlining its white, sheer sides. A contingent of soldiers scouted the mountain and said that Elijah was not there. I wondered if this was a cruel trick and he would not appear. I looked at Ahab beside me and saw how hard it was for him to hold up his head. I did not know what we would do if the prophet was not here.

We quickly pitched our tents, and soon the whole camp was asleep. Thunder rumbled in the distance, but as always, rain did not fall. I tossed and turned even though I knew my couch, heaped with cushions, was much more comfortable than the hard ground most of the people slept on. Finally, I got up and was about to leave my tent when Sapphira lifted her head. "Bel?" she said, rubbing her eyes.

"I'm going for a walk."

"I'll come," she said, and I shook my head.

"Stay with the children," I motioned to them. Usually they did not sleep with me, but I had kept them close to Sapphira and me during the journey, not wanting them to come to any harm in the mass of people. "I will be back soon."

When I walked out of the tent, David, the head of my guards, was awake, and he moved to wake the other guards, but I shook my head. "I'm taking a walk on my own," I said.

"It's not safe," he said, shifting from foot to foot. "The king will be displeased."

"The soldiers said there is no one on the mountain, and I do not live at the pleasure of the king. I just want to take a walk on my own," I said, moving past him and disappearing into the camp. The air was cool, and when I lifted my head to the wind, I thought I could smell rain. As I walked further out of camp, I could hear the rustles of small animals, but I didn't see anyone else awake until I reached the tents of the priestesses. I had seen Minta from a distance a few times on the journey. She had been one of the few who had been animated, riding her tired, old mule as fast as he would go and singing at the top of her voice. She was sitting now outside the tents, alone by the small campfire, and when she saw me, she jumped up. She looked so young, with her hair braided back, wearing a simple linen shift. Her eyes were wide and shone in the moonlight, and she began to walk beside me. I found her company welcome, and I let her stay by my side as I began to climb the mountain. She was unusually quiet as we climbed higher and higher, her long braid swinging lightly in the breeze.

The air grew tight as we climbed—thin, like the last note on a flute. Our pace slowed, and our breath grew ragged. Finally, when we neared the summit, Minta asked, "Are you afraid of what the prophet will do when he arrives?"

I laughed. "I am not afraid of the prophet." I knew that he would not want to approach me alone. He wanted to humiliate me and my gods in front of an audience. It was why he'd called us to the mountain in the first place.

"I forgot that you know him," Minta said, eyes wide.

"I *knew* him," I said shortly, thinking of Elijah with his ink-stained hands and questions about the gods. "But he is different now."

"How is he different?" Minta said, voice tight with exertion.

I hesitated, unsure what to say. No one but Sapphira knew the truth about my relationship with Elijah. "He was the king's scribe when I met him. Not a prophet. I used to read his reports each day. We were . . . friends."

Minta sucked in a breath. "You were friends with such a man?" Her voice was disgusted.

I smiled sadly. "He was different then. More curious. He was not Yahweh's chosen one yet. Being chosen by a god changes you."

Minta shook her head. "I would not change if I heard the voice of Astarte. I would be as I have ever been."

I nodded. "It takes a rare person, to be unchanged by such a thing."

"I am a rare person," Minta said, chin high. "You plucked me off the street as a child and gave me in keeping to the temple. I am destined for greatness."

If anyone else had said it, I would have thought them a fool, but when I looked at Minta, I did see someone with greatness, someone who could be more, as I had always wanted. "We are alike," I said softly, as we reached the summit.

We could see all of Israel spread out before us because of the full moon. The sea was far away but still glinted in the moonlight. The Kishon Valley was below, and though it was as barren as the rest of the land now, I imagined that it once had been green and lush, fed from the empty river gulch that wound its way up the mountain. I wondered when the river had last been full and prayed that by this time tomorrow it would be a raging torrent. The air smelled different up here, still holding the scent of the few scrub trees that remained in defiance of the lack of water. It was heady to stand on top of the mountain, so high that I could see a few night birds hunting below us, and I spread out my arms as though I might be able to jump off the mountain and join them.

"It's . . ." I turned toward Minta and saw that she had tears in her eyes. She wiped hastily at her eyes with her sleeve. "I've never left Samaria," she said quietly.

I took her hand and led her a few paces away. "Now you've been to Tyre." I pointed to the ground beneath her feet. I knelt and pressed my hands into the earth, feeling Tyrian soil under me for the first time in fifteen years. I stood after a long moment and pointed off the mountain, to the sea below. "The city is that way," I said. "It's the most beautiful city you'll ever see. It rises out of the sea like a great shell, white and shining. And no one there curses the name of Astarte."

"I want to see it," Minta said, face shining. She spread her arms wide. "I want to see it all."

I smiled, feeling a weight lift from my shoulders. "My father recently wrote and said they are lacking well-trained priestesses there. I think perhaps I know one I could send him."

Minta swallowed and turned toward me. "Oh, Bel," she said. "It is all I have wanted."

I put my arm around her shoulders and squeezed her to my side.

⊚⊚⊚⊚

The entire camp was up with the dawn, and though I hadn't slept much the night before, I too felt restless. Ahab squeezed my hand as we began the ascent up the mountain. Sapphira was by my side, holding Ahaziah's hand and carrying Athaliah on her back, but we did not speak. I saw Minta dressed in her white robe as we passed, leading a bull that would be used as a sacrifice.

We had nearly reached the summit when I saw him looking down on me, standing on a ridge a little above everyone. For a moment the whole world went still and quiet. The birds that were screaming above me made no noise, and the sound of thousands of people was silenced. We were far apart, but I felt as though I stood right in front of him, as if the air between us stirred with everything we had once been. Everything we could never be again. I no longer loved him, but I could not help but *know* him, as he knew me. We still had an intimacy we could not shake, would never be able to shake, any more than we could shed our skins.

Elijah averted his eyes first, and I sucked in a shuddering breath. The world grew loud with voices and the squawks of clamoring birds. Until, at the sight of him, the camp grew silent, staring up at him with hungry eyes. The sky was sharp and pale against his white robe, and he threw his arms open wide as he began to address the crowds.

"How long will you waver between opinions? If Yahweh is God, then choose him. If Astarte is god, then choose her. As it is, I am the only prophet of Yahweh left."

I rolled my eyes in disgust. Five priests had been killed years before, yet he and the rest of Israel seemed to think I had searched out all the priests and slaughtered them myself. There were still priests in Israel, but they were cowards who would not appear before me or even assemble on the mountain now.

"There are four hundred and fifty priestesses here—" Elijah pointed to them, disgust filling the gesture. "Have them pick their choicest bulls, one for Astarte and one for Yahweh. Let them cut their chosen bull into pieces and prepare it as they will. Then lay it on Astarte's altar, but do not light the wood. I will do the same with the other bull; then we will call on the names of our gods. Whichever god is the true god will consume the sacrifice with fire."

"What you say is good."

I wasn't sure who had spoken, but the crowd seemed to nod its agreement, and the priestesses began preparing the bull. I saw

Minta, carefully laying stones down for the altar, and thought of how she would thrive in Tyre, where the altars were inlaid with gold and jewels. Ahab and I, along with Sapphira and the children, moved away from the crowd as the priestesses worked, standing with our guards on a small hill.

"He has some trick planned," I said to Sapphira. "Something that will make a mockery of the gods."

Sapphira nodded but said, "I don't think we can worry about trickery right now, Bel."

"But he will turn the people from Astarte with guile. He will make them think that she is nothing." Sapphira just shrugged helplessly. I knew she was right; there was nothing we could do but watch. Ahab squeezed my hand but stayed silent, and I wondered if he, in his heart of hearts, wanted Yahweh to win. I knew he still feared Yahweh, still wanted his approval, like a child seeking the approval of his father.

Finally, the altar was built and the bull carved up and laid upon it. I saw Minta standing in front of the altar, waiting, and when Elijah nodded, she and the other priestesses began to pray. "O Astarte, our mother. Hear our cry. Anat, beloved sister of Baal Shamem, intercede for us. Baal Shamem, lord of the skies, answer us. Listen as your children call to you. Listen, and send rain."

They began to dance, to sing, and as they danced they called on more of the gods. They called on El, Gula, Melqart, even Mot, the god of death, but as the hours passed, nothing happened. My children were asleep on the ground beside Sapphira, and the sun had climbed into the sky, burning the priestesses' skin, parching their throats, but still, they continued to sing. I saw tears in the eyes of some of the priestesses, and I wanted to tell them to stop, that the gods knew what a folly this was and would not respond, but they just kept dancing and singing.

Finally, Elijah smiled, a grim, mocking smile, and said, "Shout louder! Perhaps Astarte is asleep or traveling. Perhaps she is sitting at her table, attending to her hair." His mockery twisted my stomach. The priestesses continued to sing, but now they brought out their knives and gently cut their forearms. Blood dripped down Minta's robe, and I knew the priestesses were desperate now for a sign from Astarte, from any of the gods.

On and on they prayed and keened and sung, but the bull remained on the altar, decaying as flies licked at its blood and the sun began to lower in the sky. Sapphira had taken my hand, and it began to tremble the longer we watched them. I could see the exhaustion on their faces, saw how even Minta's steps had begun to falter. "Please," I said, unsure who I was speaking to. "Please."

Finally, they sank to the ground in exhaustion and despair. Minta's face was pale, and her white robes were covered in blood. *I will send her to Tyre as soon as we get back to Samaria*, I thought. *Soon she will feel the cool sea breeze on her face.*

Elijah's face was triumphant as he said, "Come here to me." The crowd moved closer until they surrounded him. The priestesses were pushed out of the center of the circle until they were at the bottom of the hill, standing in the dry riverbed. Elijah built an altar, then dug a deep trench around it. Slowly, he arranged wood on the altar, then placed the pieces of his bull on it. He stood and said, "Fill four large jars with water and pour it over the altar and the offering."

They did it over and over until water—our precious water— overflowed from the trench and altar. Finally, the prophet turned to the altar and closed his eyes.

"Yahweh, God of Abraham, Isaac, and Israel, let it be known today that you are God in Israel and that I am your servant and have done all these things at your command. Answer me, Lord, answer me, so these people will know that you, Yahweh, are God, and that you are turning their hearts back again."

I felt the fire on my cheeks as it seared the earth, consuming the bull and altar so nothing remained but smoke. I had expected some trick like this, but even I startled and moved back as the sky filled with ash.

"Yahweh is God! Yahweh is God! Yahweh is God!" the people chanted, prostrating themselves. Of the thousands who stood there, only Elijah and I remained standing. I saw his mouth stiffen, but I just lifted my chin higher. No matter what trick he played, I would not bow before his god.

But I was a fool. I thought he meant only to humiliate me, humiliate my gods. I did not think that he would lift the sword belted at his waist. I did not think he would point it at the priestesses standing in the dry riverbed, and say, "Seize the wicked priestesses of Astarte. Do not let them get away." The crowd moved as if with one mind, surrounding them and making way for Elijah as he leapt down the hill, sword raised.

I screamed and tried to rush toward them, but the guards held me back. I clawed at David's face, but still he held me so that I could not push through the crowd. They erupted in a screaming mass, and I saw Elijah's sword flash over and over and over. I saw Minta's bright face for one moment before Elijah himself cut her down. I howled and managed to escape from David's grasp, but the crowd was like a rabid dog, and I was shoved hard. My head connected with something sharp, and the whole world went dark.

⊚ ⊚ ⊚ ⊚

I woke to seabirds. I could hear them cawing above me and smiled. I must have fallen asleep on the beach in Tyre as I'd done

hundreds of times as a child. A child. I was a child . . . I gasped and
sat up, my head spinning.

I was in a tent, lying on a couch, Sapphira curled up asleep beside me. Birds were screaming, and there was a strange sound . . . I
closed my eyes again, listening, and realized the pounding sound
was rain. Rain was smashing against the walls of the tent.

I leapt up and ran outside. I could hardly see for the rain pouring
down. I tipped up my head and let it fall on my face until I was
drenched. I looked around but could see no other tents, as if all of
Israel had just disappeared.

All of Israel.

Screaming.

Rocks in their hands.

Elijah.

I let out a keening howl and dropped to my knees. I screamed
over the rain, over the wind, and Sapphira appeared in front of me.
I could barely make out her features in the rain as she wrapped her
arms around me. She held me to her, her own body racked with
sobs, but I did not weep. My eyes stayed dry until she finally released me. I scrambled to my feet. "We have to go—we have to
find her. Minta. We have to find Minta."

"There's nothing left," Sapphira said brokenly. "The people.
Elijah—" She gasped, beginning to weep again as she named her
former friend. "We couldn't stop it. There was a bloodlust on them.
A hunger."

I turned from her and began to run up the mountain even though
I could hear her calling me, knew she was following me. I slipped
and fell over and over. My bare feet were cut by rocks, and small
mudslides tried to sweep me back down the path, but I kept going
until I reached the river.

It had been dry as a bone just a few hours before, but now it was a raging, rabid river, full of debris. There weren't enough bodies on the ground, and it wasn't until I got closer to the water that I realized that the priestesses had been standing in the dry riverbed when they were cut down. When the rains had come, their bodies had filled the river. Sapphira had finally caught up to me and was grabbing at my hand even as I dove into the river because I had seen a strand of long, bright hair.

The tides around Tyre were notoriously strong, but I wasn't sure that I'd ever felt anything like this river. It was vicious, yanking at my hair, my robes, as if it were a god trying to drown me. *Yahweh*, I thought with hatred. Another god might have succeeded, but my will was as strong as Yahweh's. The bodies were so mutilated it was hard to tell them apart, but I managed to find her. Only Minta had hair so red. I lifted her from the water, cradling her light body in my arms. Minta's eyes were closed, and she was so thin she might have been the child I'd found on the streets, face bruised and bloody, covered in rags. I carefully brought her to the other side of the river, where Sapphira waited for me. Sapphira tried to help me with the body, but I would not let her, holding Minta tight against me as I walked down the mountain, the rain drenching us.

When we got back to my tent, I carefully washed her body and combed out her bright hair. I dressed her in one of my purple robes and laid her on my couch so that she might have been sleeping. I touched her cold cheek and thought of how she'd pressed it against mine only the night before, when I'd promised to send her to Tyre. Sapphira took one look at Minta's clean body and rushed outside. I heard her vomiting and walked out of the tent too, but I did not vomit. Instead, I raised my knife high, then cut my arms until the blood ran down them as it had run down Minta. Finally, I raised my knife and cut open my palm where the star-shaped mark had been hidden all my life. I saw the edge of it, red and livid, and let blood fill my palm. I let the blood drip on the ground, then lifted my hand to my lips and licked it. "As Anat bathed in the blood of her enemies, so too will I bathe in the blood of Elijah before my life ends," I said, teeth smeared with blood. I turned to Sapphira. "You will send out a proclamation throughout the land. Say that while he—Elijah—might be the great prophet of Yahweh, *I* am Jezebel. May the gods deal with me, be it ever so severely, if I do not make his life like that of those he slaughtered."

PART III

⊙⊙⊙⊙⊙⊙⊙⊙⊙⊙⊙⊙⊙

"How can there be peace . . . as long as all the idolatry and witchcraft of . . . Jezebel abound?"

—2 KINGS

CHAPTER 16

As we journeyed home, just us and the contingent of guards that had been left behind, Sapphira slowly related the tale to me. It had been Ahab who had shoved his way through the crowd to my side after I fell. He had carried me back to my guards, had tried to stop the crowd from murdering the priestesses, but we had not had enough soldiers with us and the crowd would not listen, not even to their king.

"It was over very quickly," Sapphira said. "Once it was done, Elijah stood . . ." She hesitated.

"Go on," I said. "I want to know every detail."

"He looked like a general after a battle. He was covered in blood and gore, his white robes red. He did not look triumphant, though. He looked . . . stricken. As if he was a different man than the one who had ordered the killings. He looked down at his hands, which were dark with blood, and for a moment I thought he might weep. The crowd had quieted down by then, and most were looking dazed, as though unsure of what they'd done. Elijah turned toward Ahab and said, 'Hitch up your chariot and go down before the rain stops you.'"

Ahab had not wanted to leave me, but his advisors had been so terrified that not obeying the prophet would mean losing the rain that they had convinced him to leave me with Sapphira and the troop of soldiers. The people followed Ahab as he left, trailing off the mountain until it was only us left with the dead.

By the time we returned to the palace, we were all filthy and exhausted. As soon as we returned, Sapphira left me to go find the children, and I let her go, knowing that they would bring her comfort.

I went out to my pool and found that the rain had filled it again and I could see my reflection in its smooth surface. I lifted a foot but could not bring myself to dive into the cool water. All I could think of was Minta standing beside me on the mountain, her delight as I told her that I would send her to Tyre. I tried to picture her standing beside me, happy as a bride in her robes, as I bade her farewell before she went to Tyre, but my vision swam and all I could see was a rushing, grey torrent. Arms, bright with blood. Fingertips that rose above the water, nails pink as a sunset. The dead eyes of women that looked the same as the dead eyes of fish, staring and filmy.

I vomited into the pool as I remembered finding Minta in the water. Her body had floated near the opposite bank and her hair had come free of its plait and trailed around her like a bronze ribbon. Her eyes had been closed, and I realized suddenly that I would never see their brightness again.

I vomited once more, and Ahab was suddenly at my side, holding a cloth out to me. I nodded and took it from him, wiping my mouth with it. He cradled me into his chest for a long time and then said, "It is common for soldiers after their first battle to feel . . . desolate. No matter if they won or lost."

I had forgotten that he had seen war before. Forgotten that he had seen people he loved cut down in front of him. "It wasn't a battle," I said. "It was a massacre."

Ahab nodded and sighed. "I have heard reports that people around Israel are waking as if from a dream. The famine has begun to lift and so has their hunger, and they wonder . . . they wonder what they did that day. If their own hand dealt a killing blow."

"They did evil," I said slowly. "But none of them would have lifted a hand without the prophet's direction. He tricked them with the fire that seemed to fall from heaven. After that, they were like children. They looked on him as if he were a god himself."

Ahab didn't say anything, just slipped his hand into mine. Just as we were about to enter the palace, I turned to him. "You said that soldiers feel desolate after a battle. But they recover? Eventually they become themselves again?"

Ahab hesitated and finally said, "Some do. Some begin to laugh again, to joke with their friends and kiss their wives."

"And the others?"

"Not all men are made to handle war, Bel. Some men who see such suffering . . . something inside them breaks. They crack open like a seed and eventually wither and rot away."

◎◎◎◎

The country recovered slowly from the famine and drought. Crops grew again, and the rivers overflowed. Many had turned back to Yahweh, but many also returned to the temples of Astarte, even as they cursed me for bringing her to Israel. They blamed me for the drought, the famine. For the dead. But I no longer cared what the people thought of me. I cared for little, in the days after Minta was killed.

There were stories of Elijah too, but none of where he was in Is-

rael. He had fled for Judea and reportedly never stayed more than
a few nights in one place, afraid that I would kill him. Some said he
had taken on an apprentice, a man named Berel, but I did not care.
It was as easy to kill two men who traveled together as it was to
kill one.

My chambers soon resembled a war room, covered in maps and
letters, all my focus fixed on the prophet. "Here, General," I said,
circling a point on the map with a pen. "He was last seen in the hills
above this town. By now he must need food. He will make his way
down there eventually." I had taken a whole unit of the army for
my pursuit of Elijah, sent them on hunt after hunt. Ahab had protested this, said that they were needed somewhere else, but I did
not listen to Ahab. He did not understand why I needed Elijah
dead. He'd never said it, but I wondered if he was glad the priestesses were dead. If he thought they were a needed sacrifice that had
ended the drought and famine. I wondered sometimes, when I lay
in bed and tried to sleep, what I would do if Ahab ever said such a
thing to me.

The general nodded, and I wondered vaguely when I had last
seen Ahab as I poured another glass of wine. I had a hazy image of
him standing in my rooms, perhaps arrayed in his armor? I did not
know why he had been dressed in armor. He had not been needed
on the battlefield in years, but I had not cared enough to ask.

"Bel," Sapphira said, entering my rooms silent as a ghost. I did
not know how long it had been since the general had left, but I was
already busy searching out the next place Elijah might be. I took a
long swallow of the wine by my side, draining the glass, and then
pointed to the map.

"Look," I said, reaching for the bottle once more. "He was in the
east just a few days ago; he usually moves east to west, so I could

trap him in this valley next. Perhaps I will send some of the hunting dogs after him."

"Bel——" Sapphira said again, but I ignored her sharp tone. "The king needs you for the war council."

"I'm too busy." I waved a hand. "Tell him to do whatever he thinks is best."

"Jezebel," Sapphira said, reaching out to touch my cheek as she had when we were girls and she wanted my full attention. "He sent several servants. It's important."

"Not more important than this," I said.

Sapphira moved quickly, sweeping everything off my table. Scrolls and animal skins crashed to the floor, and a jar of ink began to pool on my latest map. I jumped up but couldn't save the papyrus, and I turned to her, furious. "You forget yourself," I said, voice hard.

"No," Sapphira said. "I don't." She squared her shoulders. "I have been your scribe since we were girls. I have been your friend for longer. And I have never seen you like this. You barely sleep; you spend all your time poring over maps and devising new tortures for the prophet."

"The prophet killed Minta," I said. "And hundreds of my priestesses. Women we knew in Tyre. Girls we played with."

Sapphira nodded. "It was terrible," she said.

"How do you know what it was like?" I said, palm thudding like a drum. "You weren't there."

Sapphira stared at me. "I was there, Bel. I was standing beside you when it happened."

I blinked, feeling caught like a fly in a trap of honey. "No," I said. "It was only me. Me and Elijah."

"No——" Sapphira shook her head. "We were all there. All of Israel saw what he did."

"All of Israel tore them apart," I whispered, remembering the screams of the crowd, the hunger in their faces as they rushed forward.

"Not all of them," Sapphira said. "Not Ahab. Or me."

"I know," I said, "otherwise both of you would be dead." Sapphira flinched, and I was sorry for frightening her, so I said more gently, "I cannot punish all of Israel. So, he, their prophet, must be the one to suffer. You understand, don't you, Sapphira? He needs to be afraid. He needs to be afraid like Minta was."

"I understand," Sapphira said. "But now everyone else is afraid of you too. Haven't you noticed how your maids flinch when you address them? Even your own children are afraid of you."

"Don't be a fool," I said, turning to gather the fallen scrolls.

Sapphira took me by the shoulders. "Listen to me, Bel. We are at war," she said. "Ben-Hadad has surrounded the city."

I stared at Sapphira—was she trying to make a fool of me? I walked out to my balcony, and the breeze on my face felt strange, as though I had not been outdoors for some time. I dimly thought of my pool, full once again, and wondered if I had stood by it since that day I'd returned to Samaria. It was the middle of the day, but the city was quiet as a tomb. I looked out and saw the sun shining on something in the distance. I recognized the glint of armor and gasped, turning to Sapphira, beginning to shake. "I don't remember, I didn't realize . . . how long has it been? Since"—I swallowed—"since that day?"

Sapphira ran a hand through my hair. "It's been months," she said quietly. "You don't remember?"

"I do," I said. "I remember everything, but it all seemed . . . everything else seems like sand, slipping away. Nothing else felt important." I put a hand to my hair. It reeked of oil and was full of snarls. I wondered how long it had been since I'd last bathed.

I suddenly remembered other things too. Screaming at servants who tried to get me to bathe, to dress. Ahab begging me to eat, to sleep. My children, turning away at my blank face.

"How did Ben-Hadad surround the city so quickly?" I said. "I was at the temple only the other day, and everything was normal."

"You haven't left your rooms in weeks, Bel," Sapphira said. "You're always here, poring over these maps."

"Why did Ahab allow an army to surround us?" I said. "Why didn't he send for me before this?"

"He did," Sapphira said. "He asked you to come last week. They surrounded the city yesterday. Today, he asked me to come to you one last time."

She clasped my hand for a long moment, and when she drew away, my eyes were full. I reached for the fresh wine that stood on my table. But before I grasped it, I pulled my hand away. I remembered one thing about the past months very clearly. I was always drinking wine. Cup after cup until my head swam and the world became soft and muzzy. I drank so much that I forgot about everything—everyone—but the prophet.

Sapphira gave a small smile when she saw me turn from the wine. She took it and poured it off the balcony so that it splashed onto the stone below. "The army was greatly depleted from the famine and drought," she said. "Many of the horses died, and the men were weakened. And Ahab has been more focused on building schools and grain silos in the past years, using your own plans, than building up the army. We think Ben-Hadad must have spies at the court who saw our weakened state. And now we're besieged from all sides. Ahab has tried to reason with him instead of fight; he even sent him a message saying, 'One who puts on his armor should not boast like one who takes it off,' but Ben-Hadad is young and eager to make a name for himself. They're preparing to attack the city." Sapphira's voice was even, but I could see how pale she was. Her shoulders were bowed as if she'd carried a great weight for a long time.

"I'm sorry," I said softly, clasping her hand. "I'm sorry that I have been . . . absent." I looked down at the maps. "After her death. It was the only way I could sleep. If I knew that he could not. I think—" I paused, my throat thick. "Ahab told me that some who face such—such horror, they break. Rot and wither away."

Sapphira looked at me for a long moment. "You are Queen Jezebel of Israel, Princess Royal of Tyre. You have never broken before." She lifted my bent head and forced me to look her in the eyes. "And you won't do so now."

I blinked, then nodded. "Tell Ahab that I am getting dressed and then will join him at the war council."

◎◎◎◎

When I arrived, I walked in carefully, shoulders straight even as I heard Ahab's advisors whispering. Ahab looked up when I entered, relief in his eyes, but he didn't say anything, merely took my hand and squeezed it hard under the table.

"Now that the queen is here, we can continue." He nodded to a man standing in the middle of the room. The man paled when he saw me looking at him, and Ahab said, "This is Aaron. A prophet with word from Yahweh."

I stiffened but did not say anything, and Ahab nodded for the man to continue. The prophet said, "This is what Yahweh says: 'Do you see this vast army? I will give it into your hands, and then you will know that I am the Lord.' "

"But who will do this?" Ahab said, leaning forward. "And who will start the battle?"

"You will," the man said, pointing a finger at Ahab. "You yourself will lead your men into battle today, and Yahweh will deliver them into your hands."

Ahab leaned back in his seat for a moment, moving his gaze to me in a silent question. I nodded, and he inclined his head. "Assemble the army," he said, standing. He turned to me and gave me a quick kiss, then left the room.

After the meeting with the war council, I did not want to return to my rooms. I knew they would smell stale, like old wine and uneaten plates of food, so I sent my maids to clean them and decided to walk to the temple. I nearly left when I entered the courtyard where I had agreed to let Minta travel with us to Mount Carmel, but Tanith, who was sitting there in a chair, rose. She walked toward me slowly, strangely, and it took me a moment to realize that she walked as the old did, with shuffling, careful steps, even though she was barely older than I was. She stood in front of me for one long moment, then enfolded me in her arms like a mother comforting a child. I did not weep, but I held on to her for a long, long time. When we finally released each other, Tanith gestured to the place where she'd been sitting.

"No," I said. "You sit. I have done enough sitting."

"Where have you been?" she said, once she'd sat back down. "I was worried. I haven't seen you in many weeks."

I felt heat rise in my cheeks. I did not want to tell Tanith what I had been doing, did not want to tell her that while she'd been continuing to run the temple, suffering the loss of the priestesses alone, I had been locked in my rooms, wine-drunk and vengeful. "I have been searching for the prophet," I finally said.

Tanith's hands tightened on the arms of her chair. "What will you do to him?" she said softly.

"Kill him, eventually," I said, the words sounding dull and lifeless. Was that truly what would happen? I was no longer sure. What had my obsession won me? An army surrounded our city. I had forsaken Israel to nurse my own vengeance. I would no longer.

Tanith nodded. "I'm sorry I let them go," she said, looking down at her hands. "I am sorry I was not with them, at the end."

I put my hand over hers. "I was the one who let Minta go. You would have had her stay behind, with you. She would have been safe if only I had listened to you." I thought of the excitement on Minta's face when I had told her she might come with us. "But it was the prophet who killed them. Not us. All we wanted was rain."

I sat with Tanith for some hours, and by the time I returned to the palace I found Ahab returned from the battle, calling for a feast.

"I routed him as easily as the prophet said," Ahab told me that night at dinner. I listened as he told me the details of the battle, but mostly I fell on the food as soon as it was brought to me. I did not know how long it had been since I'd truly eaten, and I was ravenous. I had just reached for another piece of bread to dip in oil when there was a disturbance by the door. A soldier came in, dragging a man wearing sackcloth with a rope tied around his waist. The man looked young, younger than Ahab, with dark hair and a thin face. He fell on his knees before us and said, "Your servant Ben-Hadad says, 'Please let me live.'"

Ahab looked as startled as I felt to have the man who had just surrounded our city bowing at our feet. Ahab frowned down at him, and I knew he was thinking of Yahweh's commands to kill the leader of every army that fought against Israel. His hand moved to his sword, but before he could draw it, I pulled him away and spoke quietly in his ear.

"He is young," I said. "He will be under our control his whole life if we spare it. We could make a treaty with him. It would help us recover more quickly from the famine."

Ahab pressed a hand to my cheek. "I have missed you," he said, voice full of emotion. He turned back to Ben-Hadad and said, "Get up, brother."

Ahab embraced him, and Ben-Hadad began to visibly tremble with relief. "I will give back the cities my father took from you. Damascus will welcome your merchants and give them the choicest place in our markets."

He continued to babble, and Ahab set a hand on his shoulder. "We will create an alliance between us. Then I will send you back to your city."

◎◎◎◎

The treaty did not take long to complete, as Ben-Hadad was willing to give us anything we asked for. During those days I worked over the treaty with Ahab and Ben-Hadad, and at night I swam in my pool.

On the day Ahab went out in his chariot to return Ben-Hadad to his men, I watched for him to return from my balcony, wishing only for the exchange to happen quickly so that I could go to my pool. Finally, I saw the cloud of dust that meant he was nearly at the city and was surprised to see his chariot stop just on the outskirts. It was not stopped for long enough for me to worry, but still, I ran out to meet him and saw that his face was grave and stern. His men gave him a wide berth. "Did Ben-Hadad try to trick you?" I said when I reached him.

"No," Ahab said shortly. He threw his reins to a servant and climbed out of his chariot. His armor was coated in dust and his face and beard were as well, so that he looked more like a spirit than a man. "I returned Ben-Hadad to his men and watched them leave. I don't believe they will be a trouble to us anymore."

"Then what happened?" I said, putting a hand on his forearm.

Ahab frowned again, then sighed. "I suppose it is better if you hear it directly from my mouth. I was stopped on the road, just as I neared the city. I thought the man needed help. He was covered in bruises and had a bandage over his face. I didn't realize it was him till he spoke."

My heart began to pound in my chest. Elijah. Elijah had returned to Israel.

"He is gone already," Ahab said before I could call the guards. "Yahweh guards him well."

I gritted my teeth but nodded. "What did he say?"

Ahab sighed. "He said that I had set a man free who Yahweh had determined should die. Therefore, it is my life for his life. My people for his people." Ahab took out his sword and looked at its clean, bright blade. "I should have killed him," he said. "But I was too afraid. Too afraid of what Yahweh would do to me if I cut down his prophet." He turned to me. "You would have done it. You would have killed him. You are more a king than I'll ever be."

CHAPTER 17

The day was hot, and the air was thick as honey. My head had begun to swim after the third supplicant, and by the end of the audience my back ached and the hair at my temples had curled in spirals. I should not have been in the throne room at all. It was Ahab's place to listen to the supplicants and decide on their complaints, but ever since the prophet had pronounced judgment on him for letting Ben-Hadad go, Ahab had become more and more disinterested in the doings of the court. He sent me to council meetings in his stead and even gave me his seal so that all would know that the decisions I made were in his name. Instead of sitting beside me now, he was in the courtyard, playing with the children. Usually I would have relished the control he gave me, but I missed him more than I thought I would. I wanted to discuss the new temple I was building, instead of him merely nodding and telling me to do what I thought was right. It was lonely, ruling alone.

My loneliness does not matter, I thought, pinching the inside of my arm so that I would sit straighter. I had come to Israel for a reason: to be remembered. Everyone knew my name now, knew I *was* the throne. The things I did would be remembered as the achievements of Queen Jezebel of Israel.

I gritted my teeth and refused to let my head bend under the weight of the crown on my head, did not let myself sink into the throne even though my back ached as the hours passed, but as the last supplicant spoke, my attention finally began to wander. I had been having terrible nightmares again. They were not of blood, as they'd been when I'd been losing my first child, but of demons. Evil, leering faces with gnashing teeth that tried to bite at me as I ran down a long corridor, trying to get to my children, to Ahab, Sapphira. They came each night, and I had started staying up as long as I could, trying to outlast them, but eventually I always fell asleep and woke screaming. Sapphira had begun to sleep beside me the last few weeks, but she could not prevent the nightmares, could only hold my hand and soothe me when I woke from them.

The audience finally ended, and I went to my pool, hoping to soothe myself, but the cool water did not help me as it usually did. I kept my head underwater for as long as I could, even when I felt someone jump in the pool beside me.

"Bel!" The voice was distant with my head underwater, indistinct enough that I could ignore it, I kept my eyes closed, hoping that whoever it was would go away. "Bel!" the voice shouted again urgently. "Bel, she's struggling." A part of me, a heavy, hot part of me, could not make sense of the words. Why was I being bothered? Why couldn't I be left alone to float? I felt strange, as if my thoughts and body were entirely separate entities, as if they had been split in two by the gods, and I did not know how to join them again. There was another splash near my head, a shout, and my body moved of its own accord. My eyes snapped open as I swept Athaliah into my arms. The girl felt heavier than usual, and clung to me, shivering.

"You cannot jump into the pool until you know how to swim properly," I said to my daughter.

"You would catch me, Mama," she said, wrapping her arms around me and throwing her head against my neck.

Ahab, now that he'd seen that I held Athaliah, began racing around the garden that surrounded the pool with Ahaziah, even though he was really too old for such games. I climbed out of the pool, still holding my daughter, and stood on the edge. "I will not always catch you," I said, angry that she had not learned this lesson yet. She was too old to need protecting. "You must learn how to survive on your own." I threw her into the pool and watched as she came up sputtering, wailing. "Move your arms and legs," I said, raising my voice over her screams.

Ahab rushed over and was about to jump into the pool when I put out my arm.

"Wait," I said. "She can do it." And after another moment of panic, she did, beginning to move her arms and legs as I'd shown her before. She bobbed up and down in the water like a dog until finally I let Ahab pull her from the water. She was hiccupping and looked frightened, but she had not drowned. She had learned how to do it on her own. "I won't always catch her," I said to Ahab. "She is a princess. She needs to know. I can't catch her." My voice snagged like a loom catching on a burr of wool and I looked into the setting sun. It was orange and reminded me of bile. My stomach heaved at the sight. I wiped at my mouth, though I hadn't gotten sick, and I heard Ahab sigh behind me. "Let's leave Mother alone," he said.

I sat on the edge of the pool after they left, dangling my feet in the cool water, utterly spent.

"Bel." The blue evening light made Sapphira spectral as she walked toward me, but I did not flinch away from her. She sat beside me, pulled off her sandals, and dangled her feet in the water too.

"I just wanted to teach her how to swim on her own," I said slowly, knowing Athaliah would have run right to Sapphira for comfort. "I knew by her age that no one would catch me if I jumped."

"Athaliah does not have your strength," Sapphira said quietly. "Most children don't."

"Minta did," I said, thinking of the tiny girl I had picked up off the street. She and Athaliah had looked very alike, with their light hair and lithe young bodies.

Sapphira sighed. "Minta was not your child," she said softly.

"Minta was like me," I said quickly. "She was *me*. If I hadn't picked her up off the street that day, she would still be alive. They all would." I thought of the children the temples had taken in on my orders. So many of them were dead now.

"Bel——" Her voice was tentative. "It is easy to live in the past. But it is time, don't you think?" She placed a hand on my arm, but I shrugged her off.

"I don't know what you mean," I said, swirling my feet in the water.

"You do," she said. "It is not befitting a queen. To not make announcements. Preparations."

I looked down at my stomach. I had purposely worn loose clothes for months, fooling everyone, even myself. I should have known I could not fool Sapphira. Only she and Elijah had ever been able to see past the adornments and purple robes to the bones beneath.

"You are with child," she said. Her voice was firm but placid, as if what she was saying was ordinary, as if it did not fill me with dread.

I had dreamed of the child the night before. I could not remember what it looked like, I only remembered that it was a boy and that I had held him in my arms and then looked up to see the hills around Samaria burning. Then I too had burned, still holding the boy child, who smiled sweetly while my skin turned black and fell away. I had told myself that it had only been a dream . . . but when I thought back to the months after my other children had been born, I shuddered. They had broken my body, my blood had poured out for them, but even worse, they had seemed to take my mind with them. I had looked up each night and found no stars, no moon, only the wail of a child in the dark.

"I took a potion," I said. "One that my old nurse told me about. I thought perhaps . . . perhaps I did not have to have this child. Isn't two enough? Ahab has so many from the other women. He has an heir. A daughter to dote on. There is no need for another."

"The potion did not work," Sapphira said. "You will have the child soon."

I gagged at her words, vomiting into the pool. Sapphira held back my hair until I was done and wiped my mouth with her sleeve.

"I feel . . . different," I rasped slowly. "Ever since Mount Carmel—and lately, the dreams, Sapphira—I do not feel myself."

Sapphira clasped my hand in hers. "I am here with you, Bel," she said, voice fierce. "I will not let anything happen to you or your child. I promise. And . . ." She softened her voice. "After you have the babe, we can make it so you will not have another child."

I leaned my head against her shoulder, and we sat there for a long time as darkness gathered around us and bats began to swoop over our heads, looking for blood.

CHAPTER 18

The child came early. Easily. I broke no bones; blood did not pool on the floor. And he screamed when he was born, screamed as the others had not. I laughed at the fury in him, opening my arms for him. Perhaps this child would be as angry as me. As angry as Minta.

When the baby was hungry, he howled and waved his fists in the air. I put my own hands in his way, letting him pummel them over and over until he quieted down. After the wet nurse fed him, she would hand him back to me and he would furrow his brow and look on me disdainfully, as if asking who I was to him, what I would do for him. Ahaziah had been a gentle child, and Athaliah had been ill for so long after being born that she barely had the strength to suckle her nurse, let alone scream, but from the moment Joram had come into the world, he'd known he was a prince with rights.

I gave the other children to their nurses for the night so I could sleep, but I kept Joram with me, sleeping in a basket by my bed. On the tenth night after his birth, I woke to his screams and could not find his wet nurse anywhere. I lifted him from his basket, trying to soothe him, but he continued to scream and scream. His face was red, and his body arched in fury at being denied food, so finally I let him suck on my already-dripping nipple. He gripped it so firmly I winced, wondering if he'd been born with teeth. His face was still indignant even as he sucked, and he rolled one eye toward me and I thought suddenly of Anat, dripping with the blood of her enemies.

The little prince has many enemies.

I flinched at the voice and twisted around, trying to see in the dark corners of the room. Joram fell off my breast and began to scream, but still I searched for the voice. The shadows seemed to pulse in one corner of the room, and I knew, suddenly, that my nightmares had come to life and a demon was standing there, ready to devour my son. I bared my teeth at it, trying to find the dagger I had kept by my bed ever since Elijah had killed the priestesses at the temple. I knew I was no longer beloved in Israel, knew that some—many, perhaps—wanted my blood. My family's blood.

"My lady?" The wet nurse appeared in the room, holding a torch that tore at the shadows in the corner, showing nothing but a wall covered in lapis lazuli flowers. "The child needed new swaddling," she said, holding a stack of white linen. "I'm so sorry he woke you." She held out her arms, but I flinched away from her, holding Joram closer to me.

"I don't need you anymore," I said, trying to keep my voice steady.

"My lady?" she said, taking another step toward me.

"No!" My voice was little more than a gasp. "Leave me—" I said harshly, and she ran from the room as Joram continued to scream. I held him to my chest as I looked at the corner, at the shadows that began to twist and boil in the torch's absence.

From that moment I did not leave Joram's side and Sapphira did not leave mine, but I would not let her handle the baby. What if she had been turned into a demon as well? There was no way to know, so I did everything for my son myself. I changed his swaddling and fed him and held him against my chest. I tried to tell Ahab about the demons, tried to warn him that someone—some*thing*—was after our son, but I couldn't get the words out right. Halfway through, I would find myself blinking stupidly, staring at the wall where the shadows met. At night, while I watched the corners of the room and held my screaming son, I whispered Elijah's name. But not with longing. With a curse. He was the one who had brought danger to my house. He had spoken against me, against the wealth and prosperity I had brought to Israel. He had killed my priestesses. At the will, he said, of Yahweh, but I wondered if part of him relished the power, the blood, the death. Elijah finally had a name his father would be proud of, one that would be written down in the book of kings.

During the day, I strapped Joram to my chest, using a sling the women used in the fields when they were gathering grain. Then I planned. I pored over maps, sent messages to each city in Israel, even in Tyre. I told them I had increased the price on Elijah's head; I said I would give extravagant riches to anyone who brought him to me alive. I did not tell Ahab my plan, though. Did not tell him that I wanted him brought alive because I was going to kill him myself. I was going to watch the life drain from his eyes as he'd watched the life drain out of Minta's. Because the only way to keep Joram safe—to keep Israel safe—would be to *know* he was dead. But no matter where I searched, I still could not find him.

I rubbed at my eyes and watched as the moon rose red in the sky. It was the second full moon since Joram's birth, and I had not had a night of unbroken sleep since then. Sometimes I dropped off to sleep when he slept, but I would always wake with a start soon after, sure that I had missed a knife in the dark. Sapphira begged me to let her take him. She said over and over that she would defend him with her life. Some distant part of me knew that I had once trusted her, but this new self could not conceive of letting anyone else hold Joram while I slept. Sapphira would sit as close to us as I would allow, would try to put her arms around both of us, but anytime I woke and found her there I would shrink away, thinking I saw her eyes glint red.

When Ahab came to my room on the night of the red moon, I tightened my arms around Joram even though they ached and burned. Usually Ahab would want to hold the baby, tickle his fat feet and try to get him to smile, but now he just stood beside me on the balcony, looking at the sky.

"I'm not sure what to do about Naboth's vineyard," he said, and I had to dredge through my muddled thoughts to remember that Ahab had wanted to buy the vineyard from a wealthy Jezreelite who had land near the palace.

"It is the perfect place for the garden I've been wanting to build, the one that you suggested, for the widows and orphans of the city. It needs to be near enough the palace that none bother them as they garden or gather, but most of the land near the palace has homes or businesses on it. The only viable land is Naboth's. It's overgrown and poorly tended, but I told him I would give him a good price."

I bounced Joram on my hip, and his mouth suddenly broke into a smile. He had never smiled at me before, and the sight was startling. It made me feel bruised and tender, and I took Ahab's hand and pointed at the baby, who smiled even wider when he saw his father looking at him.

Ahab smiled back, but briefly, and I frowned. Could he not rejoice in his son's smile? "And?" I prompted him, bouncing Joram on my hip again to try to get him to smile again.

"He said no," Ahab said with a sigh. "Now I'll have to find somewhere else for the garden, and I don't think there's better land in the city. And if I don't create the garden, the people will complain even more that I'm not fulfilling my promises."

"He said no?" I said, turning to Ahab. "He said no to the king?"

"He said it's the land of his ancestors, that Yahweh forbids that he sell it."

"You believe that?" I said, voice sharp. Ahab was gentle and kind, but sometimes he forgot he was king.

"It has been in his family for generations," Ahab said. "And besides, I don't need Yahweh's eyes on me again."

"You are king. He cannot disobey your commands, Ahab. It's dangerous."

"It's only a field," Ahab said. "The people can't hate me any more than they already do."

I laughed bitterly, knowing exactly how much people who once loved you could grow to hate you. "It is dangerous if your subjects don't fear you. Don't obey your commands. The people hated the king of Tyre before my father. It began with something small, a general who would not give his best purple robe to the king. By the next harvest, my father had slit the king's throat." I had pictured it with relish as a child, my father sitting on the golden throne of Tyre, his enemy dead at his feet. Now, though, I saw Ahab, dead on the floor. I saw Ahaziah and Athaliah put to the sword. I saw my baby, Joram, in Naboth's arms; I heard him scream as Naboth dashed him against the cold stone floors until he lay quiet.

"I will get you the vineyard of Naboth," I said, feeling fury sing through my blood, heating my aching bones. *Then*, I thought, looking down at Joram, *then my family will be safe*. I looked up at the bloody moon. *Then Jezebel will be remembered as Anat is remembered. As kings who destroy their enemies are remembered.*

◉◉◉◉

A hab left the next day to go to our winter palace in Jezreel. He begged me to come with him, but I refused, and finally he left on his own, taking the two older children with him. I was glad. I needed time to make a plan. I lay awake all night, until the corner where the demons usually leered at me finally filled with the light of dawn and they vanished. Sapphira lay asleep on the bed, arm curled around Joram, and so I rose and dressed slowly, though I did not turn my gaze from them. I had not allowed maids into my rooms in weeks, so I could not bathe properly, but I doused my face and washed my hands with a pitcher of stale water, steading myself.

I was about to pluck Joram from the bed when I stopped suddenly, my hand curling into a claw. *Perhaps this is what Naboth wants. Perhaps he wants me to come to him with my child so that he can kill us both.* My heart pounded, but I left Joram beside Sapphira and ran from the room, sure that this was the only way to keep my son safe.

I felt afire as I left the palace. My hands were burning, my chest crackling with heat. I had not been able to protect Minta, but I would no longer be defenseless. I would protect my family.

I had walked these roads many times, but they seemed to twist and turn as I walked into a great labyrinth. I bared my teeth at them as they tried to keep me from Naboth, but I kept walking forward even as my head spun and the world turned and turned around me.

I arrived at the vineyard just as the sun rose over the hills. Even the sunrise could not turn it into anything beautiful. Tangled vines that had long been left uncultivated meandered over the walls; grapes that should have been harvested weeks before lined the ground and burst when I stepped on them, leaving a bloody trail. The air smelled sharp as vinegar, and I had to put my nose to my sleeve to keep from retching. Still, I could tell that the land, if cultivated, would make a good garden as Ahab had said. It was near enough to the palace that our guards could keep anyone from bothering the widows and children, and the soil looked moist and soft. A large fig tree shaded the western corner of the field and would make an ideal resting place for the women. I could picture them sitting there, their tired faces cooled by the shade, the weight of their widowhood lifted from their shoulders as they looked at the garden the king had provided for them. I could picture the orphans too, the way they would creep about the place until they realized they would not be ousted from the land. I could see a girl with red hair and dark eyes take a bite out of an olive, spitting the pit gleefully into the ground. *If we had started this garden earlier, Minta would have had a source of food. She would not have been so small. I would not have found her and brought her to the temple. She would be alive.*

The vision made me twist my hands together and close my eyes. When I opened them, I saw an old man hobbling toward me. His back was bowed as an old tree, and his robe was a yellow so pale it was almost white.

I felt fury thrum in my chest like a just-plucked string. He could only be Naboth.

He stopped a few paces from me, far enough that I could not just stab him and be done with it. "Your Majesty," he said with a bow, voice low. I took a step back when I heard his voice, fear mixing with my anger. His voice rang like a bell, even in the field. He sounded so much like Elijah that for a moment I wondered if he *was* Elijah, if the prophet of Yahweh was trying to trick me. Then he raised his head and I saw that he had pale eyes, grey like smoke, nothing like Elijah's black eyes. "You honor me by coming to my vineyard."

I tilted my head. He had said the words without inflection, but I could hear the teeth in them. He was mocking me. I once again saw him dashing Joram against the floor, casting aside my baby's lifeless body. Fury rose through my chest and flooded my head, and I saw Naboth's eyes turn from grey to red.

"The king commands you to give him this vineyard," I said, some small part of me still trying to be diplomatic. "He will reward you handsomely for it. Enough that you can buy three other vineyards besides."

Naboth bowed his head again and took a step toward me. I slid a finger down the sharp edge of my dagger, but he was still too far away. "I am honored His Majesty requests this vineyard, but I cannot sell it."

I cast my eyes over the vineyard again, crushed a rotting grape under my foot, then said, "It is for the widows and orphans of the city." I knew widows and orphans meant nothing to a demon but felt I had to try.

"It is the land of my ancestors. I am unable to work it anymore," Naboth said, hunching over even more, perhaps trying to excite my sympathy, "but I cannot sell it."

"The king has commanded it," I said, wishing I could make my voice as lovely as Naboth's, thick as honey, sweet as cream.

"Yahweh has commanded that I keep it," Naboth said, and I saw his eyes glint red again.

"The king speaks for Yahweh," I said, but as soon as the words were out of my mouth, I knew they were a mistake.

"The prophet speaks for Yahweh," Naboth said quietly. I could hear the truth in them. Elijah *was* behind this. He had told Naboth that he was to disobey the king. After all, Elijah had lived at court for more than half his life. He knew the best way to topple a king-dom.

I had the dagger in my hand, was already picturing how I would knock the demon to the ground when I realized that perhaps *this* was what Elijah wanted. Perhaps he *wanted* me to kill Naboth my-self so that he could call the queen a murderer.

"The king's will cannot be ignored," I said to Naboth, a warn-ing he did not deserve.

He bowed his head. "Neither can the will of Yahweh."

I stepped so close I could feel his breath. "*My* will is stronger than Yahweh's," I said, before leaving him alone in his rotting vineyard.

I ran all the way back to the palace after talking to Naboth, sud-denly terrified that I would find Joram dead, but when I got back to my rooms, he and Sapphira were still asleep. I sat at the small table in the corner, the one where Elijah and I had spent hours together. I never used it anymore, but I had not been able to force myself to remove it. I rubbed a finger over its smooth surface, stopping when my fingers caught on an indentation in the wood. It had been carved into the side of the table that faced the shadows and I'd never noticed it before, but as I ran my fingers over it, my breath caught as I recognized the way the characters sloped and curled. *Jezebel* was carved there in Elijah's hand. *Jezebel Jezebel Jezebel.* It was how they used to sing my name when I walked through the city. How he used to say my name when we lay together in the dark. Was this a blessing from a lover or a curse from the prophet?

I sat there tracing my fingers over the carving for a long time, forcing my muddled thoughts together until a plan finally formed itself. While Sapphira and the baby continued to sleep, I dressed. I put gold in my hair and on my wrists. Lined my eyes with kohl and painted my lips, dabbed almond oil on my hair and neck and breasts. I needed to look like a bride before him.

I arrived at the pool after Jude—a courtier who had recently joined Ahab's council, and who I had seen watch me with lecherous eyes more than once—so that he would have the pleasure of seeing me approach. I walked slowly, my head bowed, docile as a cow, and I stood before him for a long moment so that his eyes could linger on my body. Finally, I raised my head, and his body stiffened when I put one hand to his chest.

"My lady," he said, but he did not bow before me. A man need not bow before a woman dressed as I was.

"I trust you more than all the men of the court," I said, hating the lie as I said it but dipping my head again so that he might think I was blushing. "I come to you to ask for your help."

"Of course, my lady." He took my hand and brought it to his lips. His tongue darted out and tasted the top of it, but I did not wipe his touch away. I did not sink my dagger into his chest and watch him die for touching his queen in such a manner. Instead, I smiled demurely, like a girl, and let him keep hold of it.

"Naboth the Jezreelite has cursed both the king and Yahweh." Jude flinched slightly at the hardness in my voice, and I dropped my eyes and softened my voice. "My lord the king is away, and I know I cannot let this insult stand. I need a champion to stand beside me, to take the place of the king and protect me."

Jude's eyes brightened when I spoke of him taking the king's place, and I knew then he would do anything I asked.

By the time I told him my plan, the sun had set and the pool we stood beside was bright with moonshine. "You must let me escort you back to your rooms," he said, eyes tracing my lips and breasts. I lowered my head demurely again, knowing that I had to allow him to bring me back or my plan would not work. Just as I knew that he would press himself against me in a darkened corridor until I could feel the hardness of him against my thigh. Just as I knew that he would sweep his tongue into my mouth and swish it around as if he longed to take from me. I knew that I had to give myself to protect my family, to keep them safe, but when I finally arrived back in my rooms and washed the kohl from my eyes, removed the gold from my ears, I looked at my face in my polished bronze mirror and wept.

◉ ◉ ◉ ◉

Jude worked quickly. He announced a day of fasting for the next morning at dawn and promised to gather all the elders of Samaria for it, including Naboth. I kept Sapphira in my room all that day so she would not hear of the gathering, and the next morning at dawn, I left her asleep with Joram again. After I did this, he would be safe.

Jude had had a simple wooden platform constructed where I sat. The elders and other people gathered around the platform, and I saw Naboth arrive almost last. He bent when the prayers began, and when they ended, he lifted his head and saw me for the first time. I wanted him to shake, to pale and tremble, but he merely looked at me, then away as though I were nothing to him.

"Naboth is a man of great renown in Israel," Jude said, silencing the crowd with his loud voice. His black hair gleamed with oil, and I nearly retched as the scent wafted toward me. I looked back at Naboth and saw the way his eyes gleamed red. I stiffened as Jude recited the lies I had told Jude about Naboth's sins, lies about his blasphemy of Yahweh. Lies that I knew would keep Joram safe.

Jude continued to speak, his voice rising in righteous anger, his words riling up the crowd such that when he said, "What should we do to this blasphemer?" I knew they would have only one answer.

"Stone him!" they screamed, rushing toward Naboth and carrying him off. They marched out of the city, and I went with them, through the market, past the temples of Yahweh and Astarte, until they reached the city limits. They threw Naboth to the ground, but Naboth did not cry out or scream for his life. Somehow, he found me in the crowd and watched me with eyes that turned from red back into grey as children, men, and women threw stones at him, cracking his tender flesh, splitting him open like a slaughtered pig until his blood ran in rivers on the ground at my feet.

CHAPTER 19

After Naboth was killed, I took to my bed and slept for days, Joram beside me. The terrible nightmares I'd been having faded when I held my young son close to me. Sometimes when I woke Sapphira was by my side, holding a bowl of broth that she spooned into my mouth as though I were an ailing child. I did not protest this as I normally would have. Instead, I just swallowed the salty broth, sometimes crying into it because the salt reminded me of Tyre.

"It will be all right, Bel," Sapphira said, wiping away my tears. "I am here. It will be all right."

One day, I woke to sunlight and saw that Joram was not in his crib beside me. I smiled into the sunshine, pleased that I had slept a whole night without waking. Sapphira walked into the room then, holding Joram in her arms, and her face went white when she saw me. "Bel—I'm so sorry, I just took him out for a moment; he was whimpering, and I didn't want him to wake you."

I laughed as Joram waved a fat hand and grinned at me. "Thank you," I said, running a hand through my hair. "I feel as though I have not slept so well since he was born."

"Bel?" Sapphira said, putting Joram down on the bed beside me and gently touching my arm. Her face went slack as though she had finally set down a great rock. I remembered suddenly, how Naboth's face had done the same thing when he'd been killed, his face collapsing into furrows. I reached for Sapphira's arm and held it tightly.

"Naboth," I said slowly, trying to sort through the past days. I remembered everything I had done, but suddenly I saw everything differently. I saw how Naboth had stooped with pain, not artifice. I saw how his eyes had shone in the sunlight, not red, just the pale eyes of an old man who did not want to sell his land to the king. "He's dead." I remembered how the ground had turned dark with his blood. "I thought—" I said, my breath becoming ragged. "I thought he was going to hurt Joram. I thought he had been sent by Elijah to hurt my family."

Sapphira's eyes were soft, tender as a bruise. When she spoke, her words were halted, tentative. "It's not your fault, Bel. Something took you over. It was like you were possessed." She paused. "I've heard stories of women who have gone . . . mad after having a babe. They hear from demons, telling them to kill themselves and . . . and their children. Then one day, the woman wakes and it's as if . . . as if she was not the one who . . ." Sapphira did not finish her sentence, but she did not have to. I knew what she had been about to say. She took a breath, then said, "I didn't know what to do." She reached for my hand, but I moved away from her. "I was afraid to take Joram from you, afraid that you would jump from the balcony if I did. But I was also afraid that you would . . ." She looked down at Joram on the bed beside me, and when she looked back at me, I could see the terror in her eyes.

I shuddered, moving away from Joram so that his skin would not touch my own. Would I have hurt my son eventually? If I had

not killed Naboth? *No*, I thought. *Of course not.* But what if the demons had told me to? What if I thought it was the only way to truly
save him?

I would not kill an innocent, I thought, even as I said, "I killed Naboth." I looked down at my hands. I could feel the weight of the
sunbaked stones in my hand, though I had not thrown a single one.
"I killed him for a vineyard. Why didn't he just sell it to Ahab?
Then none of this would have happened. Then . . ." I stared at my
hands. "He said Yahweh would not let him. This is Yahweh's
doing. Elijah's."

But even as I tried to blame another, I knew I would feel the
weight of those hot stones in my hands until I took my last breath.

◎◎◎◎

Ahab sighed deeply. The vines had been pulled up and the
ground furrowed, ready for planting. The fig tree was heavy
with fruit, and the air smelled sweet. "I don't think you should
have killed him," he said, plucking a ripe fig from the tree. He
pushed his thumb into it but did not eat it.

I swallowed, feeling the stones in my hands, on my chest. "No
one can disobey the will of the king and live," I said, feeling sour
bile rise in my throat. Sapphira and I had agreed that it would be
better for everyone to believe that Naboth had been killed for his
vineyard. It would do more harm to Ahab, to me, if they knew that
I had killed Naboth because I'd gone mad.

We had turned to leave the garden when a figure appeared. I
froze as I stared at his pale-yellow robe, his bent figure, sure that it
was Naboth returned as a ghost, here for vengeance. Then, the figure threw off his hood, and I saw that it was not Naboth, but the
prophet of Yahweh—Elijah.

"So you have found me, my enemy," Ahab said softly.

My heart was pounding with hatred toward Elijah, but also toward myself. I still knew him so well. I could tell with a glance that he had not slept well recently, had drunk too much wine the night before. I wondered if I would die and still know him, as I would die with the weight of stones in my hands.

"I have found you," Elijah said, voice ringing even in the empty garden, "because you have done evil in the eyes of Yahweh by killing Naboth. He says, 'I will cut you off from every last male in Israel—'"

Ahab sucked in a breath at the curse, and I knew he was thinking not of himself, but of his sons. We had two sons together, and he had five with his other wives and concubines. I pictured Ahab on the day he'd built a little ship for Ahaziah and sailed it around the pool with him. He'd missed two meetings with his courtiers and been burned red by the sun, but he'd returned grinning and happy, with Ahaziah in his arms.

"'Because you have aroused my anger and caused Israel to sin,'" Elijah finished, though now he was looking directly at me.

I looked at him and saw Minta. I saw Athaliah. Sapphira. Saw my sons, Ahaziah, Joram, their bodies felled at his hand, and I screamed my rage, my fear. I ran at him, attacking him like I had attacked my brother as a child, without care of how hard I hit or what I broke, as long as I could feel his flesh give way beneath me. Elijah was a tall man, but I matched him in height, and I knocked him to the ground as I howled like a dog, scratching him, throwing my fist into his nose so hard I heard the bones in his face crack. I would have killed him then, with my bare hands, if Ahab had not reached us and pulled me off him.

Elijah stood and wiped the blood from his nose with the back of his hand.

"And also concerning Jezebel," he pronounced, his voice weighty, as if he could feel the cost of his many portents, "Yahweh says: 'Dogs will devour Jezebel by the walls.'"

Ahab gasped, but I laughed. "You think to frighten me, prophet of Yahweh?" I said, showing all my teeth. "I am queen of a great nation. Thousands have cried for my blood in the past, and thousands more will after. I am not frightened of you, and I am not frightened of your god. You will die eventually and be known only as the voice of another. But my name will still be spoken, long after my bones have turned to dust."

Elijah stared at me for a long moment before turning away. He was gone before the guards came and I realized that Ahab was no longer holding me back. I turned and saw him kneeling on the ground, his robe torn, as he said, "I have sinned against Yahweh." He raised his eyes to me. "We cannot have another drought, Bel. We will not survive another. We have sinned against Yahweh. We must repent."

"I have sinned," I said, feeling the weight of the stones settle around me once more, "but not against Yahweh. And I will not kneel and make myself humble before him."

◎◎◎◎

After we met Elijah in the vineyard, Ahab put on sackcloth and ashes and proclaimed days of mourning and fasting. The whole court followed his example except me, and I knew it was remarked on, knew I was not helping my reputation by flaunting the king's decree, but I would not humble myself again before Yahweh—before Elijah, the man who had brought so much destruction to me.

On the last day of mourning, Ahab came running into my rooms, holding a sheaf of papyrus against his breast like a child. I knew it was from Elijah even before he spoke. "We are saved," he said, handing it to me and pulling Joram from my arms to dance him wildly around the room.

"*So says Yahweh: because Ahab has humbled himself, I will not bring this promised disaster in his day. But I will bring it on his house in the days of his son.*"

"You rejoice in this?" I said, holding the letter like it was a snake about to bite.

"Yahweh will not bring destruction on us because we—I— repented," Ahab said, looking confused.

"Instead he will bring it on our son!" I shouted. "Why would your god punish a child for the sins of his father?"

Ahab's mouth hung open. "It doesn't have to mean Ahaziah. It could be generations from now."

"You want your sons to lose Israel, even if it is generations from now? What kind of king are you?" I said.

"It is wearying, Bel, to keep fighting." Ahab looked down at his hands. "I don't want to anymore."

I looked at him for a long moment, wondering if when he had told me that story long ago, of the men who never recovered from battle, if he had been talking not about me but about himself. It would be easy to join him, easy to crack and break under the weight of Minta's death, of the people I'd killed—the priests of Yahweh, Naboth—but if I bent, then who would be left standing? Who would remember our names? There was nothing I could do except walk away from him, shoulders back, chin up, refusing to bow under the weight of the crown.

CHAPTER 20

Disaster did not befall us immediately. It left us alone at first, as our children grew and the years passed. Ahab seemed to forget the prophet's words, but I did not. I still searched for Elijah, but after my fight with Ahab in Naboth's vineyard, he seemed to disappear. I didn't even hear word of him performing miracles in other lands, and I wondered if he was dead or had just lost his taste for being the voice of a god.

I sank back in my chair after hearing supplicants all morning and rubbed my temples, looking around the throne room. It looked very like it had when I'd first arrived. A broad chamber with wide windows that overlooked the city, trimmed in gold. It was the one place Ahab would not let me change, as he said it had been designed by his father and reminded him of the man. Ahab did not sit at my side. He stayed with our children, teaching all three of them, telling them the history of his family and mine, and often walked with them around the city and the hills. Most of his time, though, was spent in Naboth's vineyard. We had indeed turned it into a large garden for widows and orphans, but Ahab tended it more than they did. He seemed to find great pleasure in digging around in the soil, planting and weeding, and mostly spoke to me about the beetles that had gotten into the melons or the lack of figs on the new trees.

"Mother, it's too hot to be indoors," Ahaziah said, a whine in his voice. I frowned as I turned to him. He was a man now, and I had been trying to teach him the things a king should know. The things his father should have been teaching him. Unfortunately, Ahaziah did not have a mind for statecraft. His focus drifted quickly, and he spent most of the time sketching. He was a talented artist, but it would not endear him to his subjects if they knew the drawings he made of them.

"It does not matter if it is too hot," I said, refraining from wiping the sweat from my brow. "We hear supplicants the same day each month. It is not fair to the people to forgo their chance to speak to us simply because it is uncomfortable."

"But Papa promised to show me the place where the raptors make their nest today. He said there are eggs in it!" Ahaziah beamed, his smile still holding the sweetness of a child. I sighed. He was gentle and kind, very like his father. Too like his father.

"He has time," Ahab said, whenever I brought up Ahaziah's disinterest in matters of the kingdom. "He won't be king until I die, and I am still hale and hearty." He smiled, then pulled me toward him for a kiss.

The last supplicant finally left, and Ahaziah frowned. "You were too hard on him," he said.

I raised an eyebrow at him and said, "In what way?"

"You told him we would not provide aid to him and his family."

"And so we won't."

"But they're hungry. You saw how thin he was. We have enough to spare."

I heard whispers around the room and knew it was Ahab's advisors. At Ahaziah's age, Ahab had already proven himself in battle, but Ahaziah had grown up in a time of peace and had never had to shed blood. I'd left Tyre and married Ahab at three years younger than Ahaziah, and at his age, I was already changing Israel for the better. *With Elijah in my bed*, I thought, before flicking the thought away like an errant fly.

I stood up, gesturing for Ahaziah to follow me. "Let's walk to the garden and find your father." I didn't say anything else until we had left the palace behind, our feet kicking up puffs of red dust. The sun shone on us as we walked and showed the prosperity that had once more returned to the country. The green olive groves, the golden grain, the merchants who filled the market with their rich wares once again.

"Do you remember the famine?" I put a hand to my temple. Sometimes the throbbing reminded me of the drums the priestesses had played that day on Mount Carmel.

Ahaziah frowned. "A little," he said. "I remember Athaliah crying because the cook didn't have any honey cakes."

I thought of how I'd held him to me, how I'd gone to the temple of Yahweh for him, so desperate to end the drought that I humbled myself before the prophet's god.

"All of Israel ran out of food," I said. "People were dying of starvation on the streets, their bodies piling up. I saw a man collapse there once." I pointed to the wall beside us, and Ahaziah flinched. "More would have died, much more, if we had not had grain stored up before the famine started. What would have happened if we had given that grain out before the famine to every supplicant who said they were hungry? Israel would not have survived."

"But won't that man and his family starve now? How is that any different from them dying of famine?"

"You know that the scribes speak to each supplicant before they see us?" I said, raising my voice above a flock of sheep someone had just driven into the market below us. "They record each person's tale in a book. Before each supplicant comes, I read their story and find out the truth. The man who spoke to us today is not starving. He is lazy, refusing to work for his family, instead sending his wife and children out. I will not reward such behavior."

I waited for Ahaziah to ask if it was fair that the man's family had to work instead of him, but he just accepted my explanation without question. He nodded, and though his chin was strong and square like his father's, his shoulders broad and voice deep, I wondered if he could ever truly be king.

He quickened his pace but didn't say anything until we reached the garden. Ahab often brought the children with him, and I saw Sapphira sitting with Athaliah under a fig tree, reading something to her from a scroll. Jehu was there too, Joram's closest friend. I did not like the boy; there was something hard and sullen about him, but no one else agreed with me, not even Sapphira, and so I merely ignored him when he was in my presence.

I smiled to see my youngest child, only six years old but hitting a stick against a fence with the fire and bearing of a warrior. *He would be a better king than Ahaziah*, I thought, though I knew it was disloyal to my older son. Joram constantly asked questions, but even more, he constantly challenged his father and me. When he was little, he would scream and arch his back when he did not get what he wanted, throwing his body against the floor and beating it with his fists. It had worried Ahab, but each time he did it, I just laughed, picked up my writhing son, and threw him into my pool as my father had done to me. He would come up sputtering, and afterward we would sit together and talk. Even now, he was the only person in the court who was unafraid to question me. After Naboth, even

Ahab seemed to shrink from me. Sapphira was the only one who'd known what truly happened, but even she did not understand what it had been like to be under the thumb of . . . something else. It had been like being under the grip of a demon. Or a god.

Only Elijah would understand. Lately, I had begun to think of Elijah again. Not the man I knew as the prophet of Yahweh, but Elijah the king's scribe, who I had loved, who had known me so well long ago.

I still remembered what Sapphira had told me about the massacre on Mount Carmel all those years ago; how after it was over, Elijah had looked at the dead on the ground and almost wept, as if he were not the man who had raised his sword, who had cut down Minta. Though I lay my head down at night, I had trouble finding rest. Perhaps he too tried to sleep but could not because of the weight of the dead.

"Look, Mother!" Joram saw me approach and leaped off the stump he'd been balancing on, twisting his body in midair and decapitating a vine with his wooden sword so that a melon fell to the ground and cracked open, showing a deep red interior. Jehu laughed from where he sat on the ground, watching.

"Joram," Ahab said wearily, "I told you not to cut off that melon."

"I'm hungry," Joram said, picking up a piece of the broken melon and tossing another to Jehu.

"This garden is not for us. We tend it for the widows and orphans of Samaria."

"It is still ours." Joram began to suck at the melon, dripping red juices all over his face. "Everything in Israel is mine."

Ahab sighed. "No," he said. "How many times have we talked about this? Ahaziah will become king, not you."

Joram threw down his melon. "I will be king too," he said, his voice strangely resonant in the air. Enough that both Ahaziah and Athaliah looked up. His voice was melodic, as if he were reciting a song or poem. Something that had already come to pass.

"The only way you become king is if you kill me," Ahaziah said with a little laugh, ruffling his little brother's hair. "And you wouldn't want to kill me, would you?" It was meant as a joke, but for a moment we all paused and leaned toward Joram. I remembered how I had attacked my brother when I'd learned I would not become king, and for a moment I could picture Joram decapitating Ahaziah as neatly as he had the melon.

Finally, he said, "Of course not." His voice was its usual timbre, and he seemed confused.

"Perhaps you had a dream that you were king," Athaliah said. Athaliah had a great interest in dreams and badgered all of us to tell her what we'd dreamed the night before so she might interpret them. "Maybe you'll marry a princess who will become queen and then you'll become king."

Joram nodded but looked around the surrounding countryside with confusion still writ large on his face, as if it *was* his land, and all of us were playing a trick on him.

"I am king," Ahab said finally, his voice light, cracking the tension in the air. "And I don't think any of you can kill me yet." He dove at Joram, who whooped and began to wrestle with his father, making us laugh. Only Jehu still sat, silent. His piece of melon devoured, juices dripping down his wrist and onto the ground.

◎ ◎ ◎ ◎

I continued to try to teach Ahaziah how to rule—when to listen, when to act—and even though he heard me, I did not think he truly learned anything. "What would you have done today?" I said

one evening when I ate dinner with my family in my rooms. "If the
supplicant we heard today came before you and you had to decide
his fate by yourself?"

Ahaziah sighed. "I would have done what you did, Mother," he
said, popping a grape into his mouth before throwing one at Joram,
who caught it neatly in his own mouth. The two brothers grinned
at each other, pleased with their game, and I was about to reproach
Ahaziah when Athaliah said, "I would not have given him the full
portion of the grain." I turned toward my daughter, surprised, as
she continued. "It might make good sense now, but he will only return later for more. I would have given him a small portion of grain
and then found a job for him in the palace kitchens."

I looked at her appraisingly. It was a good idea, one I had thought
of myself, though I had discarded the idea, as I knew the cooks in
the kitchen were tired of the untrained men Ahab kept sending
down to them when he did not know what else to do with them.

"That is an excellent idea," I said to Athaliah, and her cheeks
flushed pink with the praise. Athaliah was sixteen years old now,
but I often forgot about her, in between trying to train Ahaziah and
dealing with Joram's temper. She was beautiful, I realized suddenly, with long shining hair and large dark eyes. She was more
beautiful even than my mother, and had not inherited my height,
so she had the delicate look that men preferred. Ahab and I had idly
discussed her marriage before, but as I looked at her now, I knew
we should have made plans before now. Sapphira, who sat at the
table with us, caught me looking at Athaliah and I saw her face
pale—she had always been able to know what I was thinking. She
did not leave the table when everyone else did, and for a while we
sat in silence, drinking our wine slowly, neither of us wanting to
broach the subject. Finally, I broke the silence. "You know—

you've always known that she cannot stay here. That she will have to leave."

Sapphira took a long swallow of wine, but when she set down the cup, I saw her hand trembling. "I hoped . . . I hoped that you would not send her away. That you would not want her to feel what you felt."

"There is no one good enough for her in Israel," I said. "I want a king for her husband."

"You want a king so that you might have a new alliance for Israel. Just as your father wanted when he sent you here."

"Athaliah is smart," I said to Sapphira. "She should not be the plaything of some minor courtier in Ahab's court. She should rule her own court."

"She has always been smart," Sapphira said. "You have only noticed now because she can be of use to you."

I did not say anything in my own defense because I knew Sapphira was right, knew that she was angry as a mother might be. As I should have been. I felt sorrow at that thought. I knew I was not the type of mother Sapphira wished me to be. But I also knew that securing a new alliance would protect my sons. And it would give Athaliah the chance to shine without the shadows of her brothers.

"I will miss her," Sapphira said, a tremble in her voice. "She reminds me of you when we were girls. When we were still in Tyre. Sometimes when I'm with Athaliah I imagine what would have happened if we had not come to Israel."

"My father was right to send me here," I said. "He knew that I could not do anything great in Tyre. That my name would not be remembered if I stayed there. Look what I have done. I have brought a country that was on the edge of disaster back to life. Our granaries are full. Trade routes that I established, that I maintain, are filling our treasury. There are temples to Astarte across the land. Look how Israel has changed."

Sapphira looked out on the rolling hills that surrounded us, the city that looked new and shining, better even than it had been before the drought and famine. The sun shone on the fertile fields, and we could hear the gentle thuds of workers gathering the fig harvest. "Your father did not send you here because he thought you would do well. He did it because it was the most valuable alliance for him. Which is what you will do for Athaliah." Sapphira suddenly reached across the table and grabbed my hand. "Bel. Please, let her choose her own husband. Even if it is not the alliance you wanted." I opened my mouth to protest, to say that women did not make decisions about their own husbands, but Sapphira spoke again. "When have I ever asked you for anything?" she said, sounding both angry and sad. "This is all I ask of you."

I leaned back in my seat and stared at her, feeling winded. She was right. She had followed one step behind me our whole lives. She had been with me during my early years as queen, had written down each word I commanded, helping build my name. She had held my hand when I lost my first child; she had kept my secret about Elijah, had pulled me back from the edge when I had been in despair over Minta, when I had been desperate to protect Joram. She had done more for me than anyone had a right to ask. And mostly I had not asked. I had assumed. I had known that Sapphira would always do as I wanted. Perhaps it had been her way of repaying the life debt we had been told she owed me from the moment of her birth. And now I looked into her eyes and nodded. "Athaliah will agree," I said. "We will go through the options together, me, Ahab, Athaliah, and you. And Athaliah will agree to it. Before we make any treaties or send any letters. Even if it is not what is best for Israel. For me."

Sapphira began to weep, and I rose to wrap my arms around her, my best, dearest friend. "You can go with her, if you want," I said. "I will not make you stay with me." I wondered if this was what Tanith had seen all those years ago, Sapphira leaving me so that she could go with my daughter.

"No, Bel," Sapphira said, squeezing my hand. "I love Athaliah. I would do anything for her. But I will not leave you. Not for anyone. Not until the end."

Before the end, I thought, but I did not say anything, just let Sapphira continue to cry softly into my shoulder.

CHAPTER 21

amoth Gilead was taken years ago," I said to Enosh, who sat beside me at dinner. "It is of no real importance." I pushed a honey cake around my plate. I could not believe that all these years later I was still arguing with Enosh. I remembered suddenly the bet that Elijah and Sapphira had placed on how I would insult Enosh years before and smiled slightly before I said, "Why should we go after it now?"

"Have you not heard the rumblings across Israel?" Enosh said, taking a long swallow of wine.

I raised an eyebrow but didn't say anything, waiting for Enosh to continue. I knew he was angry that Ahab was not at dinner with us, but of late Ahab refused to attend even feasts of state, sending me in his place. I thought of the girl I had been when I'd arrived in Israel, thinking that I could win the esteem of the people through peace. In the end, though, love and fear were not so different. If I could not have one, at least I would have the other.

"We have been at peace for years," I said. "Why would we destroy that peace?"

"People grow tired of peace," Enosh said. He took a deep breath, as if he were frightened, and then said, "As they grow tired of Ahab, my lady."

"They cannot grow tired of Ahab," I said. "He is their king. He has brought prosperity to them and their children."

"He was the one who spared Ben-Hadad." Enosh chewed on a piece of meat. "And it is Ben-Hadad's son who causes trouble now. They blame Ahab. They say that he is king in name only," Enosh said slowly. "They say that he spends all his time in the garden or running around with his children. They say that . . . someone else rules now."

Enosh looked at the place where Ahab should have sat as I crushed a purple grape beneath my fingers. I had done all I could to keep Ahab's attentions on Israel, but Ahab was not a king suited for peace. He grew too complacent under it, too sun-soaked and slow.

"Would they have preferred the kingdom was left to fall into ruin?" I said, thinking of how the people had once sung my name in the streets.

"They want their king, my lady," Enosh said, looking straight ahead. He was a tall man, taller than Ahab, but even though Ahab had not fought a battle in years, his muscles were still strong across his chest and shoulders. Enosh was technically a commander in the army, but he had never truly fought in a battle before. Not as Ahab had. He knew that it would be impossible to regain Ramoth Gilead without Ahab.

"We must consult the gods," I said.

"Let us hope they answer quickly," Enosh said, and I could hear the threat in his voice. Israel was tired of waiting. If Ahab did not return to his place beside me, they might decide they wanted a different king. One who was not of Ahab's blood. I remembered my fears when Joram had been born, his being dashed to the floor and killed, and my mouth hardened.

"I believe the gods will look favorably on this," I said. "You may tell your men to prepare for war."

"You don't need to consult with Ahab?" Enosh asked, and I saw that he too was longing for a king, wishing he was sitting by a man instead of by me. I thought of the grain silos I had built that sustained Israel throughout the famine and drought. Thought about how only with my plans had we refilled those silos after they had been drained during the famine. How I had built schools for the scribes, clothed and fed orphans, created and strengthened trade routes that had enriched the country. That had filled Israel's coffers and clothed its people in purple and gold. But it did not matter what I had done—it would never matter. Because after all of it, all that mattered was that I was a woman.

I took out my dagger and stabbed it through the heart of the small bird on my plate. "Ahab has always done his duty as king. He will be with you at Ramoth Gilead."

◎◎◎◎

Ahaziah should go with you," I said again as I helped Ahab buckle his breastplate.

"It would not do for the king and the heir to be at the same battle," Ahab said. "What if something happened?"

"Nothing will happen," I said, tapping a finger on his armor. It gave a soft *ping*. "It is only to take back what is ours. The king of Aram does not have enough men to stop you. Not with Judea on our side as well."

Ahab's hair was tied back, and his armor gleamed, but he did not have the look that I was used to seeing on his face before he went off to battle. "But Micaiah said that it will lead to disaster."

I stiffened. "You consulted with that priest? Even though I told you I had already gotten the blessings from the gods?"

"He is a priest of Yahweh," Ahab said, voice petulant. "He can intercede with Yahweh for us."

"Elijah is the prophet of Yahweh," I said. "He is the only one who can truly intercede to Yahweh. We learned that on Mount Carmel. And since we have not heard from him in years, it is to our other gods that we must turn."

Ahab said nothing, and I slammed my hands on the nearby table, making it rattle. "I told you why this must be done," I said. "The people are calling for their king. They do not want me to rule. They hate me even more than they did after the drought because I killed Naboth." I flexed my hands but knew that no matter how I tried, I could not drop those stones.

"I love you," Ahab said softly. "Is that not enough?"

I nearly laughed at the naivety of such a question, but I knew he was speaking from his heart, so I said, "It is because of your love that people fear me. They think I have entranced you. Stolen you away from them. From Yahweh."

"How could I be stolen from Yahweh when he is constantly telling me how I have disappointed him?" Ahab said, trying to smile, but I could tell that not having his god's admiration still weighed on him.

"You have not disappointed Israel," I said. "You have given them peace. Prosperity. You only need to remind them of it. Remind them of the warrior you are."

Ahab nodded and strapped on his sword, then turned to me.

"Do you ever wonder, Bel? Wonder if it was worth it? So many died during the famine, on Mount Carmel . . . there has been so much blood."

I did not pause even though I wanted to. I did not begin to weep as I thought of the bloodshed. Ahab should not doubt himself on the eve of battle. "There would have been more. If we had been at constant war like your father was. More would have died if we had not opened trade with Tyre."

"Then why am I going out to war now?" Ahab said.

"Prosperity lulls those under it," I said. "The people long for excitement. They want new stories to sing. Stories of their great king."

"They should sing of you," Ahab said. I thought of the song they had sung about me when I'd first arrived in Israel. The song that Elijah had written.

"They should," I said. "But they will sing of none of us if we and our children are killed because they do not believe in us anymore."

I held out his robes to him, but he shook his head. "Enosh and I are planning a new strategy. A blind. He will wear my royal robes. They will aim for him, and I will be able to lead the attack from the side." He tried to hide it, but I could see the glint of excitement in his eyes as he talked about the strategy.

"He will be most protected even if they do aim for him," I said. I frowned at Ahab. His beard was entirely grey. "You will be fighting in the field, then?" I said. "I do not like it. You should be surrounded by your guard."

"I will be in my chariot," Ahab said. "I haven't fought a battle in years, but I was once a feared soldier. It will be good to test out my strength again. I am not an old man yet."

I almost protested, but . . . but I liked seeing him as he'd been. I liked watching him pull on his armor and go to fight our enemy with courage instead of sitting in his garden with children.

He pulled me toward him and kissed me deeply. "Don't worry, Bel. When I return, the people will see that they still have a warrior king. And our family will be safe."

◎◎◎◎

Three days after Ahab had left with the army, I had woken to a body that ached. I knew it was probably only the onset of my monthly bleeding, but it made me feel anxious and angry all day, so in the evening just before the sun set, I escaped to my pool. I did not have the time to swim as I once had, but the water was still as great a relief as ever. I floated on my back as the sun began to slowly set, and I thought of the day Ahab had taken me to the coast just so that I might swim in the sea again. We had been so happy that day, before the drought and famine, before the massacre on Mount Carmel or the killing of Naboth. Perhaps once he returned from the battle, we could leave Samaria for a time to go and visit the sea. Perhaps then we could talk about the future of Israel again, and how we might make sure it was secure before it was handed over to Ahaziah.

I had just climbed out of the pool and was reaching for a towel when a cloud of dust appeared on the road. A lone chariot was coming down the road at speed, and I wondered why its driver did not slow down. Then I realized that there was no one driving it. The horses pulling it careened along the road and came upon me so quickly I had to jump out of the way. They nearly fell into the pool, but at the last second they stopped, trembling and foam-mouthed. I did not recognize them, but they were expensive warhorses, black as ash, unlike the ones Ahab used.

Ahab said he had a new team, I thought, as I carefully drew near the frightened beasts. My heart began to pound like a drum, but still, I drew near. It was impossible this was Ahab's chariot. His was much finer, with gold adornments. *He was hiding*, a voice in my head said. *He was pretending he was not the king, so of course he would not drive the king's chariot.*

Still, when I carefully put a hand on one of the trembling horses, I did not believe that it was Ahab's chariot. Ramoth Gilead was too far away, and his horses would have had to run themselves to death to return all this way. The horse beside me reared up suddenly and broke free of its restraints. It sprinted away but collapsed only a few paces away. I stared at it, but it did not raise its head, and I realized that it was not moving. My hands trembled as I released the other horse from its restraints. It dipped its head in the pool and began to drink noisily, as if it had come a far distance. As if it had come from Ramoth Gilead.

"He had to go," I said aloud as I climbed to the side of the chariot. "It was the will of the gods."

"Micaiah said that it will lead to disaster."

"Micaiah is not the prophet," I repeated. "And Yahweh said he would not bring destruction on Ahab. He *promised*," I whispered, as I finally saw inside the chariot. There was a man in the chariot, but he was lying on his face. An arrow was still sticking out of his shoulder. The floor of the chariot was red from a man's lifeblood, but when I bent to touch it, I found it cold, as if the man inside had been dead a long time. Long enough that not even his blood still held his spirit. For a moment, I merely crouched in the blood, the hem of my robe turning scarlet. Slowly I reached out, to try to see the man's face, but his body had already turned hard as a stone. I had to stand and wrench the body before I finally managed to turn it over and look down on the king's face.

I howled, a horrible, broken-animal sound that I heard dogs take up, before I dropped to my feet and cradled my husband in my lap.

I stroked his cold face over and over, as his eyes looked blankly to the sunset-streaked sky. "They needed a king," I said over and over, tears falling hot down my face. "They needed a king."

After a long time, I saw that I was no longer alone. A dog, who must have heard my howls and come to investigate, was crouched by the chariot, licking up the blood that dripped out of it. I stared at it but did not shoo it away, even though its muzzle was red. Instead, I painted my own mouth with Ahab's blood, thinking of his lips on mine. I cupped my hands and filled them with the pooling red, drinking of it so that his life might fill up the hollow spaces in my bones, the cracks between my teeth. So I could subsume him—become him—for however brief a time. Become my husband. The king.

CHAPTER 22

At Ahab's funeral, my children wept and keened, but I stood dry-eyed beside his body, a black veil covering my face. Ahaziah wept so much that Sapphira had to hold him, and though he was too old for such public grief, I did not chide him.

Palace guards had eventually found me, cradling Ahab's body, and they had thought I was dead too, because I was covered in his blood. I screamed when they tried to take him away and I saw the way their eyes flicked to my mouth, my teeth red with his blood. I knew they would probably spread word that I was a witch who had drunk her husband's blood to commune with devils, but at that moment I did not care what they thought. It was only later that I realized how dangerous a rumor of witchcraft could be for me. *You shall not suffer a witch to live*, the early prophets had said.

They stone witches, I thought, staring as my husband's body was shut away into darkness. *Perhaps it is what I deserve. To die as Naboth died.* As they rolled the stone over the tomb, Ahaziah whimpered, and the crowd began to murmur. They had wanted their king to fight. He had, and he was dead. Now they wanted their new king to act like the king his father had been. The king they had killed.

I will not die as a witch, I thought. *I will not allow myself to die until I have done all I can for my children. I will not die until the moment of my choosing.* I looked at the sky, wondered if Yahweh was watching, gloating at the death of the king he had so hated. The king who had chosen peace over war and been punished for it. *I will not die at your will*, I said to Yahweh, clenching my fists. *You might have been Ahab's god, but you are not mine.*

"We will now read of King Ahab's reign from the book of the annals of the kings of Israel," Ahaziah said. I was proud that he managed to keep his voice from trembling as he spoke. The king's scribe opened the book and read, "In the thirty-eighth year of Asa king of Judea, Ahab, son of Omri, became king of Israel, and he reigned over Israel twenty-two years." The scribe's voice was high for a man, nothing like the prophet's, but as he spoke, I could hear Elijah's voice in the pages. I had forgotten, somehow, that Elijah had been the one to record the early years of Ahab's life, and it was strange to hear the exploits of Ahab's boyhood, the valor he had shown in his first battle, the year he had married the princess royal of Tyre. It was probably my imagination, but it seemed that after our marriage Elijah had dwelled on my achievements rather than on Ahab's. He had written of them, of me, tenderly, and I wished, for the first time in years, that he was standing beside me as a friend. He had loved Ahab too, once.

"The king caused temples to be built across the land, established trade with Tyre, and fed and housed orphans and widows." I thought for a moment the scribe was confused, that he had wrongly attributed my deeds to Ahab, but then my mother's voice echoed in my head. *My name will be forgotten, just like yours.* And I knew suddenly that the record wasn't wrong. Knew that all my deeds would be attributed to Ahab, to my children. The good I had done would be subsumed into the good the king had done. *The only thing that will be remembered of me will be the evil I did.* The merchant who had died in my temple. The priests I had killed. Naboth. No matter how much good I did, I would be remembered for one hot summer day.

Stones flying through the air.

Blood covering the ground.

I will be the nameless wife of the king, or I will be Jezebel, the queen whose evil deeds were greater than any other.

Harlot. Witch. Or nothing.

I barely heard the rest of the recitation, but I stayed by the tomb long after everyone else, even my children, had left. Sapphira had gone with them, helping Ahaziah back to the palace, and I made my guards go with her so that I might say goodbye to my husband alone. I took off my veil and laid it on the ground, putting a hand on the stone that covered the tomb.

"It shines like the sea."

I turned slowly, somehow unsurprised to see Elijah standing a few paces away from me.

"I think it rather plain," I said, looking at the grey stone wearily. "But it's what Ahab wanted."

"Not the stone," Elijah said. "Your hair. The grey in it shines like the sea."

"What would you know of the sea?" I said. He hesitated, and I remembered. "I forgot," I said, voice hard. "You lived in Tyre after you doomed Israel to drought." I wanted to find the fury I'd felt after he'd killed Minta, when I'd knocked him to the ground in Naboth's vineyard, but I only felt worn to the bone. He had killed those I loved. I thought of the priests of Yahweh, of Ahab in his tomb. I had killed those he loved too.

"I could see the water from the widow's window," Elijah said. "Sometimes I would watch it for hours."

"I heard you raised her son from the dead," I said.

Elijah shrugged. "Yahweh raised him. I was merely the instrument in his hands." Elijah looked down at his own hands. "I am glad now to have brought one back. When I sent so many to the grave." Elijah sighed and looked at Ahab's tomb. "I was here for the burial. I'm sorry I didn't see him before . . ." He trailed away, and I saw that his eyes were red.

"You haven't seen him in years," I said. "And last time you did, you cursed him. Why should you care?"

"Are you so heartless, Bel?" Elijah said.

I laughed mirthlessly. "You've heard the stories of me. That I delight in evil. In blood."

"You have killed many," Elijah said.

"So have you."

Elijah nodded. "I have," he said. "But I loved Ahab. And I grieve his death."

"I loved him too," I said. We stood side by side in front of his tomb, quiet and distant.

"Do you think the gods care about us?" I said after a long time. "Or do you think we are just their playthings?"

Elijah didn't say anything for a long time. When he spoke, his voice was steady. "Those you killed, you killed in the name of the king. Those I killed, I killed in the name of Yahweh. But that doesn't mean their blood is not on our hands." He hesitated. "I trained another prophet to take my place," he said. "A man named Berel. Yahweh blessed him. He went with me performing miracles and speaking of Yahweh. One day, some youths from the nearby town were mocking him because he has no hair. He called down a curse on them, and the youths were mauled by a bear." Elijah's voice was bleak. "I cannot believe that Yahweh wanted those children killed. But Berel said he did it in the name of Yahweh." Elijah looked weary, old, as he said it, and I wondered if I looked the same.

"I thought Naboth was a demon," I said suddenly. "I thought you sent him to bring down my family. To bring down Israel." I knew how foolish the confession was, but I was unable to stop myself from speaking. "The crowd stoned him. And though I did not hurl one stone, I can still feel their weight in my hands."

Elijah looked down at his own hands. They were no longer ink-tipped. They had held back the rain, had held the sword that cut down innocents. Once they had been stained black, but perhaps now they should be red. For the first time in my life, I thought of my name being written down in the book of kings and shivered. Perhaps it would not be so hard for people to believe what I had asked Sapphira to write down. Perhaps the evil I had done would never outweigh the good. I looked back to Elijah, and at the look of his hunched shoulders, I straightened mine. I would not look back on my life and cower. Because no matter what this prophet—this man—had done to innocents, *he* would be remembered for the child he had brought back to life, for the bread and oil that never ran dry, for fire that came down from heaven.

"I have to get back to the palace," I said. "Ahaziah needs me."

Elijah looked as though he wanted to say something else, ask me to stay, perhaps, but instead, he just said, "I fear these next years will be hard on him. He does not seem to have the strength Ahab had."

I raised my chin. "I have what he lacks."

He did not say, "But you are not king," but I heard it nonetheless as I turned my back on him to return to the palace, to my son, and take my role as dowager queen.

"Goodbye, Bel," I heard him say softly as I left.

It was the last time I would see the prophet—see Elijah—ever again.

CHAPTER 23

Elijah was right. Ahaziah did not have the strength of Ahab. His reign did not start well. His advisors did not trust him, and even I was aghast at some of the choices he made in those early days. Soon, I sat beside him at every function, every audience, whispering in his ear when I saw him begin to flail. This too angered his advisors. They wanted him to rule alone, wanted me to disappear into the women's quarters, but I refused.

I walked over to my bronze mirror, but my face looked flat and old. There were lines around my mouth and eyes, and the grey that Elijah had noticed was like a silver river widening every day. At least my chin had not weakened with time.

My maids had painted my face and dressed me, and I was eating figs with Sapphira when Ahaziah came into my rooms. He was dressed in his royal robes, but he wore them like a child pretending to be his father. He yawned hugely, and Sapphira got up to get him more wine, ruffling his hair as she went. I frowned. It was an affectionate gesture but made him seem even more childish.

"Why can't you continue to see the supplicants as you always have?" he said, taking a grape from my plate and popping it into his mouth.

"We've talked about this," I said, forcing myself to keep eating slowly and not slap him for such a foolish question. "You are king now. I am the dowager queen. The people have the right to address their problems directly to their king."

"Can't I just tell them you're speaking for me?" Ahaziah said. "The garden has been neglected and—"

I clamped my hand down on his wrist so hard he yelped. "Listen to me, you foolish boy. *You* are king. Not I. To secure your throne, you must listen to your people. You must be seen as acting on your own. If I speak to the supplicants, the people will think I am ruling through you. That I am bewitching you into listening to me."

I let go of his wrist, and he rubbed it petulantly. "But, Mother," Ahaziah said, "I trust you. Surely you would be a better ruler than I am. I never wanted— I don't want—" His eyes filled with tears. "I do not want to be king," he whispered so quietly that I could barely hear him.

If I had been a better mother, I would have comforted him, held him to me so he could weep quietly into my chest. Instead, my eyes flicked to my maids who were still in the room, to his guard listening at the door.

"Do not weep over your father's death," I said loudly enough that the whole room could hear. It would be better if the court thought he was a tenderhearted son than a weakhearted king. "He knew that he was leaving his kingdom in the hands of one he trusted." I flicked my hand, dismissing the maids and guards, and when the doors were finally shut, I leaned toward Ahaziah.

"What you want does not matter. You *are* king. I will help you as much as I can, but I am not king. I never will be." The words were like bitter wine in my mouth. "Your father loved you. He trusted you to take care of your brother and sister. Of me," I said, even though Ahaziah taking care of me was a laughable thought. "He also trusted you to take care of the kingdom he left you."

Ahaziah wiped his nose on his sleeve, but finally he nodded. "I will do my best," he said with a smile. I smiled back but wondered even as I did if his best would be enough.

◎◎◎◎

It was strange to sit not on my throne, but in a smaller chair beside Ahaziah, and remain quiet as he dealt out judgment. He was too softhearted, as I knew he'd be, but I hoped that that quality would endear him to his people, even if it made his advisors mutter and frown.

The last supplicant of the day was a man dressed in sackcloth. He bowed before the king but did not even incline his head in my direction. "I have come to ask you for a gift, my king," he said, his voice bold for a man wearing the clothes of a beggar.

Ahaziah inclined his head. His crown shifted, and I winced. He had a smaller head than Ahab, and the crown that was worn for ceremonial occasions was too large for him. I would need to get it made smaller. "Let me hear your request," Ahaziah said, which made my stomach loosen a bit. At least he wasn't just granting gifts without knowing what they were.

"Israel was once a great nation," the man said. "But then evil came over the land. I ask that you heal that evil."

My stomach tightened. I knew what the man was about to ask for, but Ahaziah only looked puzzled and said, "I do not know this evil of which you speak."

The man laughed once then looked at me. His eyes were hard. "The evil are the gods your own mother brought to Israel. She has built temples to Astarte across the lands and torn down the altars of Yahweh."

Ahaziah jumped to his feet. "You forget yourself," he said, voice thunderous. I had never heard Ahaziah speak so loudly or with such command. "She has done nothing except teach the people of our beloved Mother Astarte, of El and Anat. She has torn down no altars, and all are welcome to worship whatever god they wish."

The man sneered. "She sentenced priests of Yahweh to death in this very room," he said. "She killed the righteous elder Naboth when he refused to sell land to her."

"I will hear no more lies! Leave now, or you will be thrown into prison." The man left slowly as whispers flooded across the room. "I have heard all I will hear today," Ahaziah said, slamming the doors as he left the throne room.

He was waiting for me in my rooms, sitting on the edge of the balcony, feet hanging into open air. He had always loved to be high up and was entirely fearless no matter how far he might fall. "I'm sorry, Mother," he said when I sat beside him. "I'm sorry you had to hear such lies."

I closed my eyes for a moment. It was time Ahaziah knew the truth. "They were not all lies," I said. "Of course, I do not believe that our gods brought evil to this land. They brought prosperity, trade with Tyre, a refuge for orphans. But . . ." I hesitated, looking at my son's open face. There was no artifice in him. He would believe whatever I told him. I straightened my shoulders. I was queen. I would not be ashamed of what I had done. "I did sentence the priests of Yahweh to death. They ignored the will of the king and would not pray for rain during the drought. And I . . ." I did not know how to finish. No one except Sapphira knew what had truly happened between me and Naboth. Perhaps if I told him the truth, perhaps if he knew that I had not been in possession of myself, he would not hate me? But by the time I'd finished the story, he'd edged away from me as if afraid.

"You had so many killed?" he said. "But why? Why did they have to die? You cannot kill everyone who does not obey you."

"You can," I said, voice hard. "And you should. Both of your grandfathers took their thrones through blood and death. From kings whose people did not believe in them. From kings who let dissidents run rampant among their people."

Ahaziah looked like he was going to be sick. "I thought Israel has been at peace. We've had peace." His voice was pleading.

"We've had peace because we killed those who spoke against us," I said quietly. "It is how all kings rule. How they keep their families safe and continue their line through the generations."

I wonder what might have happened if I had not told Ahaziah the truth. Perhaps he would have found the strength to be the king who Israel needed, but I think not. No matter what he believed about the world, Ahaziah was too good to be a good king.

He pulled away from me after our talk. He began to drink more and more and throw raucous parties on the roof for his friends. At first, I did not worry. He was a young man who was grieving for his father. He wanted to be with those his own age. It was not until I learned that he had invited Enosh to one of his parties that I realized this was how he intended to rebuke me for my past.

Ever since Ahab's death, I had refused to see or speak to Enosh. I blamed myself for Ahab's death, but I also blamed Enosh. He was the one who had brought the idea of retaking Ramoth Gilead to me in the first place. Enosh, who survived the battle at Ramoth Gilead without a scratch.

I dressed for the party as a man might dress for a battle, painting

my face white and lips red, wearing enough gold in my ears and
bangles on my arms that the metal could have stopped a blade. I
wore my purple robes for the first time since Ahab had died and
had my maids place my crown on my head, even though it was so
heavy it made my head ache. I hesitated on the stairs to the roof but
knew I had to join them. *I have to learn what Enosh is whispering in
his ear*, I thought. My hand was on the railing when another thought
hit me: *Perhaps he is here to kill my son as he killed Ahab*. I had not
thought of Enosh as wily enough for such schemes, but it was possible I had misjudged him.

I mounted the stairs quickly, determined that I should be by
Ahaziah's side all evening, whether he wanted me there or not.

When I reached the roof, I found it strewn with gold-flickering
lanterns and torches. There were ivory couches heaped with pillows sewn with gold, and a group of musicians played in the corner. Servants held out trays towering with glistening meat and
sweets and passed golden goblets of wine around.

Ahaziah stood in the western corner, holding court with the city
spread out behind him. He was balancing on the edge of the roof
while holding a goblet of wine, face smudged with food as though
he were a child. I pushed my way toward them, and when he saw
me, he smiled, but it was not his sweet smile. It reminded me of
mine. All pointed teeth and wide, red lips. "Mother!" He lifted his
goblet to me, swaying so much I thought he would fall. He didn't,
though, merely jumping from the roof to clank his goblet against
Enosh's, who stood by his side. "Congratulate me, Mother!"

"Congratulate you for what?" I said.

"On my first treaty. Enosh and I have agreed to construct a fleet
of trading ships that will build a new trade route from Apollonia to
Caesarea. We should not only have to rely on ships from Tyre but
should have our own."

I stared at Enosh. Caesarea was his home city; the new trade route would double their income. "My father has the best ships in the world," I said. "Why should we build our own?" I looked at Enosh, but he didn't say anything. We both knew that no matter what the treaty was, it would benefit Enosh more than Ahaziah.

Ahaziah frowned. "Israel is a great nation in its own right. We should have our own fleet and not rely on the goodwill of a foreign king."

I wondered if he meant to wound me by calling my father a foreign king, but I could not read his face well enough. "He is your grandfather," I said. "And after him, my brother will rule. We have always had a wonderful relationship with Tyre."

"Because of you," Ahaziah said. "But you won't live forever."

I blinked and looked at Enosh, knowing that my son would never come up with such an idea on his own. Enosh shrugged as if he could not be held responsible for his own words, and I knew that in a way he was right. Ahaziah was looking at Enosh with shining eyes, as he had once looked at Ahab. Anyone, especially a man like Enosh, would try to press his advantage with a young man so desperate for the approval of a father.

Later I tried to dissuade Ahaziah from building the ships, tried to show him the advantages it would give Enosh, how the extra income could make Enosh dangerous to the crown, but he stubbornly ignored me. "Why shouldn't we help our oldest advisor in this way?" he said. "Enosh gave good advice to my grandfather and father, and he has been my friend during these trying times. He would not recommend something that would harm me." Ahaziah was entirely earnest when he said it, his voice so hopeful and pleased with himself that I knew nothing I said would matter.

◎◎◎◎

The ships were wrecked before they even set sail. Ahaziah had built them at great expense, but a vicious storm had blown up one day before they even left our shore, tearing them from their moorings, and dashing them to pieces. Ever since he'd heard the news, Ahaziah had not left the roof garden.

A week after the ships wrecked, I was closeted in the chamber off the throne room that we used for our war councils, talking with the army commander. He had worse news to share.

"Moab rebels more each day." They were our neighbor to the east and had always been troublesome, always trying to poke at our borders, see where our weaknesses lay. "They see the king as . . ." He hesitated, but I nodded at him to continue. "They see him as weak. He is not a warrior like his father was, and so they do not fear him. They have heard that he spends most of his time drinking with his friends, rather than ruling the country."

I gritted my teeth but nodded. I had gone up to the roof that morning to try to get Ahaziah to come down after several servants had failed, but he had been in a drunken stupor when I found him, and when I tried to get him to stand, he had swayed dangerously. "It's too hard," he'd said, breath smelling of wine. "I cannot be king if it means I must betray my allies. If it means I must kill those who speak against me. I am not you, Mother."

I knew he meant the words as a reproach, and if we'd been alone, I would have slapped him and brought him down by his ear, but many of his friends were on the roof too. Such a scene would only make things worse for him. So I had let him collapse back onto the roof and left to attend the meeting on my own.

"My lady." A guard ran into the room just as the general was showing me where Moab was marshaling their forces. "You are needed at once. The king. He—he—"

"What?" I snapped. "What has happened to the king?"

"He was on the roof, my lady." The guard swallowed. "He fell."

As I ran to Ahaziah's rooms, I remembered the prophecy Elijah had spoken, how he had said that disaster would fall on my sons. I remembered how Ahaziah balanced on the edge of the balcony as though he did not care if he lived or died.

When I entered his rooms, he was surrounded by people, Sapphira already at his side. I had never seen her so pale. I looked away from her, not wanting to read what I saw in her face. I turned instead to my son, who smiled weakly. He had a long gash on his cheek, but he was alive. "I should have listened to you," he said when I clasped his hand. "I was standing on the roof and a gust blew . . . I was dizzy already . . ." He looked down, but I could see that his lips were stained purple from the wine.

"You are alive," I said, smoothing back the hair from his face. "That is what matters."

Ahaziah's face fell. "I felt something—something tore, Mother. When I fell."

I kept my face implacable. "We have the best healers. You will get better."

Ahaziah nodded his head, but he did not look convinced, and as the days passed, he did not rise from his bed, even after the bruises faded. When he sat up, he would cry out in pain and clutch his side.

"His fate is in the gods' hands," one healer finally told me. His voice was low, but I saw Ahaziah's eyelids flicker and knew he had heard.

Once the healer left, Ahaziah called me over and spoke in a weak voice. "Would you send messengers to ask Baal Zebub what my fate will be?"

I nodded, even though I did not want the god of prophecy to tell us anything. We had reached a peace between us, a softness that we had never had toward each other, even when he was a child. I told him stories of my childhood in Tyre, the dolphins I'd swum with and the fish I'd caught, and he asked eagerly after what grew on such salty shores. He would have made a better farmer than a king. He would have been able to tend his land all day, and he would not have complained about the years it added to his brow or the dirt crusted under his nails. He would have sacrificed to the gods and married a plump, pretty woman and been content.

Tanith came as quickly as her shuffling feet would allow. She stopped in the doorway when she saw Sapphira and me sitting by Ahaziah's side, and I saw her hand tighten on the walking stick she used. She took a single, deep breath then walked in the room, a soft, gentle smile on her face. She lowered herself onto a stool as Sapphira and I held tightly on to his hands, as though our strength would be enough to tether him to this world.

Tanith smoothed a hand over Ahaziah's hair. "You have done well, Your Majesty. Your father would be proud of you. And the gods . . ." Her voice broke for a second, then she continued. "And the gods are ready to receive you into their embrace."

Ahaziah's face relaxed at her words. "Thank you," he said, squeezing Tanith's hand. He turned to me, his face smooth as a newborn. "I think I will sleep now and think of my garden."

As he closed his eyes, I curled around my son like I had when he was a baby. Sapphira laid her hand on Ahaziah's hair, and Tanith held her palms out in prayer as he slowly, gently, slipped away, like a small, bright shell the tide wanted for its own.

CHAPTER 24

Joram took to kingship as Ahaziah did not. He was young when his brother died, but he did not have the gentleness of Ahaziah. He asked me for my advice and then ignored it, and when I chided him, he laughed.

It was strange, because I hated when he laughed at me, when he ignored me, but I also knew that his finding his own way was the only way he would be a true king. I had killed for Joram, to save his life from the threat I thought Naboth was, but he did not know what I had done. He only took as he had always done, like he had a right to whatever his hand touched. He was charming, smiled graciously, and was much more of a favorite of the people than Ahaziah had been.

After Ahab's death, it was Berel, Elijah's former apprentice, who was now proclaimed as the prophet of Yahweh. The miracles he performed were spoken of with awe across the land, but I did not truly understand the power he had until I found that a stone that had been devoted to El had been taken down.

"Why would you remove El's sacred stone?" I said, voice raised in anger as I walked into my son's rooms. Joram had added even more gold decorations around the room, lining his bathing tub in blue lapis lazuli, and though many lavished praises on it, I found it to be overdone for my tastes.

At twenty, Joram looked the part of a king. He was shirtless, having just climbed from the bath, and the muscles in his chest and shoulders gleamed. He was more impressive than even Ahab had been because he had my height as well, and I'd heard many a maiden in the court sigh over him and vie for his favor. I knew I should be encouraging him to marry and produce heirs. After all, Athaliah had been married seven years before and already had two children, but I knew that a new queen would only try to fight me for power, and with Israel constantly skirmishing Moab, it was too dangerous to step into the background now.

"It angers Yahweh," a voice said from the shadows. I turned and saw Jehu, sitting in the corner, peeling a fig. He had remained Joram's closest friend and was now commander of the army.

I stared at him for a long moment, but he did not flinch or turn away from me, his knife going around and around in one unbroken movement until the fruit's flesh was laid bare. I had never grown to like Jehu. There had always been a stillness about him that had reminded me of a storm the moment before lightning struck.

"Everything angers Yahweh," I said. "I would have thought you boys learned that years ago."

Joram's eyes flashed when I called them boys, but Jehu merely stared at me. "Evil angers Yahweh," Jehu said softly. "We are doing our best to remove evil from the land."

I wanted to slap the boy, to watch his head snap back and his body fall to the ground, but I just ground my teeth together and then said, "El is not evil. He is the king and father of the gods."

"The *gods*," Jehu said, softer still. "But he is no king to Yahweh. He is nothing to Yahweh." Jehu's eyes were as dark as Elijah's, and for a moment as he stared at me, I saw the prophet looking back.

Joram waved his hand at Jehu for silence, but I saw the lift of his lips, saw how my words amused him. Jehu did not smile back, merely biting into his fig so that its juices ran down his chin. "I am king, Mother," Joram said with a sigh, as if reproaching an infant. "I must remain open to all the gods, as you've always said. If removing a stone will put me in a favorable light in the prophet's eyes, then it is worth it."

I stared as he dismissed me, reducing the many years Ahab and I had ruled over Israel—how we had saved it from starvation and ruin—to nothing but the tired stories of elders. I realized my son did not remember what I'd accomplished. He looked on me, on what I'd done, as one looks on an old woman insisting on the beauty of her youth even as she stands before you a crone. Irrelevant.

"In Berel's eyes," was all I said, remembering what Elijah had told me about Berel calling bears to maul children for mocking him.

"Berel is the chosen prophet," Joram said. "He was taught by Elijah himself. And since Elijah hasn't been seen in years, Berel speaks for Yahweh now."

"Berel is nothing," I said, realizing as I spoke that I was echoing Jehu's words of a moment before.

Jehu moved fast as a snake at my words, suddenly standing before me, hand raised as though he would strike me. "Berel is the prophet of Yahweh," he said, so close I could feel his breath on my face. "*You* will give him the respect he deserves."

I wanted to gut him where he stood for speaking to me as though I was beneath him, as though *I* was nothing, but Joram moved in between us. He touched his friend on the shoulder and then pushed him gently away from me.

"It is for the best that the stone was removed, Mother," Joram said, giving me a light kiss on the cheek. "We need Berel to look on us favorably if we are to beat back Moab."

"Why not ask the blessing of our gods?" I said. "El, Astarte. The warrior goddess Anat. Surely she can guide you better than Yahweh."

"We ask the blessing of all gods," Joram said smoothly, before Jehu, who had opened his mouth, could speak. "But Yahweh is still the god of Israel. You know that your gods are foreign, Mother. They do not have the power in Israel that they do in Tyre."

Your gods, he said, so casually. As though they were not his gods too. As if they had not brought prosperity and peace to Israel for thirty years.

"I have already consulted Berel," Joram said. "He said that Yahweh will deliver the Moabites into our hands. He insulted me in doing so"—Joram's face darkened—"but I will deal with an insult if it assures us victory."

"I wouldn't trust the word of that man," I said, looking at Jehu, who had retreated once more to the corner of the room.

"I know," he said, giving me another kiss as he pushed me from the room. "That is why I am king, and not you."

◎ ◎ ◎ ◎

I stood on my balcony and watched as they approached. Their armor shone bright in the sun, and as they marched closer and closer to my city, it was like watching a silver tide move in.

After Joram ignored my caution over the fight with Moab, he'd marched the army out and been soundly defeated. I had been furious when he returned with scars on his face and a wound in his side, but I knew that one lost battle did not mean a lost war, and in this at least, Joram had listened to me, calling the entire army to Samaria so that we might protect our capital city and make proper plans for how to push Moab back. I turned my attention from the approaching Israelite army and looked down on the city. Joram was more focused on the war than he was on feeding his people, and the lack of food was beginning to show in their thin faces. I had quietly distributed grain from our last remaining granary, but it had almost run out and I did not know what I would do next.

Joram will never ignore what he sees as a slight on his kingship, I thought, remembering how even as a child Joram would attack anyone who mocked him, even if they were a great deal bigger than him. At the time I had merely laughed at his anger, thought that it was good for a boy to fight his own battles. Now I realized that Joram thought he had to fight every battle, even if his energy would be better spent on other pursuits.

I was sitting at my table poring over the letter I had just received from my brother when someone knocked urgently at my door. A priestess entered, eyes wide, panting slightly. "Your Majesty." She bowed to me. "The diviner, Priestess Tanith, has asked that you make your way to her at the temple with all urgency."

I ran through the palace to Tanith's room, worried her time had come, but when I arrived, I found her well, sitting in the courtyard where we always met. And even though she had told me I must come urgently, she seemed to be hesitant, taking time to pour me wine, get me a better pillow for my back, before she finally stopped in front of me. "I have to tell you something, Bel."

Tanith's hair was pure white now. Her hands had trembled ever since Minta's death, and she had trained another priestess to take over for her as diviner, but she still knew each priestess in the temple.

I set the glass back down. "Don't tell me Joram is destroying more sacred stones."

"No," Tanith said. "It's not that." She twisted the silver ring she wore around her middle finger. "I will be returning to Tyre soon," she said. Her eyes found mine, but I could tell that was not what she had wanted to tell me.

"How wonderful," I said, though the news of it saddened me deeply. "It will be good to feel the sea breeze on your face again."

Tanith nodded. "I had always planned to go, but I'm leaving earlier than I wanted, because——" She took in a deep breath. "Because I am afraid. I am afraid of the king."

I put my hand over hers. "Surely you know Joram would not let any harm befall you or the priestesses? And neither will I."

"It is not Joram of whom I speak." Tanith held my gaze for a long moment, eyes steady. "I have heard that Berel has . . . he has anointed a new king over Israel. Jehu, son of Nimshi."

"What?" I thought of Jehu's pale eyes, the way he'd stood so close to me months ago, as though he had the right, as though he was . . . king. I thought of Joram's hand on Jehu's shoulder, the kinship Joram felt for the man he considered a brother. "But Jehu would never betray Joram. He loves him . . . who—who told you such a thing?"

"My priestesses keep me informed of what the people are saying," Tanith said. "I've asked them to since the day . . ." She hesitated. "Since the day Minta killed that man in the temple. A priestess from Jezreel came not an hour ago. She saw Berel anoint Jehu herself."

I thought back to that moment in my son's rooms. Joram had touched Jehu, had shown his affection for him for years, but had I ever seen Jehu return the affection? Had I ever seen Jehu put his hand on Joram's arm or call him brother? Or had he always looked at Joram with that strange stillness in his body, like a snake preparing to strike an unsuspecting mouse? "He is away," I said slowly.

"He is not here right now; Jehu is gathering the army. Gathering the army he commands . . ." My voice trailed away, and I drank the whole glass of wine in a single gulp. Jehu had been out in the country for weeks, gathering the army as Joram had instructed. I suddenly remembered the silver flood I'd watched approach the city only an hour before.

Tanith's voice was steady even as she said, "I was told that Berel said, 'Thus says Yahweh, the God of Israel: "I have anointed you king over Yahweh's people, Israel. Go, strike down the house of your lord, Ahab, so I can avenge the blood of my servants, the priests of Yahweh, at the hands of Jezebel. The whole house of Ahab shall perish. I will cut down every one that pisses against a wall, wherever he may be in Israel. And the dogs will eat Jezebel by the walls, and no one will bury her."'"

By the time Tanith finished speaking, she was whispering, so I had to lean in to hear her final words. I had not thought of Elijah's old prophecy against me in so long. At the time he said it, I had laughed in his face. Then, I was still queen, Ahab by my side. I had thought that nothing could bring us down. Now the words made me cold.

"It is treason," I said softly. "Treason to anoint a usurper to take my son's place."

Tanith nodded. "Others have won thrones with treason," she said, and I thought of my father and Ahab's. Of Ben-Hadad and how it had been my choice to let him live. Had that one decision doomed us all?

I stood suddenly. "I have to warn Joram. He is at the winter palace in Jezreel, recovering from their last skirmish with Moab. Jehu is his trusted friend. He will let him into the palace without question," I said, rushing to my rooms.

I was nearly ready to leave for Jezreel when I heard screams. I ran to my balcony and saw that the Israelite army had surrounded the city. For a moment I felt relief, thinking they were here with Joram, but then I recognized the man's pale eyes, and knew it was Jehu who rode at the front of the army. His shoulders were strong and broad, and he sat on his horse proudly. Like a king. I clenched my nails into my palm at the traitorous thought and watched as they came closer. Finally, they stopped beside the garden that had once been Naboth's vineyard, and my heart began to pound. "Great goddess—" I began to pray, but when I saw the man on the horse beside Jehu, I stopped cold. "Yahweh," I whispered, my lips barely able to move. "Please, Yahweh. Please spare my son. My boy. Please."

They shoved Joram to the ground with his hands tied in front of him. "Peace, Jehu!" he shouted. My boy's voice was high and frightened as a child's, and I thought of the dream I'd had before he was born, the one where Israel burned.

"There can be no peace when your mother Jezebel's harlotries and sorceries are so many." Jehu's voice was resonant. The voice of a poet. A prophet. A king.

I was gripping the railing of my balcony so hard I thought my bones would break, but I did not let go as I watched Joram stagger to his feet. He ran, he ran so fast that for one precious, mad moment, I thought he would escape. But then Jehu drew his huge bow back and I screamed as the arrow flew. My boy turned his head toward my voice at the last moment, and his eyes met mine just for a moment before Jehu shot him in the back. Then he fell, his blood spilling across Naboth's vineyard and soaking the ground.

CHAPTER 25

They are at the gates, Bel," Sapphira said, bursting into my room a few minutes later. Her face was red and streaked with tears, and I knew that she must have seen Joram fall. "We need to leave now."

"No," I said slowly. "No, I will not go."

"You cannot stay," Sapphira said. "They will—"

"They will kill me." I lifted my chin. "I will not abandon my people or my name," I said. "I will die among them, an Israelite."

"Then I will stay with you," Sapphira said, putting the bag down.

I shook my head. "You are my best and truest friend. I will not have you raped and tortured by Jehu and his men."

She began to weep, and I wrapped my arms around her. "They will do the same to you if you do not come with me," she said. Tears streamed down her face. She looked back at the palace, then said, "You saved thousands. You gave them prosperity, and you ended famines and saved their sons from war." She took a deep breath. "My queen," she said, bowing to me. "I will not obey this last command. I will stay with you. I *will* be with you till the end."

I wrapped my arms around her. I breathed in her smell, the feel of her cheek against mine. She was my first friend. My last friend. I had kept her alive on the night of our birth. And I would keep her alive now. "When you get to Tyre," I said, "will you jump into the sea for me?" I held a cloth I'd prepared, soaked in a sleeping draught, to her nose even as she fought me, until she slumped against me. I sobbed as I straightened her robe, then took in a deep breath and called in my last two loyal guards, asking them to carry her through the corridor that led out of my rooms. I followed them until we arrived at my pool, where Tanith stood waiting with a camel as I'd instructed. The guards tied Sapphira's slumped form onto the camel, and I dismissed them, leaving Tanith and me alone together.

"You have honored the goddess," Tanith said slowly. "She will be with you. Astarte will be with you, till the end." I helped her climb onto the camel and watched until I saw them reach the caravan that would take them back to Tyre. Then I turned and slowly walked back to my rooms. Back to Israel. One last time.

My maids had fled, so I dressed and adorned myself. I braided my long hair and twisted it through with jewels that would catch the late-afternoon light. I put on my best purple robes, wound a gold necklace around my throat, and put bangles on my wrists and ankles. I filled my fingers with rings and then began on my face. I carefully whitened it, erasing the years so that I was as fresh-faced as the girl I had been thirty years before. I outlined my eyes in kohl and then slowly, carefully, I painted my lips a deep red, lining them, as if with blood, one last time.

I heard them approaching and stood, walking slowly out to the balcony. I looked one last time for the sea, which I found shining in the distance. Then I arranged my robes and sat on the edge of the balcony, waiting.

When they arrived, they knew, instantly, who I was. I looked down at them with a slight smile on my lips, and finally, Jehu nudged his chariot forward. "Have you come in peace?" I said, voice mocking. "Do you wish to treat with the queen of Israel, Jehu? Murderer of your master. Your friend."

I saw dogs had begun to gather at the feet of the men, and I smiled wide, teeth white and shining, even as my scarred palm drummed like a second heartbeat.

I had realized at Ahab's burial that my accomplishments would never be read aloud. No matter how many temples I built and orphans I saved, no matter how much prosperity I brought to Israel, I would always be a witch. A harlot. Jezebel.

It was the only way. I had told Sapphira that when she had come to my rooms the evening of Ahab's burial to find me standing alone on my balcony. She had been quiet for a long moment after I had explained my plan.

"How can you ask me to do such a thing?" she had asked softly, her eyes wide with grief and shock.

"Because you are the only one left. Because you have always been at my side, my one true friend. And I know . . . I know you will do it right. I know you will understand how." I had clasped her hands in mine. "You have been with me through everything. Will you be with me through this?"

At first she'd refused. "I do not want to do this. It will make your name—"

But I'd raised my chin. "I know what it will do to my name. But it will still be *my* name. And once it is completed, you can return to Tyre. No, no, listen." I rushed, even as I saw her face harden, saw her shake her head. "It will not be safe for you to stay with me once the story spreads. I wish for you to return to safety, to Tyre. I will have my father find you a place at the scribe school if you wish—"

"No. No, if I do this, it will be the last thing I write." She'd looked into the distance at the rolling hills and finally bowed her head. "With the children growing up, Athaliah married . . . I have grown weary of this place. You did not force me here, Bel," Sapphira had said suddenly, seeming to read my thoughts. "I knew from the time I was small I did not want to marry and that I wanted to travel. I wanted to live an interesting life." She'd grasped my hands. "Well, I wanted to *write* about an interesting life. You have given me what I wanted, a life outside of my family. But I think I will enjoy living near my brothers, helping raise their children." She'd pulled me close, holding me tightly as she whispered in my ear, "But I will tell them the *truth* of you, Bel." She'd stepped away from me with a little cough, trying to disguise the tears in her eyes. "Anyway. I will not be leaving this week or even this year. It will take me a long time to do this properly."

And it had. It had taken years, but she had written it. Not *my* story, not really. No, the story I asked her to write was the one of Jezebel the wicked, the seductress. The witch queen who had ruined Israel. The similarities in our stories would be few. But they would end the same way.

"Are there any who are on my side?" Jehu called. "Throw her down."

No one rose to his call. No one was left. I smiled again. Jehu's face was like any king's, written with every thought, every emotion, sure that what he commanded would be done. He was sure that his story would end well, his good deeds written down, his sins forgotten.

I looked at him for a long, long time.

Then I fell, as my husband had fallen, as my sons had fallen, as Sapphira had fallen only hours before. And as I fell, I smiled, because I knew that my name would be remembered. I knew that my tale would be told, as no queen's tale had been told before.

It would begin simply, as all good stories did:

In the days of kings, there was Jezebel.

Acknowledgments

I wrote the first line of Bel's story late one night in bed, a spring sticking into my back. It was just her and me. Thankfully, it didn't remain that way. Without the support and guidance of my agent, Jim McCarthy, I could not have made this book what it is. Thank you, Jim, for taking a chance on me and answering all my anxiety-fueled questions.

Nidhi Pugalia has been the best editor a girl could have. Thank you for truly *seeing* Bel, and for helping me create a book I am proud of.

I am not an artist. Just ask me to draw a shark. Thankfully, Jim Tierney is one of the best around. Thank you for a cover so beautiful it made me cry.

Without the guidance and support of Brian Tart, Andrea Schulz, Lindsay Prevette, Kate Stark, Bel Banta, Roseanne Serra, Nicole Celli, Andrea Monagle, Matt Giarratano, and Nick Michal, this book would not be out in the world. Book people are the best people.

I could write a whole book about Katie and what her friendship means to me. A true kindred spirit. Thank you for reading *Jezebel* so many times. You were with me when I got the call that *Jezebel* was going to be published. I hope I'm with you when you get the same call.

Thank you, Danielle, for being the best writer-friend I could ask for. Everyone check out Danielle Renino's books. She's gonna be your next favorite writer.

Even though my friends call me asking to see my dog instead of me, I still love them. Thanks to Jarin (especially for Jezebel's snazzy nickname, Jezzy B), Inna, and Alex (who took my author photos!). Thanks to Tess Sharpe for answering my panicky new-author questions and not being annoyed by me.

We didn't go to movies or restaurants much when I was a kid. We went to bookstores instead. Thanks to Mom and Dad for always encouraging me to read and write and dream. I still resent, however, the reading time limit I had as a child. That is a grudge I will bear unto my death.

Brendan was the first person to read *Jezebel*, and I told him he'd get his own line here. Thanks, Bren.

Thank you to April, Erin, Patrick, Fiona, Sarah, and Brendan for all somehow being available to answer my group FaceTime when I called to tell you *Jezebel* was being published. Thank you for screaming and cheering. Thanks for the love and support of Sterling, Judy, Elaine, and Marckenson.

My husband, Tyler, is my favorite person in the whole entire world. The first thing we ever talked about was books. It'll probably be the last thing we talk about too.

I always thought it was silly when authors thanked their pets in their acknowledgments. I formally apologize to those authors. Because my puppy, Pippin the Snap, is the greatest dog in creation. At this very moment, he is sitting in front of me on the ottoman I'm supposed to be using.

It is hard to talk about what Jezebel herself means to me. For now, I'll just say, *thank you* for coming into my life, howling.